I CAN'T BELIEVE THIS, Mika thought to himself. I've been in some tough spots before, but nothing like this.

I'm in trouble with a demon and have to do what he commands, even though I don't really understand what that is, or I risk being changed into a demon myself, one digit at a time.

My faithful companion TamTur, fiercest wolf in the Wolf Nomad clan, has crossed eyes, a fat tongue, and a lump the size of a fist on top of his head.

Hornsbuck, my stalwart friend, is wrapped in a blanket of confusion and thinks everyone he meets is his old girlfriend, Lotus Blossom.

The princess has been polymorphed into a wolf who will attack me when I'm not looking, the moment I drop my guard.

I must devise a plan, Mika told himself, one to benefit all. I must be responsible and uphold the Wolf Nomad code of honor. I must go bravely into the most dangerous adventure of my life. . . .

GREYHAWK ADVENTURES

Book 4

THE PRICE OF POWER

by Rose Estes

A journey into an incredible world of magic and peril

Cover art by Clyde Caldwell
Interior art by John and Laura Lakey

TSR, Inc.

GREYHAWK ADVENTURES

Book 4

THE PRICE OF POWER

Copyright ©1987 TSR, Inc. All Rights Reserved.

All characters and names in this book are fictitious. Any resemblance to actual persons, living or dead, or to actual places or events, is purely coincidental.

Distributed to the book trade in the United States by Random House, Inc., and in Canada by Random House of Canada, Ltd.

Distributed in the United Kingdom by TSR UK Ltd.

Distributed to the toy and hobby trade by regional distributors.

ADVANCED DUNGEONS & DRAGONS, AD&D, DRAGONLANCE, and ENDLESS QUEST are registered trademarks owned by TSR, Inc. PRODUCTS OF YOUR IMAGINATION, GREYHAWK, and the TSR logo are trademarks owned by TSR, Inc.

First Printing: August, 1987
Printed in the United States of America
Library of Congress Catalog Card Number: 86-51275

9 8 7 6 5 4 3 2 1

ISBN: 0-88038-458-1

TSR, Inc.
P.O. Box 756
Lake Geneva, WI 53147

TSR UK Ltd.
The Mill, Rathmore Road
Cambridge CB14AD
United Kingdom

For Tom,
as usual: stalwart and caring through thick
and, more importantly, through thin.

GNOLLS

BURNEAL FOREST

MIKA'S CAMP

FLER RIVER

ERU-TOVAR

PHANTOM FOREST

WOLF NOMADS

LAKE QUAG

SEPIA UPLANDS

MOUNDS OF DAWN

VESVE FOREST

PERRENLAND

CLATSPUR RANGE

PROLOGUE

THE DEMON MAELFESH was angry. He could not remember the last time any of his minions had dared to oppose him. It had been several millennia at the very least. Maelfesh did not like being disobeyed. And never, never before had his will been subverted by a mere mortal!

Yet the unthinkable had indeed happened. A mortal, a human, no less, one Mika-oba, a member of the Wolf Nomad clan on the world of Greyhawk, had bested the demi-demon Iuz and sent him packing, banished to the ethereal plane, where he would remain for a very long time if Maelfesh had anything to say about it. And he did.

Iuz would not be missed; Maelfesh had a multitude of demi-demons on hand to do his bidding. But this mortal could not be allowed to escape unscathed. Already he had heard unhealthy murmurings and caught sideways glances from slitted eyes as his minions watched and wondered whether he could possibly be fallible.

11

No, the mortal would have to be punished, but not slain—at least not too easily or too soon. The human would have to realize the depth of his transgression before he died. His fear and his punishment had to be spectacular. Maelfesh had no idea what that punishment would be. But he had absolutely no doubt whatsoever that an idea would come to him.

Chapter 1

MIKA KNELT BESIDE the great wolf TamTur and watched the blood flow from the wound in his chest. He had tried applying pressure, but the blood continued to pour through his fingers. He had tried healing herbs—in fact, he had tried every herb in his pouch, grabbing great handfuls and pressing them against the gaping hole. But nothing had worked, and as Tam's breath grew even more faint, it seemed likely that he would die.

"Damn it, Tam, don't you dare die on me!" Mika screamed, filled with frustration and panic, not knowing what else he could do to prevent the inevitable.

Desperate, he picked the wolf up in his arms, carried him across the cracked paving stones of the ruined temple, and laid him gently on the broken slab of the altar.

Mika's dazed companions offered little encouragement. Hornsbuck, Mika's loyal clansman lay slumped against the walls of the temple, slobbering in a catatonic state; his eyes blank and fixed ahead. The venerable scout was watched over by his vigilant wolf RedTail, who lay curled at his side. Mika's faithful roan and Princess Julia—who had recently become a most ill-tempered wolf—were nowhere to be seen, and were doubtless foraging nearby, unconcerned over Tam's fate.

Mika fumbled in his pouch and pulled out his book of spells, the book that had been his father's. The book of spells that he should have learned by heart years earlier but had somehow never quite found the time.

Mika flipped through the pages, turning them rapidly as he sought a spell that he could accomplish with his meager abilities and yet would be strong enough to save the wolf's life.

"Charm . . . confusion . . . fire . . . fumble . . . polymorph, hmmm, polymorph . . . wizard eye . . ." No, none of them would do. Except, maybe, just perhaps . . .

Polymorph . . . powerful spell . . . changes form and ability . . . may change personality and mentality . . .

Mika stopped reading and looked at Tam. He could scarcely see the rise and fall of the wolf's chest and, even as he watched, the blood began to drip slowly onto the stone altar instead of spurting thickly as before. Tam was nearly drained. If Mika were going to save him, he had best do so immediately.

Mika began to panic. All right! He would do it! He would try a polymorph spell. He could do it. He hoped. He'd done it twice before, hadn't he? All right, so he'd done it wrong once. That didn't count. This time he'd do it right.

But what was he to change Tam into? Anything the wolf became would die just as easily as Tam himself. Except a troll. Trolls didn't die. Not even when you lopped off their heads and limbs. They lived through the very worst of wounds by regenerating, replacing the fallen parts and healing wounds with ease, appearing as good as new afterward, if a troll could ever be termed good as new.

But a troll? Trolls were hideous, gruesome things, and no one would turn into one willingly . . . unless their life depended on it.

Mika's mind was made up. He could think of absolutely no other way to save the wolf who was closer to him than anyone in the world . . . except maybe Celia, oh, and Amber, and Alyssa, and that girl in the bar in Yecha . . . what *was* her name?

Mika shook his head, dispelling the thought of nubile bodies from his mind. He read through the spell quickly, memorizing it faster than he had ever memorized anything before, except maybe the combination of knots binding Melanie's door that her brother foolishly thought would keep him out. . . .

The spell called for the cocoon of a caterpillar. Mika spied a cocoon fortuitously attached to the wall behind the altar and pried it loose with the tip of his sword, hoping that it had been spun by a proper caterpillar. The Great She-Wolf alone knew what other strange creatures had inhabited this temple of evil.

Tam would have to take his chances; he was so close to death now that worrying about what kind of web it was seemed ludicrous. Far more likely was the possibility that Mika would botch the spell and turn Tam into a turtle or a toad. Well, he could but do his best.

He looked at the spell one last time, gripped the cocoon in his left hand, and placed his right hand on Tam's chest just above the terrible wound. He took a deep breath, closed his eyes, and began to chant.

Halfway through the spell Mika felt Tam's body tremble. Abruptly the wolf stiffened and his legs jerked spasmodically. Mika kept his eyes closed and kept on reciting.

As he reached the end of the spell Mika heard a strange sizzling sound and smelled the stink of burning blood. Uttering the last few words, he racked his brain worriedly, trying to think of what he had done or said to produce such results. Sizzling blood was not supposed to be one of the effects of the spell.

Then, just as he pronounced the very last word of the spell, there was a thunderous crash, and something struck him full in the chest. He felt himself thrown backward as though from some terrible explosion. Almost before he realized what was happening, he struck one of the many broken marble pillars that had once supported the lofty bell-shaped dome of the temple. His head struck the stone with great force, knocking all the breath out of his body. His back and his chest were a blaze of pain, and he saw a brilliant display of sparkling stars before his eyes. He gasped for air, but his lungs refused to work. He gagged and heaved, but the band of pain just grew tighter across his chest until it seemed that he would never breathe again.

The stars before his eyes were sprinkled on a crimson background, and he writhed on the ground trying desperately to get his breath. Just as the stars began to fade from view, winking out one after the other, Mika felt something brush his face, lighter than a feather's touch. Suddenly the pain was gone. Completely.

Mika lay there, eyes still closed, the cessation of the terrible agony as sweet as pleasure. He drew air into his lungs and savored it as though it were a rare wine. He was content to lie there for a moment, grateful that he was still alive. He sighed deeply and resolved to study the spell book more carefully. Another mistake like that one, whatever it was, might kill him the next time. He'd been lucky.

Tam! What had happened to Tam? He opened his eyes and shot to his feet, only to fall back in horror. There, leaning against the edge of the altar was a . . . a . . . a something horrendous. It looked like a man being burned alive . . . being consumed by flames . . . except the thing was twice as big as a man! It was hard to see. Mika held up his hands and shielded his eyes against the abnormal brilliance of the flames, and as he did so, the figure shifted and stood upright.

Mika stared at the figure, transfixed with terror. It couldn't be human. Nothing human could live wrapped in those terrible flames. Even at a distance, Mika could feel the heat of the fire. He felt his eyebrows shrivel and the hair on his scalp began to steam. But if it wasn't human, that meant that it could only be . . . *not human*. Mika felt his soul cringe with fear. He tried to scuttle backward but was brought up short by the pillar.

The frightening apparition lifted its arm and pointed at Mika with a long, blue, flame-tipped finger.

"Mika-oba!" it proclaimed in a deep, hollow voice that somehow vibrated deep within Mika's skull and the hollows of his bones and turned his insides to jelly. "Mika-oba!" it repeated, and Mika was sure he felt his teeth starting to melt.

"Mika-oba!" it thundered yet a third time, and Mika realized that it was waiting for him to reply.

"Yes-s-s-s?" he quavered in a small voice.

"Mika-oba, you have dared to defy me," roared the creature, and the flames shot out in all directions in shades of deepest red that crackled and spat angrily.

"I . . . I didn't mean to, sir—your worshipfulness," croaked Mika. The hair of his nostrils tingled with every inhalation as he tried desperately to remember how he might have offended this being. But try as he might, Mika could not remember any way in which he might have angered the being, and even worse, he did not even know who or what the thing was. He just knew that it was very, very real and could probably turn him into a crispy nomad chip with one wave of its fiery hand.

"It was an accident," Mika whimpered, hoping that the thing would accept an apology. "I didn't mean it. It'll never happen again, you have my word."

"Of that, I am quite certain," said the fire-thing. "You have dispatched Iuz to a place from which he will not return. But you have disrupted my plans, and that makes me very, *very* angry."

The creature lifted its hand and started to point at Mika again. Mika didn't know what was about to happen, but neither did he wish to find out.

"Wait!" he screamed. "I'm sorry. I'm sorry! I didn't know you had plans. I mean, of course you had plans. Of course you're upset. I can understand that. Why don't you let me fix it? I can do that! I can do anything if you'll let me. Let me help fix the plans. Please! I'd be glad to. All right? Yes? All right! Tell me what you want. Just don't fry me!"

Mika heard the pleading words pouring from his lips in an endless line of pitiful drivel. He hated himself. But he also hated the idea of being turned into a fried wolf chip. He could drivel for hours if it kept him alive.

The thing lowered its arm, and the blue flames wrapped themselves around its wrist, coiling in sinuous bands like a gold bracelet. It put a fiery fist beneath its flaming face and pondered Mika's suggestion; its eyes gleamed a deep carnelian red like molten rock. It stared at Mika, unblinking.

Mika was transfixed by the thing's gaze. He felt naked to his very soul and beyond. He knew that the thing, whatever it was, could see into the heart of his being and knew all of his flaws. He suddenly felt with certainty that the creature would find him wanting and kill him on the spot.

If Iuz, the demi-demon whom Mika had helped dispatch to some netherworld, had belonged to this creature, that meant the fire-thing was a full-fledged demon, far too powerful for Mika to even ponder killing. Mika realized that he was as good as dead. He wilted visibly, too frightened to attempt to flee, too frightened to do anything but stand there and wait for the end which he hoped would be quick and merciful.

"All right," the demon said pleasantly, creasing its

face in what Mika took to be a smile, the crimson flames licking around the edges of its lips. "Allowing you to set matters right could prove amusing. I will permit you to live for the time being . . . as long as you do as you are told. I will know, of course, if you deviate from that path, and retribution will be swift and final.

"Do not think your friends can help you," added the demon. "Your large friend, Hornsbuck, still sits against the far wall of the temple, his few brains quite addled by his encounter with the umber hulk. Your wolf, as you can plainly see, is near death. And the girl, the Princess Julia whom you cleverly turned into a wolf, is skulking over there in the shadows, still waiting for the chance to kill you. Nor will the magic gem that you obtained from the princess help. No, your only chance for survival is to do exactly as I bid. Do you understand?"

Mika shivered in spite of the heat emanating from the demon. His hand rose to clutch the great blue-green jewel that hung from the fine-spun chain around his neck. He gulped, trying to swallow the huge lump that was stuck in his throat, and nodded his understanding, unable to speak.

"The princess was but a pawn, her malady conveniently contrived," said the demon, referring to the enchanted sleep that had felled the princess. Before she had been mistakenly transformed into a wolf, that is. And before Julia—for that was the princess's name and now the wolf's name, of course—before Julia, in a misguided pique, tried to kill Mika. And before, in all the confusion, the earthly form of Iuz had been destroyed . . . Oh, what a muddle! Mika shivered again.

"My business was with her father," continued the demon, its voice still reverberating in Mika's bones and making him feel quite ill indeed. "The princess was but one insignificant portion of his payment."

"Payment?" asked Mika in a gravelly voice, all of his spittle dried to dust. "Payment for what?"

"Why, the price of power, of course," replied the demon. "You don't suppose that power is given freely, do you? The man had a pact with me. I gave him power, and in return he gave me whatever I wanted."

The demon crossed its legs leisurely, planting its heel in a shower of sparks that skittered across the pavement toward Mika like iron to a lodestone. The demon laughed as Mika shrank back and gusts of burning air buffeted him, singeing the edges of his leather tunic and lighting tiny fires on his cape in a half-dozen places. Mika frantically beat out the flames, feeling the fire scorch his palms.

The demon's laughter diminished to a chuckle, which produced no new flames.

"So what happens now?" asked Mika, grimacing at the pain in his hands. "What happens to the king? What happens to the Princess Julia? Do you still want her?" he asked hopefully. "Will that set things right?"

"Oh, I don't want the princess," said the demon. "I never did. That was Iuz's business. I have no need of a princess. And I already have her father since he defaulted on his payment."

"Where is he?" asked Mika, wondering if he really wanted to know. "And what do I have to do to set things straight?"

The demon tapped its crimson chin with a long, tapering finger of flame and stared at Mika with its terrible carnelian eyes. Mika felt himself growing nauseous.

"That might be interesting," the demon replied at length. Then, standing upright, it walked around the far side of the altar and, resting its fiery palms on the broken slab, leaned over the silent body of the all but forgotten wolf.

"Go to Exag, the walled city. That is where you will find the king, where he awaits my displeasure."

"What am I to do once I get there?" asked Mika as he eyed Tam nervously, wondering if the wolf was alive or dead or if the nearness of the fire demon were cooking his poor, helpless flesh.

"I haven't decided yet," replied the demon. "I will let you know when I think of it. The price of power is quite costly, as is my forgiveness."

Forgiveness was something the demon had never granted to anyone or anything, but Maelfesh saw no need to mention that little fact to the human. The fire demon quite liked the manner in which Mika groveled. It was refreshing. It had been a long time since Maelfesh had been anything but bored. Living forever had its drawbacks. After you saw and did everything a few dozen times, things tended to get a little dull. It just wasn't any fun when you always knew the end of the story.

Maelfesh had ceased dealing directly with humans several millennia ago, having graduated to demi-demons and the like, higher life forms, according to its way of thinking. The demon had regarded it as a promotion at the time, but had forgotten how predictable demons were, being programmed to accept leadership of the hierarchy. Humans were quite unpredictable and were seldom, if ever, willing to accept the existing hierarchy of power, human or otherwise.

Even now, this miserable, half-literate, over-sexed brute of a Wolf Nomad was contemplating the odds of successfully double-crossing the demon and escaping unharmed. Maelfesh felt the flicker of hope as it rose in the human, mirrored by the gem that hung from his neck. The demon smiled to itself as it pictured what was to come. Maelfesh was almost glad to have been thwarted; it was going to be great fun playing with this nomad. I might even miss him when he is dead, Maelfesh thought. But not for too long.

"Don't even think about trying to break your word," said the demon as a corona of white-gold flame shot out and formed a gleaming diadem around its head. "I will know what you are thinking, and should you deviate from my strategy, revenge will be swift."

"I would never do that!" said Mika, trying to stifle the thought that had crept into his mind unbidden, wondering how the demon had known. Surely it was but a lucky guess.

The demon seemed to fade for the briefest of moments and then it flared up brighter than before as it stretched to its full height.

"It was no lucky guess, human. To demonstrate my abilities, I will help you with the wolf. You did the spell wrong. You used the cocoon of a vampire moth, not a caterpillar. Details are very important, Mika. Had the spell worked, you would have been faced

23

with a vampire wolf. However, I, Maelfesh the munificent, will help you this once and give you what you think you want . . . a troll wolf."

The demon gestured over the body of the wolf with its long, flaming hand. Unreadable runes burned in the air, glowed brightly, then disappeared, leaving only a smudge of black smoke to tell of their passing.

As Mika watched, Tam stirred. The demon laughed, causing every molecule in Mika's body to dance as though possessed. As the bile rose in Mika's throat and he clutched at the marble column for support, the demon turned into a pillar of fire that spouted huge spires of sparks and flames which cascaded down on Mika, setting his cape and even his hair afire before disappearing from sight.

Chapter 2

MIKA HOPPED ACROSS the floor of the temple, frantically beating out the fires that sizzled and burned his hair, clothes, and body. His hair was the worst; he could feel the flames as they chewed through his thick brown mane and reached for his scalp. Smacking himself on the head with the flat of his already scorched palms, he managed to extinguish his burning locks, but not before he was nearly choked by the thick clouds of acrid smoke that smelled like burning feathers.

Ignoring the pain in his palms, he slapped at the flames on his cloak, flames that seemed to grow taller with his every movement. Finally realizing that the air was fanning the fire, he disengaged the hasp that held the cloak at his throat and dropped it to the floor where it burned merrily until it was but a pile of ash.

As he beat out the last of the stubborn embers that had eaten their way into the thick leather of his tunic, he heard an ominous growl. Startled, he looked up and saw a sight so frightening that his heart lurched in his chest and then palpitated wildly.

Standing on top of the altar, head lowered, ready to spring, was Tam. Or what had once been Tam. Now it was some dreadful parody, some horrible apparition that looked like Tam, but wasn't.

The creature had nasty greenish-gray skin, with only the barest hint of fur growing in a few meager clumps on its body, between its ears, sprouting between its spavined ribs, and at the very end of its tail. Even these few small bits of fur were ringed with scrofulous, flaking skin.

The terrible chest wound still gaped wide, and the flesh beneath was a sickly shade of gray. A pale, watery ichor dripped from the wound, and where it fell upon the altar it hissed like acid and ate its way through the stone.

Its teeth were bared, showing corpse-white gums thick with foamy spittle that dribbled over its lips.

But the creature's eyes were the absolute worst, for they burned with a dreadful intensity that showed no sign of recognition.

"Tam?" Mika said in a quavery voice, hoping that his friend, the wolf, would come to his senses. The creature's ears pricked at the sound of Mika's voice, but it did not have the desired effect. Instead of recognizing him, the wolf lifted its dewlaps and snarled, a deep, throaty sound that rose from the animal's chest. Mika knew that sound all too well; he knew that it signaled an impending attack.

"No, Tam! Look, it's me, Mika, your old pal!" Mika said fervently, a sick smile on his face.

But even that failed to work, and the wolf that had once been Tam dropped into a crouch and hurled itself at Mika.

Mika dove aside as the troll wolf lunged past, its teeth snapping futilely at the spot where he had been. Quicker than Mika had expected, the creature landed, twisted, and flung itself at Mika again. Mika threw up his hands, deflecting the wolf as it attempted to rip out his throat, causing it to fall to the ground, momentarily off balance.

Mika seized the opportunity to run, placing a marble pillar between himself and the troll wolf while he tried desperately to think of what to do. He had wanted to turn Tam into a troll wolf, and he had gotten what he had hoped for. Now the problem was to stay alive until the wound healed and he could turn Tam back into a normal wolf.

The book! Mika felt for the spell book, hurting his burned hands in the process. But the book was gone, as was the pouch it was kept in. Mika chanced a brief look out from behind the pillar and spotted the book where he had left it, on the ground halfway across the temple on the other side of the wolf, who was even now getting to its feet and looking around for Mika.

Their eyes locked; Mika felt a shiver of fear run down his spine as the cold, dead eyes stared into his own.

Mika swallowed painfully and ran his fingers through his hair as he tried to think of how he might evade the troll wolf and reach his spell book. Perhaps there was some other spell he could try, some other way he— Mika stopped in mid-thought and looked down at his hand. In it was a large, brittle clump of frizzled threads. Except it wasn't thread, it was his hair. He dropped the awful stuff as though it were a handful of maggots and touched his head gingerly with his other hand. Another brittle clump broke off and, as he stared at it sorrowfully, he realized that all of his hair had been fried by the intense heat of the demon's passage.

Hardly had he taken in the thought when the troll wolf made its move. Padding softly toward him, it paused no more than a man's length away and eyed Mika, obviously wondering which way he would move around the pillar.

Deciding, the troll wolf slunk around the right side of the column, the side closest to the fallen spell book. Moving more swiftly, the troll wolf dashed forward, its teeth clacking together sharply, and Mika yelped and ran from behind the pillar with the wolf in close pursuit. He pounded across the pavement, bellowing with every step, not only from fear but from the awful pain of his burned feet which were already beginning to swell inside his badly charred boots.

Mika ran for the edge of the room, hiding behind each and every pillar, hoping to confuse the wolf, throw it off the track. But the troll wolf was not deceived and followed Mika every step of the way, snapping at his heels and trying to slice his hamstrings.

"Tam! TAM!" screeched Mika. "Stop! Don't you recognize me? It's me, Mika. Tam! Stop!"

But the troll wolf, undeterred, continued to do its utmost to catch and kill him, all the while growling and snarling in a most hideous manner.

No matter what Mika did, he could not shake the wolf who seemed to divine his purpose and who came between him and the spell book at every turn. The spell book was his only chance. Without it he would never be able to change the troll wolf back into a normal wolf, and he himself would be troll meat. Already he could feel his strength ebbing, and the pain of his burned body was growing acute. And every time he moved his head, bits of hair and eyebrow fell off.

There was only one good thing to be said of the situation; the awful wound in the wolf's chest appeared to be closing. Already the lips of the wound had drawn closer together, and less raw, pink flesh could be seen. If Mika could only last long enough, the wolf would be cured.

The thought cheered Mika considerably. Hobbling along with an awkward gait quite similar to that of a child with full diapers, he wobbled across the open space between yet another set of pillars.

The troll wolf was pacing him now, licking its grinning jaws in anticipation. There was no need to hurry, the human was his.

As though sensing the troll wolf's thoughts, Mika picked up a large chunk of marble fallen from the roof overhead, grunting with pain as his swollen fingers curled around the stone. If the wolf came for him, he would brain it, friend or no friend. You had to know where to draw the line at a time like this, and being eaten by a friend was where Mika was drawing the line.

Now they were pacing together, step by step, Mika walking backward, holding the chunk of marble above his head; the troll wolf followed close behind, watching for its chance to catch the human off guard.

Slowly, slowly, they circled the perimeter of the

ruined temple, slowly coming within sight of the precious spell book. Mika gauged his steps carefully, eyes glued to the troll wolf's chest, watching for the moment when the terrible wound would close completely.

The troll wolf drew nearer. Slaver foamed around its teeth and dripped off its tongue. Deep snarls erupted from its throat, thick and heavy with menace. Its dark eyes seemed to glow with hatred, and never once did they leave Mika's face.

In spite of himself, Mika was frightened. Knowing that it was really Tam didn't help one bit. Being killed and eaten by your best friend was somehow worse than being killed by an enemy.

As they crept within reach of the spell book, two things happened at once: the edges of the wound came together, and the troll wolf made its move.

As though realizing that Mika was about to end its existence, the troll wolf sprang for the man who had once been his friend. But hoping to catch him off guard, he leapt only to groin height, jaws open wide, teeth gleaming in the soft, filtered light that streamed through the broken dome.

A very real shriek of terror poured from Mika's lips. Leaping backward, he brought the hunk of marble down as hard as he could, smashing it on the top of the troll wolf's head.

The troll wolf staggered back drunkenly, its eyes crossed and its tongue lolling out the side of its mouth, which was, for once, closed. It tried to focus and took several additional steps before it keeled over and fell directly on its muzzle, sprawled in a half-kneeling position, its scrawny, hairless rump stuck in the air.

Off balance, Mika tumbled to the ground himself, crying aloud as he struck the flat of his burned palms against the gritty paving stones. Blinking back the tears of pain that came to his puffy, lashless eyelids, he scooted across the distance to the spell book and grabbed it in his shaking hands.

Breathing deeply, he pulled himself into a seated position, trying to find a spot that did not hurt. He flipped through the pages of the book quickly, looking for the spell that would return Tam to his normal state.

Puffy fingers pointing out the words, he mumbled his way through the spell, committing it to memory between frequent groans of pain. This time he concentrated on the spell totally, trying to get it right, wanting no mistakes. Yet he was forced to hurry, fearing that the troll wolf would regain consciousness and try to kill him before he could memorize the spell.

Just as Mika had feared, the troll wolf raised its ugly head, stared Mika in the eye, and snarled. Mika snapped the book shut, met the troll wolf's gaze evenly, and began to chant.

The troll wolf snarled, and the sound turned into a choked, garbled whimper that seemed to stick in its throat.

Other changes occurred simultaneously. Even as Mika watched, hair began to reappear on the troll wolf, pushing through the greenish-gray skin like a needle through cloth. The dead look faded from the wolf's eyes, replaced by one of puzzled concern. Soon, the last vestiges of the awful troll wolf were gone, leaving the welcome vision of Tam in its place.

With the return of Tam came pain. Mika became aware of just how terrible he felt. Every last bit of his body was either burned, scorched, or blistered, and in some instances, all three. His eyelids were thick and puffy, and his lips were grotesquely swollen, fat imitations of themselves that protruded far out in front of his face, as did his nose, which, when viewed through crossed eyes, looked like a bulbous over-ripe rutabaga. Even the spaces between his toes and fingers hurt. As he sat there feeling pitiful, the last of his hair broke off and fell to the ground.

It was too much. Mika felt a tear tremble on the edge of his fat eyelid and trickle down his burned face. In his imagination, he heard it sizzle as it dissipated on his hot skin. He sighed deeply, echoed in turn by Tam whom he had almost forgotten in his misery. He glanced up.

Tam looked almost worse than he did! There, square between the wolf's eyes, on the very top of his head, was an enormous lump which seemed to grow bigger even as Mika watched in amazement, making Tam look like some kind of hairy unicorn. The lump appeared to throb as it rose until it nearly equaled the wolf's ears in height.

Tam whimpered and pawed at his head, but as soon as his paws touched the incredible lump, he howled aloud. Mika noticed with interest that the wolf's eyes were still crossed.

There was nothing that Mika could do for him; all of his healing herbs were strewn on the floor of the temple, mixed and trodden underfoot. Nor did he have the strength to perform another spell.

Mika put the spell book down, then sagged slowly

and very carefully to the ground. Cradling his head on the spell book, he closed his eyes with a deep sigh.

Later. I'll fix the eyes later, he thought as he drifted into an exhausted sleep, Tam's whimpers, as well as his own, echoing in his ears.

Chapter 3

IT WAS NIGHT WHEN Mika wakened. For a moment he just lay there, too stiff and too sore to even contemplate moving. Tam was still whimpering occasionally, interspersed with low groans. It wasn't like Tam to show his pain; usually he was grimly stoical. Mika doubted that the bang on the head had broken any bones. Quite probably Tam just had a terrible headache that would go away in time. Considering the way that the wolf had tried to kill him, Mika did not feel too sorry for him.

If anything, he felt sorry for himself. Every single bit of his body throbbed with pain. His clothes were in tatters, and his hair was burned down to a rough stubble. He didn't have to check himself in a glass to know that he looked awful.

Even worse than looking awful, a demon was angry with him and had charged him with an impossible mission that he had no interest in performing. How would the demon know if he disobeyed? At that moment, filled with pain and self-pity, Mika resolved not to do as the demon had told him. Why should he go to Exag? He didn't even know this king. Furthermore, he didn't even like the king's daughter, the Princess Julia. After all, hadn't he nearly gotten himself killed trying to help her? She'd been enchanted before he'd even met her and had fallen into a deep sleep.

He and his fellow Wolf Nomad, Hornsbuck, had been attempting to bring her to Eru-Tovar, where a cure could be found, when their caravan had come under attack. It wasn't his fault that everyone else had been slaughtered by the gnolls and hyenas and the dread Iuz. He and the princess and Hornsbuck and their two wolves had barely survived themselves.

Mika turned his head painfully and looked across the temple. Yes, Hornsbuck was still there and still appeared to be deep in the miasma of the confusion spell he had received from his encounter with an umber hulk. Mika wondered if the spell would ever wear off. Since the moment of his affliction, Hornsbuck had spoken rarely and thought everyone he met was some long-lost love named Lotus Blossom.

The Princess Julia had indeed been roused from her enchanted sleep, but far from viewing Mika as her rescuer and showering him with gratitude as he had hoped, she had tried to kill him. It had been her knife, meant for Mika, that had struck Tam and so nearly cost him his life.

He did not turn his head to look for Julia. He did not care where she was. For all he cared, she could run away and stay a wolf forever.

Mika's resolve hardened as he thought back over the events of the past several moons. No, he would not do it. He would not do as the demon had bidden him. The Princess Julia could go hang, she was no longer any of his concern. He would take Hornsbuck and the wolves and just go on his way and be long gone before the demon ever figured out that he had disobeyed him.

But no sooner had he made this decision than something strange began to happen. At first he merely thought that the skin on his hand was itching, due to the burn he had sustained, a common enough reaction to sunburn. But the skin began to tingle and then hurt.

Mika gripped his wrist and hugged the hand to his chest, gasping with the intensity of the pain. The ache grew worse. He clenched his teeth and felt the muscles in his jaws creak as the flesh and skin of his pointer finger swelled to mammoth proportions and then began to split and peel like an over-ripe gapa melon left too long in the sun.

He clutched his wrist and stared at his finger in open-mouthed horror, wondering what was happening, too frightened to make a sound.

The flesh peeled back completely and dropped away like the useless husk of a gorney nut. The pain was terrible now, a raging agony that burned at the base of what had once been his finger.

Mika stared down at his hand, too shocked to even blink, the horrible pain momentarily forgotten. For something . . . something was there where his finger had once been. Tears of pain veiled his eyes; he blinked to clear his vision, almost too frightened to look closely.

He moved his hand and felt the pain move up his

arm, dissipating slowly. He twitched his fingers, starting with the littlest one and moving up. They all worked. He stopped at the pointer finger and, with a numbed mind, commanded it to bend, to move, to work. Which it did.

Mika gripped his wrist tightly and felt the nausea rise in his throat. He looked away, leaned his head back against the ground, and closed his eyes. His body was covered with cold sweat, and he felt sick. He wanted to look at his hand, to find out what it was that had taken the place of his finger, but he was afraid.

Slowly the nausea passed and the sickness was replaced by a feeling of dread. Mika stared up at the night sky through the broken dome of the old, ruined temple.

He could avoid looking and hope that it, whatever it was, would go away, but somehow he knew that it wouldn't. Sooner or later he would have to look, to see what had happened to his hand.

The feeling of sickness lay heavy in his stomach, but there was nothing to be gained by waiting. He rolled on his back and held his hand up in front of him in a shaft of soft-white moonlight. But not even moonlight could lessen the shock of what he saw.

The nausea rose in his throat unbidden, and he twisted to the side and retched onto the pavement, heaving until his stomach was emptied of all but bitter bile. This it continued to spew out, as though by emptying itself it could somehow purge his mind of the awful vision.

But it was useless. The vision burned bright in his mind, remaining vivid long after he had closed his eyes to it. What had once been his finger was now covered with dark green scales and tipped by a thick, curved, horny talon.

Weakened, he rolled to the far side and cradled his head in the crook of his arm and took in a deep shuddering breath, holding the awful finger as far away from him as possible.

The demon. It had to be the demon. He had said that if Mika disobeyed him, he would know; that his revenge would be swift. He had dared to think, to merely *think* that he might do other than obey the demon, and the demon had punished him by replacing one of his fingers with a demon digit.

Suddenly a terrible thought popped into Mika's head. What if he's inside my head somehow and he knows everything I'm thinking? I'd never be able to do anything again without the demon knowing about it! There was a funny prickling at the base of Mika's neck, and then he knew with total and complete certainty that he was right.

Mika didn't think it was possible to become any more depressed than he already was, but in the hours that followed, he managed.

Somewhere in the very darkest hours of the night, Tam crept over and lay at his side, his muzzle stretched across Mika's chest. But that only served to depress Mika more thoroughly, for the bump on the top of the wolf's head had not shrunk but had grown even larger. Further, Tam's eyes were still crossed and his tongue protruded a good knuckle's length from the end of his mouth, swollen where he had bitten it. Air whistled in and out as he struggled to breath, and he whimpered between every breath. He sounded and looked as bad as Mika.

I can't believe this, Mika thought to himself as he lay there throughout the long night, staring up at the sky and patting Tam on the back with his one good hand. I've been in some tough spots before, but nothing like this.

I'm in trouble with a demon and have to do what he commands even though I don't really understand what it is, or else risk being changed into a demon myself, one digit at a time.

My faithful companion TamTur, fiercest wolf in the Wolf Nomad clan, has crossed eyes, a fat tongue, and a lump the size of a fist on top of his head.

Hornsbuck, my stalwart friend, is wrapped in a blanket of confusion and thinks everyone he meets is his old girlfriend.

The princess has been turned into a wolf and, if I'm lucky, she's run off somewhere. I haven't seen her since the demon appeared. But then I haven't looked.

The only one who seems to have escaped unharmed is RedTail, Hornsbuck's wolf. But he won't obey me; all he cares about is Hornsbuck.

And the horse, amended Mika, mentally adding the gallant and brave roan who had carried him through much danger till they reached this fateful spot. It wasn't his fault that everything had turned out so poorly.

He tried to devise a plan. One that would benefit them all. Somehow he would have to restore Hornsbuck. He didn't want to even contemplate taking such a dangerous journey without someone along to protect his back. He wasn't sure if he could do it, but he would try. At the least, he felt responsible for Hornsbuck, who had been doing his best to get them out of the underground catacombs when he was felled by the umber hulk. What a muddle.

He couldn't even imagine what would happen when they got to Exag. Mika shrugged the question away; it was too far distant to think about. Here and now was the issue.

Lulled by the constant whimper-whine-gasp of the wolf and almost overwhelmed by his problems, Mika closed his eyes as dawn filled the chamber with pearly fog, and he fell into an exhausted sleep.

Chapter 4

MIKA AWAKENED, feeling only slightly better than death. It was obvious that Tam felt no better, for his eyes were still crossed, his tongue still swollen, and the bump on top of his head was even larger than before.

Mika groaned as he crawled to his knees and slowly stood up. He felt awful but knew that nothing was to be gained by staying here. Anything would be better than staying. Well, almost anything.

Mika glanced down at his hand, hoping he had imagined the awful occurrence, but the demon finger was still there, each circular scale gleaming bright green in the morning light.

He sighed deeply, knowing that there were many things to be done. *Town.* He had to get to town to buy provisions so they could begin the demon's mission.

Mika walked across the temple slowly, grimacing with every step as the tender, swollen flesh of his soles grated against the broken pavement. The roan had finally materialized and seemed glad to see him, having eaten all the weeds and grass within its reach. It whickered happily and, tossing its head up and down, nudged Mika painfully on his burned chest. Mika untied the reins and drew the horse behind him as he made his way toward Hornsbuck.

The big Wolf Nomad sat with his back against the wall of the temple, staring vacantly into mid-air. His green eyes focused on Mika without much interest. "Lotus Blossom?" he asked querulously, yet without seeming to really expect an answer.

Hornsbuck's huge, ham-sized fists lay idle in his lap. His great, reddish blond, bristly mane and enormous, full beard hung limp and bedraggled. It seemed to Mika that Hornsbuck's skin had lost its tone; it hung from his bones like the flesh of an old man who had been much heavier in his prime. It seemed that he who had always been so full of the flavor of living had given up and, if left alone, would soon drift off into death.

Mika was alarmed. How could he ever succeed on this devilish journey without Hornsbuck! Forgetting his own problems, he knelt down beside the man and pulled him to his feet. Hornsbuck did not help Mika, nor did he resist. It was like dealing with a child.

RedTail, Hornsbuck's big male wolf, circled nervously, whining softly, seeming to understand that Mika was trying to aid the man he followed. Under normal circumstances, RedTail would never have allowed Mika to touch Hornsbuck. But these were not normal circumstances.

Once he was on his feet, Hornsbuck mounted the roan with Mika's help. RedTail watched anxiously.

Tam staggered to his feet and tried to join them.

He took two uncertain steps and then lurched off drunkenly to the left. His momentum carried him for a short distance, whereupon he lost his balance and fell to the ground, whining.

There was only one thing to do. Mika trudged over to the wolf's side. Closing his eyes, he repeated the words to one of the few spells he knew by heart, a sleep spell. He had found it useful when meeting young women. Awakening from unexpected naps, they found themselves cradled in his arms. Sometimes they stayed there.

Tam stopped whining and began snoring, a peculiar snorting-wheezing-whistling sound, but anything was better than looking at his poor, crossed eyes. Mika picked the wolf up in his arms and, grunting under the weight, carried him over to the horse.

The roan shied and rolled its eyes as Mika neared, but it held fast. He draped the wolf over the horse's hindquarters, behind the saddle, and tied him securely like a sack of oatmeal.

Mika looked around the temple, checking to see if he had left anything. His leather pouch lay crumpled on the stones at the base of a pillar, the horns and vials of healing ungents crushed and ruined. His sword and the Princess Julia's knife lay in the center of the room where the battle with the demi-demon, Iuz, had taken place.

Mika lifted his hand and stroked the blue-green gem that hung from his neck. The princess. There was no avoiding it. He knew that he had to find her.

Mika scanned the temple, searching, but the princess was nowhere to be seen. Could she have left? For a moment his heart leapt within his breast and he hoped with all his being that it were true, that she had left and gone off on her own. But then he was overcome with worry that she might have done so. The princess was part of the mission and, like it or not, she was needed to unravel the mess and put things together right.

Mika crept around the edges of the temple as quietly as his swollen feet could manage, looking in all the darkened nooks and crannies where she might have hidden.

He found her at last, huddled beneath the great stone altar, her eyes, one green, one blue, glowing out at him from the darkness. As he held his hand out toward her, she growled and bared her teeth.

"I should have known," Mika said with a sigh. "Unpleasant as a woman, unpleasant as a wolf. Why would I expect anything different?" He turned aside as though to leave.

While Mika was fairly adept in dealing with women, he excelled at handling wolves. He was a Wolf Nomad, after all. And while the princess was familiar with being a woman, she had been a wolf for only a short time.

As Mika drew back, the princess lunged forward to bite him, the hatred glowing bright in her eyes. That was what Mika had been waiting for. In a motion almost too fast to follow, he seized the princess behind her neck and, pinching the skin at the base of her neck, lifted her clear of the altar as easily as if she were a small kitten.

Mika carried her, as she snapped futilely and snarled loudly, back across the temple to the patient roan. He rummaged in the saddlebags, whistling cheerfully through swollen lips, not allowing the princess the satisfaction of knowing how much his arms ached and how much he longed to set her down. Finally he found what he was looking for, a sturdy length of smoked rawhide. It would not last forever, but it would do for the time being. He tied it firmly around her neck and knotted the other end around the horn of the saddle. Try as she might, she could not free herself quickly.

Everything was ready—well, almost everything. Mika removed Hornsbuck's cape from around his massive shoulders and fitted it around his own. It covered most of his body, having been made for a much larger man. Falling to his ankles, it hid his burned flesh and singed clothes from sight. But his boots were badly charred and tattered. Muttering an apology to the bemused Hornsbuck, he removed the man's boots as well and placed them on his own feet. They were so enormous that he had difficulty keeping them on, but if he shuffled, it would be all right.

His head and hands were another matter. His hair had been burned away to mere stubble, and his face was puffy and peeling and scarlet red in color. And then there was the little matter of the demon finger.

Mika was at a loss. What could he do to hide his head and hand? One glance at him and people would run, screaming. His eye was caught by something pink which lay crumpled on the stones. The princess's dress! The one she had been wearing when he turned her into a wolf!

"Aha!" cried Mika as he picked it up off the ground and looked at it, studying it carefully.

"I can wind it around my head like so, tuck the

edges in all around, and everything will be fine. Well, RedTail, what do you think?"

Mika spread his arms wide and modeled his new headgear for the wolf. RedTail looked away and whined, seemingly embarrassed by the pink silk turban.

But Mika was pleased. There was little or nothing he could do about his hand except keep it hidden from view beneath the voluminous cloak, but now he was fit to go out in public.

He grabbed the roan's reins firmly and, making certain that the princess could not reach him, he made his way through the carved set of double doors and left the temple of Iuz.

Chapter 5

THE SUN WAS HIGH in its passage, blazing down on the strange little caravan as they picked their way over the multitude of broken steps that had once streamed with worshippers of the dark one, Iuz. Now, nothing remained but broken stones and bleak memories.

Mika led his charges across the broad, flat plain that separated the temple from the great walled city of Eru-Tovar, the capital city of the Wolf Nomads, wondering how quickly he would be able to find what he wanted and leave.

As he trudged across the barren plain, clenching his toes inside the large, over-sized boots in an effort to keep them on, he began to wonder if he mightn't be able to undo some of the damage to Hornsbuck's addled brain. It could scarcely get worse. Digging in his pouch with his free hand, he pulled the spell book free and began to leaf through it, looking for an appropriate spell.

So involved was he in studying the book that he

failed to notice another Wolf Nomad caravan on its way out of the city until it was nearly beneath his nose.

The caravan master, a pompous man of advanced years, was taken aback by the strange sight that greeted him: a man, oddly muffled in a red cloak large enough for one twice his size, shuffling in too-large shoes, and wearing a bulbous pink silk turban on his swollen, hairless head, leading the strangest entourage imaginable.

An enormous fellow rode atop the single horse, his bare feet dangling nearly to the ground. Tied behind him was a wolf with a lolling tongue who snored loud enough to wake the dead. And dragging behind the horse on the end of a leash was another wolf, with one green eye and one blue eye, that snapped and snarled and fought the rawhide restrainer. The only normal member of the party was a stocky wolf with reddish blond fur and a short, scarred muzzle who trotted off to one side as though trying to appear unconnected with the rest of the group.

"Ho!" said the caravan master, Wolf Nomad protocol overcoming his misgivings.

"Huh?" said Mika, shoving the turban back from his eyes with a cloak-wrapped hand, allowing the spell book to cover as much of his face as possible. "Oh, uh, ho! Ho!" he replied, unable to see clearly because of the sunlight glaring in his eyes, yet recognizing the ancient wolf clan greeting. To not respond would be an insult and a breach of acceptable conduct which could result in a challenge, and, perhaps, even a duel.

"Whartan of the Wolf Nomads, born to the Blue

Forest Wanderers, out of the Pine Lodge clan," said the caravan master, reciting his lineage and demanding, without so saying, Mika's credentials.

"Mika of the Wolf Nomads, born to the Burneal Forest Hunters, out of the Far Fringe clan," replied Mika, knowing full well that the man was correct in asking his identity, for no one was allowed within distance of Eru-Tovar unless he could account for himself either by birth or by business.

"Who is your companion?" asked the man, still highly doubtful of Mika.

"One Hornsbuck by name, a mighty warrior," answered Mika, pushing back the turban which had once more slid forward over his eyes. "Also of the Far Fringe clan."

"Success be your reward," said the man after a long pause, unable to think of what else to say.

"And peaceful be your journey," replied Mika, relieved that he had not been forced to fight. He nodded at the man, holding his turban on with the spell book.

The man gave him one last penetrating look and then signaled his caravan to continue. Mika stood quietly as all twenty wagons passed by, trying to ignore the curious looks of the outriders. Just then the last of them approached, a great burly monster of a fellow with ropelike muscles and two long blond braids. Hornsbuck straightened in the saddle and held out his arms. "Lotus Blossom!" he cried joyously, his blue eyes brightening visibly. The braided rider smacked his lips, producing a long, vulgar kissing sound, and rode on. Hornsbuck attempted to leap down from the saddle and follow the rider, and it was all Mika could do to subdue him.

Finally, Mika was able to persuade Hornsbuck to stay where he was, but not before the princess darted in and delivered a painful bite to Mika's heel. Fortunately, the immense boot protected him from serious injury so that he merely limped a little bit more than he had before.

Mika pulled himself up to his full height as they drew near the city. He let his eyes rove over it, impressed as always by the sheer size of Eru-Tovar.

The city had been built on a tall rise, surrounded on all sides by the open plains. The entire city was walled, in most places four times the height of a man. The wall was made out of huge, polished squares of black marble, quarried from the nearby hills. Mounted atop the walls at regular intervals were realistically carved wolves' heads, mouths open and snarling. Banners flew above the guardposts, black wolves on a crimson ground, and fluttered on either side of the massive gates, the main entrance to the city.

Mika led his party through the gates, answering all queries correctly, satisfying the guards' suspicions by mention of inter-clan connections. He also added that he was seeking medical attention for his friend, who even at this moment was drooling onto the horse's neck. It was Hornsbuck who convinced the guards. Waving their lances, they passed Mika through the gates and into the city.

Eru-Tovar was a marvelous place indeed. Boasting a permanent population of some five thousand inhabitants, it often swelled to three times that number on feast and festival days, during the peak moments of timber harvest and during the autumn hunt, drawing far-flung nomad clans, as well as those who sought to purchase their wares.

The city reflected a cosmopolitan air, the direct result of the many cultures who had passed through its gates and left their mark. There was little that could not be found in Eru-Tovar.

There were streets filled with shops that sold nothing but fresh meat and others that sold only smoked and dried meats. There were streets filled with alchemists and others that boasted magic-users. Woven goods, leathers, precious metals and gems, produce, livestock, money-lenders and booksellers, each enterprise had its own section of the city.

But Eru-Tovar also gave space to a huge open-air market for vendors whose business was of a less permanent nature; and of great interest to Mika was a sprawling, active, red-light district. It was to this last that he directed his attention, for it seemed that few of his problems could not be soothed by a soothing glass of wine or two. He also felt that he had earned it.

Following a path he had taken many times before, Mika entered the huge market that fronted the red-light district, giving it an air of decency that it did its best to live down.

Mika led the roan between the rows of sturdy stone houses which were shuttered against the heat of the day. Following the babble of voices, he soon found himself in a broad thoroughfare lined with tall, multi-storied buildings constructed of cream-colored stone and accented by brightly painted windows and door frames of red, green, and blue.

Spread in front of these buildings were wagons, two-wheeled carts, semi-permanent stands, and in some instances, mere blankets spread on the ground.

Vegetables, fruits, wheels of cheeses, jewelry, weapons, clothing, skins and furs, as well as cobblers, tooth fixers, healers, and a variety of other services were offered to passersby in loud tones.

Mika's eye was caught by a shimmering bolt of cloth, blue-green with tiny flecks of silver shot through the weft. He turned aside to finger the material and held it out to admire the play of sunlight on its soft folds.

"For your lady?" the vendor asked, and with great shock Mika realized that he had not been thinking of a lady at all. That idyllic part of his life seemed remote now. He tossed the material aside in confusion and strode off down the street without looking back.

Using a pouch of coins that he had taken from Hornsbuck, Mika purchased hard twists of stringy, white cheese still wrapped in the yellow-green leaves of the galda tree that gave it its salty flavor. The seller, a large, buxom woman with a bronzed, pock-marked complexion, threw in a leather sack of nutritious galda seeds for good measure and pinched Mika on the thigh as she muttered a bawdy suggestion on garlic-scented breath.

Mika blanched beneath his turban and, kissing the woman's hand gallantly, begged forgiveness, citing time as a factor for his refusal.

Mika took his leave of the woman and forced his way through the dense crowds, most of whom gave his party curious looks. RedTail followed close on the roan's heels, stopping occasionally to visit and sniff out one of the many wolves that thronged the streets. Even the princess had stopped dragging at her leash and was looking about her with interest.

"Probably thinking up some new plot to murder me," mumbled Mika.

Wolves were no unusual sight in Eru-Tovar as they were in other cities, for every adult male nomad was required to obtain a wolf pup shortly after its birth as part of his formal initiation into the ranks of the clan. Even those members of the clan who chose to live in the cities were required to adhere to this dogma or risk having their manhood questioned.

Obtaining a new-born pup was no easy matter, and many nomads wore their scars, as well as their honor, proudly. Recently, Mika had heard rumors that some town-born nomads, strangers to the forest and without personal knowledge of its workings, had resorted to purchasing pups from those who were willing and able to obtain them. But Mika found the tale most difficult to believe, for even he with his strong desire to protect his body from harm, found such cowardice distasteful in the extreme.

Mika glanced behind him and smothered a grin as he noticed that several male wolves were following the princess, sniffing at her tail and hindquarters with interest. Aloof and unpleasant as a human princess, she was proving far more popular as a female wolf. Mika would see to it that no real harm came to her, but in the meantime, he had to admit to a certain amount of pleasure at her discomfort.

Salt, spices, ground and roasted yarpick coffee beans, flour, a sack of kara fruit, a large pouch of dried vegetables, and leather-hard strips of smoked meat filled Mika's saddlebags to bursting.

A metal gauntlet, large enough to cover his deformed hand, was his next purchase. He smoothed it over his fingers and held it up to the sun to admire the smooth symmetry of the tiny, metal-mesh links as they shone in the sun. Strange how he had never noticed how beautiful chain mail could be. He clenched his fist and smiled.

A new tunic of soft, gray doeskin, not very practical but quite lovely, tall, knee-high boots with a border of thick fringe, and a swirling cloak of turquoise-blue silk, completed his new wardrobe.

At the last moment, unable to resist, he replaced his old, thick-leather sword belt with a new one of gray snakeskin inset with turquoise and silver. It was not like him to spend money on clothing, but somehow it seemed both appropriate and necessary.

The only false note was the pink turban which he was forced to continue wearing because the cloak's hood refused to remain on his head, the slippery silk sliding off the burned stubble.

Enjoying the feel of his new clothes, Mika walked through the busy streets, taking in the sights of the city he visited all too infrequently. Unfamiliar with the many twists and turns, he soon found himself in an unfamiliar area.

Tiers of wooden cages of all sizes lined the edges of the street and were filled with animals, some as rare and exotic as the tiny pseudodragon, less than a foot tall but able to deliver a fatal blow with its sting-tipped tail. Other more common animals were the norm, and rows of cattle and sheep and pigs filled the air with their barnyard stink.

Smaller creatures, rabbits, marmots, pocket weasels, and poultry comprised the length of the next section. Mika's neck began to prickle. Turning, he saw a pair of baleful, black eyes staring at him from the confines of a small cage. Curious, he walked closer and looked in. He drew back in horror and disgust as he saw an infant harpy crouching within, tiny pinfeathers barely covering its lower half, whitely naked from the waist up.

Mika hurried away, not even answering the sellers' comments, for he knew that whomever was foolish enough to purchase the harpy would eventually die, killed either by the creature itself or by its mother, who would track it relentlessly.

Chapter 6

HIS PURCHASES MADE, Mika led the roan through the myriad of curling streets that led from the marketplace to the street of wine merchants.

Bedlam struck as soon as they turned the final corner. The narrow street was packed with people crowding in as though hurrying toward some irresistible attraction.

The noise was tremendous; loud screeches and terrible moans filled the air like bees droning around a pot of spilled honey. Arms and legs waved everywhere, and even as Mika watched in bewilderment, a large, armor-clad body flew past him and landed in the middle of the crowd, smashing several unfortunates beneath it.

"What on Oerth!" Mika wondered aloud.

"Probably a drunk," said a woman who leaned out of her window, her eyes bright with curiosity. "But it won't last long. Here comes a complement of the guard," she said, nodding toward the street Mika had just left. "Some poor soul will sleep in the dungeon for the next fortnight."

Another body went flying. Mika and his motley band were hemmed in by the crush of people crowding behind them. Curious by nature, Mika was not averse to finding out what had caused such an enormous ruckus and seeing the person who was able to toss such large men so high into the air. There! There went another one, the poor fellow landing head-first on the canopy of a mead-seller's wagon, bringing the vehicle and its contents to the ground in a splintering crash.

Mika's height permitted him to view the proceedings better than most of those who filled the street, and the press of those behind his group brought them closer and closer to the site of the disturbance.

" . . . teach you to lay your hands on a lady, you thug!" bellowed a deep voice and a large, beetle-browed man arced overhead. The crowd roared its encouragement to the unseen assailant, and Mika could see grushniks passing hands as people wagered on the eventful outcome of the fray.

" . . . Sell me bad wine, will you?!" roared the voice. "I'll teach you to pick on a poor, defenseless woman!" The crowd ducked as another body was hurled into its midst. Suddenly, Hornsbuck leaned forward and his green eyes grew bright. Standing up in the roan's stirrups, he began to scan the crowd, seemingly searching for someone or something. Concerned, Mika tugged at his leg, but it was like pulling on a hundred-year-old oak and had about as much effect.

"He watered down the wine, the pig-dog!" roared the deep, bass voice, and the crowd roared back its approval.

A wide smile crossed Hornsbuck's face. Following some unspoken command, the roan began to push through the densely packed crowds with Mika, who was unable to stop him, and unwilling to be separated, following behind.

It was difficult to move, but faced with the choice of moving aside or being crushed beneath the hooves of the huge horse, the crowd parted. Mika, the princess, and RedTail brought up the rear.

At last they reached the center of the maelstrom. And to Mika's astonishment, a woman proved to be the cause of all the noise and trouble. A large woman to be sure, a very large woman.

She stood at least a hand taller than Mika's own six feet and was as broad as Hornsbuck. She had white-blond hair woven into two hawserlike braids and was dressed in a thick, leather tunic, similar to Hornsbuck's, which covered her huge body from neck to mid-thigh.

Her legs—massive, treelike limbs—were not bare, but were encased in rough, blue cotton trousers. Her boots were of thick, heavy leather tied off below the knee. Her arms were bare and as muscular as Hornsbuck's. As Mika watched with awe, she picked up the last of her attackers, a man easily as big as she, squeezed him in an immense bear hug till his ribs could be heard to crack, then lofted him above her head and threw him at a large, white, pasty-faced merchant who stood wringing his hands in despair among the broken remains of his wine cart.

The bully crashed into the wine merchant, and both of them collapsed on the ground. The man crawled to his feet, stumbled over the fallen body of his employer, and then, panic written on his face as he looked back at the angry woman, ran off amid the jeers and catcalls of the boisterous crowd.

"Who else? Who else would seek to subdue a poor, helpless female?" shouted the woman, hands on her broad hips as she turned around slowly, scanning the crowd.

"Lotus Blossom," Hornsbuck crooned into the sudden silence.

"Hornsbuck, be quiet! Not now!" Mika whispered in alarm, punching Hornsbuck on the leg. "The woman's a lunatic, leave her alone!"

Ignoring Mika completely, Hornsbuck placed his hand on top of Mika's turban and leaned forward, resting his entire weight on Mika's head. Mika staggered under the weight, unable to say a word as he tried to keep his legs from buckling. Hornsbuck sat back, releasing him as the woman whipped around, her face purple with her exertions.

As Mika struggled to pull the turban up over his eyebrows, he saw the woman's fists clench and the muscles in the great arms bulge. He edged backward, wondering if he could get away before the woman pinched their heads for daring to speak. Then he heard the welcome sound of the guard as they trudged forward, pushing through the crowd. Maybe all was not lost, maybe the guard would arrive on the scene and arrest the madwoman before he and Hornsbuck were killed.

"Hornsbuck!" cried the woman, the rage fading from her face, replaced by a huge grin. Her brilliant cornflower-blue eyes sparkled when she smiled at the nomad as he dismounted from the roan and stumbled toward her with open arms.

"Lotus Blossom," he cooed warmly, folding her into his vast embrace, and the two leather-clad bodies merged like bears in heat.

"Here comes the guard," Mika called hoarsely, almost unable to believe that this enormous woman with the bulging biceps was Hornsbuck's infamous inamorata of whom he had spoken so often.

"Hornsbuck, he tried to cheat me," said the woman, her lower lip trembling as she nestled her head on Hornsbuck's shoulder. "I bought a liter of wine to drink with my dinner. It was watered! When I complained, he laughed and turned his bullies on me. I defended myself and managed to hold my own."

Hornsbuck did not answer, seemingly content to hold the woman in his own mammoth arms.

Mika looked around at the broken jugs, the wine merchant's entire inventory, the smashed wagon, the bullies, all four of them lying unconscious with more than a few limbs twisted in unnatural positions, and thought that Lotus Blossom could probably hold her own against an entire squad of guards. Judging from the sound of marching feet behind them, she might just get the opportunity to prove it.

"Quick, the guard!" he said, repeating the warning even more loudly.

"Come, my sweet, let us remove ourselves from this unruly mob," Lotus Blossom said with great dignity, offering Hornsbuck her arm.

Hornsbuck responded rather slowly, linking his arm through hers as though uncertain of what he was doing or why. Lotus Blossom batted her eyelids coyly and smiled a shy, dimpled smile, her grapefruit-sized cheeks glowing red with vibrant health.

"Here, merchant, this should cover your damages," Mika said as he half-emptied his sack of money, showering the recumbent form with a sprinkling of grushniks which would not have begun to make good the damage.

"But do not let us hear of any further complaints, or we will return and mark paid to the business that the lady began."

The sight of Hornsbuck, coupled with the mighty woman, was more than the poor merchant could bear, and he sank back on the wine-wet cobbles and groaned.

The crowd began to disperse, confusing and inhibiting the guards' progress. Mika seized the roan's reins and, whistling for the wolves, slowly followed the leather-clad pair as they sauntered down the street, foreheads touching, Lotus Blossom murmuring soft nothings in Hornsbuck's ear.

Halfway down the street, the captain of the guard trotted up alongside Mika and touched his wolf-tail-embellished cap in greeting.

"Good brother, it seems we have come too late to break up the fight that has disturbed this street. Did you see what happened? Can you describe the ruffians?"

"Indeed," answered Mika, touching his turban in turn, thankful that it was he who had been asked. "It was two men, dark they were. One had a ring through his left nostril. The other had a knife scar running the length of his face. They looked like Blackmoorian cutthroats. I think they tried to rob the wine merchant. They ran off down that side street yonder. If you hurry, you can catch them still."

"Many thanks, brother," said the guardsman. Calling to his men, he rode off down the street, bypassing Hornsbuck and Lotus Blossom without a second glance.

Lotus Blossom stopped in front of a slope-roofed, evil-looking dive. Foul fumes speaking of lost evenings and wasted lives wafted out of the open door. A ragged, reeking wastrel lay sleeping in the doorway, his snores and exhalations containing enough alcohol to drug a wolf.

Lotus Blossom pushed the fellow away with the toe of her boot and ushered the still bedazed Hornsbuck inside. Mika stood outside, trying to think of what to do. It seemed unlikely that he would be able to persuade Hornsbuck to leave. Although his friend had recognized the woman, Mika knew that Hornsbuck was still bereft of his senses.

Mika liked to lift a drink as well as the next man, maybe even more, and having a drink had been part of his plan, but he did not like the look of the place and did not care to watch Hornsbuck drool in public. But since he could not propound an alternative, he sighed and tied the horse to a nearby post, leaving the soundly wheezing TamTur strapped over the roan's back. Then he entered the dark doorway, dragging the princess behind him. RedTail entered without hesitation, and Mika surmised that he had followed Hornsbuck into many such a place during their years together.

It took a while for Mika's eyes to adjust to the dark, and when they did, he was not overly encouraged, for the interior looked much the same as the exterior.

A long, low hearth, constructed of fieldstones, ran the entire length of the left-hand side of the building. An ox was spitted over the glowing embers, turned by a filthy, rag-clad urchin of indeterminate years and sex. Rabbits, pheasants, guinea hens, and marmots sizzled and browned on stakes suspended over the coals, and potatoes baked on flat rocks.

The wholesome smell of the cooking meat competed with the stench of whiskey, wine, and mead which had been spilled on the wooden floor until it could absorb no more and formed a tacky, sticky surface that gripped the foot in an unpleasant manner.

Mika made his way across the dark room, bumping into the occasional chair and table, all but unseen in the murk, for a dense cloud seemed to fill the upper level of the room, a permanent stratocumulus of smoke from the hearth and pipes of now-absent customers.

The woman had seated herself at a smallish table. Hornsbuck, still gripped by his confusion, stood alongside, not understanding what was required of him, his eyes vacant and foolish.

Mika slid into the chair meant for Hornsbuck. The woman stared at him with open displeasure and then glanced up at Hornsbuck, her eyes narrowing as she noticed, perhaps for the first time, that something was wrong.

"Who be yourself, and what be wrong with Hornsbuck?" she asked in a tightly controlled voice.

"My name is Mika, and I am of Hornsbuck's clan," Mika replied, kicking out at the princess as she tried to bite the underside of his thigh. "Hornsbuck tangled with an umber hulk and was bravely felled. He was powerfully stunned and has failed to come out of the magical confusion, though it happened some time ago. I keep hoping he'll get better, but he hasn't yet."

"Looks like you've got a few problems yourself," said Lotus Blossom as she eyed Mika critically. Mika clutched his new cloak and straightened the pink silk turban with a chain-metaled hand, trying to look dignified.

"Hornsbuck's always been a bit confused," said the woman. "Needs me to take care of him. You leave him to me. I know something that'll fix him right up. Make yourself at home, Mika, we might be a while."

Lotus Blossom rose from the table and, without another glance at Mika, slowly led the bemused Hornsbuck off by the hand. The last Mika saw of them, they were vanishing up a flight of stairs.

Mika heaved a large sigh and settled back in his chair as he examined the rest of the room, noting that on his right a large bar ran the length of the room. Shelves covered the walls and were filled with jars and bottles of every size and shape. Mika felt certain that they contained a wide variety of interesting and unusual liquors. Given the large number of foreigners who visited the city, such an assortment was probably necessary. His interest in the place began to quicken.

The room was barely lighted with a number of thick candles set in cheap pottery bowls. The tables and chairs were constructed of rough wood and were none too comfortable. RedTail pressed against his leg and began licking a spill of burgundy wine that had puddled on the table and dripped onto the floor.

The princess crouched beneath a chair, a grimace of distaste replacing the snarl that had become her one expression, as she lifted one paw and then another as though wishing she could levitate. Mika laughed.

The look of hatred returned, and then the princess leaped up onto a chair and began licking her footpads gingerly with obvious displeasure.

Realizing that he was likely to be there for a while, Mika went outside, untied Tam, carried him inside, and placed him beneath his chair where he would draw the least amount of attention. Then, raising his hand, he shook the money pouch in the air, clinking the few remaining coins together. A heartbeat later, the charcoal-smudged waif appeared at his side. Mika ordered food and a skin of wine. The princess sneered.

The food came. Mika ate his fill of sweet marmot meat and a bowl of stewed ground beans and onions. He ate till he could hold no more and then tossed the bones to the waiting wolves. Then he stretched and waited and looked toward the stairs, wondering when Hornsbuck would come back.

"Best be forgettin' them, laddie. You'll not be seein' them agin afore mornin', if then," said a gravelly voice.

Mika turned around and saw a small man dressed in faded blue cotton seated at the table next to him. For a heartbeat, the very briefest of time, Mika thought that the fellow's eyes glowed an eerie shade of carnelian red. Mika started! He leaned forward, but it was gone—the man's eyes were brown.

"Take my word for it," the man said, gesturing with a long-stemmed, white clay pipe. "Our Lotus Blossom has strong urges."

"You mean Hornsbuck and that . . . that . . . creature are, are . . . ?" Too overcome for words, Mika rose to his feet, his hand reaching for his sword, his mind blanching at the horrible thought.

"Best hush, laddie," said the man, laying a hand of caution on Mika's arm as he glanced around to see if any had overheard Mika's comments. "Them as come in Jayne's think highly of Lotus Blossom. She's their champion. It would be unwise to insult her in their hearing. Also, yon nomad could do worse. She's a lot of woman."

Mika fought back a shudder and forced his mind on to other thoughts. "Jayne's, you say. That's the name of this . . . establishment?"

"Aye, finest international drinking parlor in the city. You'll find folks here from all over the known Oerth. I, myself, am from the ocean of Solnor.

"My captain and I, we come to bargain for a load of amber and hornwood. We stopped for a drink." The man's eyes grew cloudy with remembrance. "See there," he said, pointing to a spot behind Mika.

Mika turned his head and saw a large wicker basket positioned beneath a small table. Squinting to focus, he saw that it was filled nearly to the brim with human arms that had been wrenched off at the shoulder. Mika felt the bile rising in his throat, but he fought it down as he stared at the fly-covered basket in helpless fascination.

"My captain accepted the woman's challenge,"

continued the man, not appearing to notice Mika's discomfort, "and now, here I am, stranded. She won all our money, as well as his life. I do odd jobs around the place to earn my keep."

Mika choked down a cup of wine, too overcome to speak.

"Don't mind if I do," said the fellow, pouring himself a cup. "Nyr Baba's the name."

"Forgive me, but your news has shaken me," said Mika, who proceeded to introduce himself and pour another cup of wine as well.

Just about then, the ceiling began to shake, vibrating in a most frightening manner, rumbling like a herd of thunder ox on the rampage, showering the room with an accumulation of dust and debris that set the inhabitants to coughing. Mika shuddered and looked away as Nyr lifted his cup with a sly grin and toasted the unseen lovers.

They drank the remainder of the skin, and then Nyr ordered a second which Mika insisted on sharing with RedTail. Princess Julia continued to hold herself aloof, aside from glaring at Mika with her usual degree of hatred. Late in the evening, she was forced to give up her chair by a patron who ignored her snarls and dumped her unceremoniously onto the sticky floor. Tam snored on, oblivious to all around him, although Mika was pleased to notice that the lump on his head seemed to be subsiding.

Mika and Nyr shared tales of their lives and exploits, both real and imagined. As the hour grew later and the level of wine lower, they sank into confidences and Mika told Nyr the story of his last adventure. To his surprise, the man broke into laughter and collapsed on the table, holding his head and wheezing for breath.

"By the blood of the Great She-Wolf, mother of us all, it's true. I swear it!" sputtered Mika, swaying in his chair. "Look, I'll even show you my finger."

"I believe you, laddie. I believe you," shrieked Nyr, almost helpless with laughter.

"No, you don't," said Mika, reaching for his sword.

"Yes, I do, laddie," said Nyr, wiping his eyes and looking at Mika with sudden compassion. "Indeed I do, for I have heard parts of this story before. Be a good lad, and I'll tell you about it."

Chapter 7

"YOU SAY IT'S A blue-green stone and it belonged to the princess," Nyr gasped, tears running from his eyes as he forced himself upright and wiped his streaming eyes with shaking fingers.

"Aye," said Mika, now almost sober from rage. "What's so funny about that? It's magical, I tell you."

"I know, laddie. I know," said Nyr. "And you've used this stone, right? How many times?"

"Twice," growled Mika. "And it worked fine."

"Unfortunately," said Nyr. He looked at Mika with sympathy. "Did the princess not tell you anything about this stone?"

"I didn't give her much of a chance," said Mika, growing more and more uneasy. He glanced at the female wolf and saw her staring at him steadily, a satisfied gleam in her blue and green eyes.

"Ah, laddie. I hate to be the one to tell you," said Nyr, "but you're in real trouble. My advice is to find a hole and throw the damned stone in it, or best of all, crush it beneath your heel."

"I cannot do that," said Mika, and he felt something twist deep inside at the thought of destroying the stone. To be honest, he had hoped to keep the gem even after returning the princess to her home.

"Then it is already too late," said Nyr. "The stone has seized hold of you."

"Tell me whereof you speak," demanded Mika, reaching across the table to grab Nyr's shirt and pull him half out of his chair. "What is wrong with the stone?"

"There's no need for violence," said Nyr, freeing his shirt from Mika's grasp and seating himself once more. "I will gladly tell you the story, only you may wish that I had never spoken."

Mika glared down. The female wolf sat with her odd-colored eyes fixed on Mika's face, her tongue lolling out of the corner of her mouth in a wicked grin.

"There are two kinds of stones," said Nyr. "One is blue-green, and one is red-purple."

"Yes?" said Mika, frowning as he failed to grasp the significance of the man's statement.

A look of pain filled Nyr's brown eyes. He looked down at his scarred and calloused hands, his wrinkled face drooping with discomfort. "One is a female stone. The other is male," he muttered.

Mika's heart sank in his breast like a stone through water. Even without understanding the full import of Nyr's words, he knew that he was in trouble.

"A man must use only the red stone," said Nyr, drawing the courage to finish the tale. "He may use the blue stone as well, but only if he possesses the red and uses them at the same time. Used separately, they are powerful, used together, they are all but invincible."

"What . . . what happens if a man uses a blue stone by itself?" asked Mika, his mouth almost too dry to form the words.

"Each time he uses it, he becomes more and more female," Nyr said softly.

Mika gulped, remembering how drawn he had been to the cloth in the marketplace; he glanced down at his new finery in horror. "Can the damage be undone?" he asked gruffly, almost afraid to hear the answer.

"Yes," said Nyr. "But it would take a red stone to do it, and such a stone would be difficult to acquire."

"Why so?" asked Mika, determined to have the stone no matter what the cost.

"Because the stones are few in number, coming as they do from the princess's own island, which is small and easy to guard. Such stones are not sold or traded on the open market like other gems."

"No," said Mika in a low tone. "But how is it that you know so much about the stones?" he asked, suddenly suspicious.

"I am a sailor," said Nyr. "I have spent my life upon the water and have heard tales of every ocean and sea.

"I saw one such fellow who was unlucky enough to have successfully stolen a blue stone. Though most womanlike, he was cursed with a male appearance, still sporting a huge beard and mustache. He was quite ugly." Nyr shuddered at the memory.

"He had tried without success to purchase a red

stone. . . . Last I heard, he, uh, she, had fallen in love and married a pirate."

"Why did he not simply throw the thing away?" asked Mika, already knowing the answer.

"The stones seem to call to the soul," said Nyr, "much like the song of a siren as she lures sailors to their deaths. You yourself have said that you could not give yours up."

Mika nodded, for he knew that it was true.

"Come, laddie, 'tis not the end of the world," said Nyr in a kindly voice. "I'm sure you'll think of something. Here, let me buy a new skin. Maybe it will help us think!" And holding up two coins, he summoned the serving boy and they set about their drinking in earnest.

Mika drank so much that night that Jayne's actually began to look good to him. The customers no longer seemed boorish slobs, unfit to groom his wolf. No! Indeed, he thought them to be boon companions, one and all. Fine, intelligent fellows with marvelous gifts for humor and storytelling. In fact, everything each said seemed as though it should be carved in stone for the world to read and admire. He himself was equally witty and amusing and uttered many wise thoughts. The more he drank, the more he thought so.

RedTail agreed with him; that was easy to see by the way the wolf looked at Mika with his marvelous amber eyes. As RedTail's reward for being such an astute judge of character, Mika shared his ale with the wolf, drink for drink. At length, however, RedTail ceased agreeing with Mika. In fact, he ceased agreeing with anyone, for his eyes were closed and his nose was stuck in his cup, wolven snores echoing and rumbling out of the tumbler.

Tam still snored beneath Mika's chair and, as far as Mika could tell through bleary eyes, the lump atop his head had shrunk still further.

Princess Julia, however, still sat a few paces away, staring at Mika with a malicious gleam in her eye as though delighted that he had learned the horrible truth about the gem. Mika's lip lifted in a snarl of his own, and he and the female wolf glared at each other with hatred.

Periodically throughout the long night the ceiling had rumbled and thundered and, at every occasion, the inhabitants of the bar had lifted their cups and cheered. Well into the evening, the walls began to shake and even the floor boards began to bounce, causing tables and chairs to dance across the floor, spilling food and brew.

As patrons clutched their cups and covered their heads against the rain of dust, there was a tremendous bellow that rang through the building.

It was at this moment that a fat merchant dressed in multi-colored silks wobbled over and sat down at Mika's table.

"Fine wolf you have there!" he said as he stared at the princess.

Mika nodded glumly. "Yeah, terrific wolf," he echoed.

"I could use such a wolf," said the merchant, taking care not to stain his silk cuffs in the pools of spilled wine.

"Then go out and get one," said Mika, trying to picture the smarmy fellow squeezing himself down a wolf run into the den. He snickered at the thought.

"There are other ways," said the merchant. "Allow me," he said as he poured Mika a cup of wine from a flask which he drew from a finely tooled leather pouch.

Mika, who was reaching the bottom of his wineskin as well as his coins, had no objections. He downed the wine in one gulp, noticing vaguely that it tasted rather strange and left a bitter taste on the back of his tongue. Just as he started to say something, he felt his head grow numb.

The paralysis crept downward at a rapid rate. As he crumpled forward onto the table, he realized that he had been drugged and wondered if he were going to die. Gripped completely by the paralysis, he could do nothing as he watched the merchant reach down and untie the princess's leash and drag her away. The last thing he heard as his eyes closed were the sounds of snarling and snapping and an enraged curse. Then there was nothing but darkness.

Chapter 8

DAYLIGHT WAS ATTEMPTING to make an indentation on the shadows of the place when Mika felt the earth move. He clutched the table and hung on for dear life. The world shook again, harder this time, rocking his chair from side to side.

"Run, Tam, save yourself!" he hollered as he gripped the edges of the table and closed his eyes more tightly.

"MIKA!" roared the loudest voice in the world. And then Mika knew that he had died and had been called for judging by the Great She Wolf, mother of them all.

"I always tried to be good," he whined. "I didn't do half the things I was blamed for."

"Right," grumbled the voice. "You did more than half, but they couldn't prove the rest."

"Hornsbuck?" Mika said querulously as he turned his head painfully and tried to open his eyes.

"Who did you expect, the Great She-Wolf?" Hornsbuck asked sarcastically.

Mika opened his eyes blearily and saw Hornsbuck standing before him, larger than life and seemingly in full control of his senses. Lotus Blossom hung coyly behind him a few paces.

"Hornsbuck!" Mika cried joyously, more glad than he would have thought possible at seeing his old friend restored to vigor.

"You're repeating yourself, boy," said Hornsbuck as he thumped Mika on the back. "Looks like you've had yourself quite a night. Well, so've I. Methinks we could do with a little something to put in our bellies, then you can fill me in on what's been happening." Hornsbuck turned and put his arm around Lotus Blossom's ample waist, hollered for the servant, and then sat down at the table with the basket.

Mika ordered two rabbits and a marmot, as well as a skin of honeyed-ale, Hornsbuck's favorite, thinking that it would be more than ample as a morning snack. But Hornsbuck had other ideas and requested a whole haunch of ox as well.

"How about a test of strength before we eat?" he said to the woman, a smile of some pleasant remembrances playing about his lips. But even though he smiled, Mika could tell that he was of serious intent; his heart trembled at the thought.

"Oh, Hornsbuck," Lotus Blossom said, her own lips curling with laughter. "I don't think so. It makes me feel bad when I beat you, and you know how you hate it."

"I been practicing since I saw you last," Hornsbuck said with a grin as he flexed a massive bicep. "You won't beat me again."

Mika gaped at him. Hornsbuck beaten in a contest

of strength by a woman? Never would he have thought it possible!

"I'm sure you have, dear," Lotus Blossom said demurely, "but so have I."

"Hah! Afraid to lose. I knew it!" Hornsbuck said with satisfaction. "You know I'm better than you!"

"Well, it's possible, I suppose," said Lotus Blossom, "but I've won an awful lot of trophies since you were last here. Yon basket's almost full. We'll have to dump it soon."

Mika followed her gesture in spite of himself and looked again at the awful basket filled with arms. He felt the gorge rise in his throat and looked away quickly.

Hornsbuck placed his elbow on the table, hand up, and grinned at the woman.

"Oh, all right," she sighed, "if you insist." And she positioned her own massive arm on the table next to Hornsbuck's. They gripped hands.

For a time nothing happened, nothing at all, so evenly were they matched. The two hands and arms were so alike in size and shape. Hornsbuck's was tanned more darkly, owing to his extended exposure to sun and wind, but both were covered with blond hair and freckles, both were bulging with muscle and sinew.

They grinned at each other, teeth gleaming whitely in the dull candlelight, masking their true emotions. They stared intently into each other's eyes. And still the locked hands and arms did not move even the slightest.

The haunch of ox arrived and was placed on Mika's table, along with the marmot and rabbits.

Mika settled back with a mug of honeyed-ale to nurse his throbbing head and await the outcome of the contest.

The late afternoon sun was trying its tentative best to enter the doorway before either hand moved. Mika had long since grown bored with the non-event and sprawled in the chair, the jar of honeyed-ale considerably diminished. RedTail had helped himself to a rabbit and consumed it quietly. Tam still snored beneath the chair, slumbering peacefully. Mika looked around for the princess but did not see her. Her absence troubled him vaguely, but his head ached too much to think very hard. He tried to tell himself that she hated him far too much to leave him for long.

The tavern had filled slowly during the long afternoon as word spread about the contest. The room was nearly full, as nomads, short stocky dwarves with enormous beards and rings in their ears, sharp-eyed merchants, and ordinary hangers-on—the dregs of society who comprised the tavern's steady customers—ringed the table wagering loudly. Much to Mika's dismay, the odds were greatly stacked against Hornsbuck.

Every grimace and frown, every small waver of a fist caused money to change hands. Lotus Blossom and Hornsbuck were no longer smiling. Hard looks of fierce concentration turned their faces into harsh masks. There was no trace of their previous softer expressions.

Their arms were rock-hard, the muscles seemingly carved from marble. Their fingers were white and bloodless, so tightly were they gripped. The very air seemed to quiver around them, and the table vibrated visibly.

Then, incredibly, the locked limbs moved! The crowd gasped and surged closer. Yes! The arms were moving, as Hornsbuck forced Lotus Blossom's arm toward the table!

Whispers flew like angry hornets, and money changed hands rapidly with soft clinks. Then, almost imperceptibly, Lotus Blossom forced Hornsbuck's hand upright, and as it paused at the zenith, began pushing it downward.

Eyes bulged from their sockets; Lotus Blossom's blue eyes were fringed with thick, white lashes and Hornsbuck's bright green eyes blinked back the sweat that trickled through his bushy eyebrows.

Teeth were bared in snarling grimaces, and their faces gleamed with beads of moisture. Their breath rasped harsh in their throats as they grunted and snorted, trying to lever a better position.

The two wavered back and forth for many long hours, first one taking the advantage, then the other. Mika began to doubt that either would ever win. He began to picture them dying, still locked in position, atrophied into withered caricatures of themselves. He heaved an ale-scented sigh and rearranged himself on the hard, uncomfortable chair for the hundredth time.

Then, all at once it ended. Growling like a rabid animal, Lotus Blossom slammed Hornsbuck's hand down on the table, pinning it firmly to the wood. Quicker than a snake strike, Lotus Blossom wrenched Hornsbuck's arm, forcing it back toward his body and out. Hornsbuck was unprepared for the maneuver and choked back a cry of pain.

Mika leaped to his feet and struggled to free his sword from the sheath between his shoulder blades, his actions somewhat slower than usual due to the amount of ale he had imbibed and the unfamiliar feel of the metal gauntlet. He cursed his laxness, seeing in an instant how easy it would be for the woman to rip Hornsbuck's arm from its socket and add it to her grisly collection.

Just as Mika's sword finally cleared the sheath, the crowd roared its approval, for Lotus Blossom had released Hornsbuck's hand. For a moment, they just stared at each other, heaving great gasps. Abruptly Hornsbuck's face relaxed and he bellowed out a mighty laugh.

"By the gods, you did it again!" he roared, gathering the woman to his leathery chest and looking into her eyes with fondness. She in turn wrapped her arms around his great girth and hugged him back, an embrace that would have killed a grizzly. "You almost had me there," she roared in return, thumping him on the back.

"Honestly?" growled Hornsbuck, peering at her closely.

"Well, no, but I thought I would say so to make you feel better," said Lotus Blossom, blushing at being caught by the falsehood. "But you lasted longer than anyone, 'cepting that Solnorian Sea baron. But I got him in the end. That's his arm there, the one with the maggots."

Ignoring Mika's grimace of disgust and the cries of the crowd, the two combatants sat down at the table once more. Lotus Blossom accepted a heavy pouch placed on the table by the proprietor of the tavern. Mika guessed that she received a portion of all money spent on food and liquors during such contests.

Lotus Blossom dropped the pouch down the front of her tunic without even counting the coins and then looked around as though seeing the place for the first time. Spotting the haunch of ox on Mika's table, she seized it and placed it in front of her. Touching it with a finger, she frowned.

"This meat be cold," she said, perhaps forgetting that it had been ordered more than half a day earlier. Seemingly out of nowhere, the ragged youth instantly appeared at her side and removed the offensive cut of meat. He returned almost immediately bearing a new haunch that sizzled and popped with heat. Following a hand signal from the woman, the youth brought a second for Hornsbuck. Bowls of ground beans, stewed fruits, steamed whole onions sprinkled with garlic, and a platter of marmots stuffed with wild mushrooms soon filled the table. An immense skin of burgundy, unwatered, was placed beside each plate.

Without speaking, the combatants fell to eating and did not stop until every last scrap of food had been consumed. Their tunics bulged, and their hands and faces were shiny with grease. At last, Lotus Blossom pushed herself back from the table and uttered a deep, rumbling belch. Putting his hands to his midriff, Hornsbuck echoed the thunderous sound.

Mika could do naught but drink and watch them until he was nearly green with discomfort. But it didn't matter, for they paid him no mind. It was as though he had ceased to exist.

Rising together at some unheard signal, Hornsbuck and Lotus Blossom wrapped their arms around each other's waists and began to wend their way toward the staircase again.

"Hornsbuck, wait!" Mika cried, leaping to his feet. "Don't leave, there are things we must discuss!" For a moment it seemed that Hornsbuck might ignore him, intent on lust rather than duty, but at last he turned. Making his way back to the table, he and Lotus Blossom glowered down at him. "Well?" he said in a forbidding manner.

Mika's heart sank. Try as he might to think of the right words, they did not rise to his tongue. Speechless, yet knowing that he had to do something to prevent Hornsbuck from leaving, Mika held up his gauntlet and took off the glove.

Hornsbuck and Lotus Blossom stared at his hand in absolute horror, their eyes wide, their faces pale. Slowly, without a word, they sat down at the table. Mika looked down at the hand, his own eyes drawn to it, even though he dreaded the sight. There . . . there where once there had been one, were now *two* scaly, green demon fingers!

Chapter 9

MIKA THOUGHT that he might throw up. He clutched his wrist and rose half out of his chair. He stared at his hand, blinking his eyes rapidly, hoping that there was some mistake, that the finger would go away if only he wished hard enough. But the finger remained.

To be more specific, it was his thumb. It was, if possible, even more hideous than the pointer finger, for it was wider, more spatulate than a thumb, and the talon four times thicker than a fingernail, ridged and lumpy and dull yellow in color. The talon curved back over the tip of the thumb and ended in a sharp, vicious edge.

"Mika, tell me what has happened," Hornsbuck said, severely shaken by the sight of Mika's deformity.

Mika told his tale in a dull monotone, scarcely able to take his eyes off his hand, picking up the story at the point where Hornsbuck had lost his wits to the umber hulk and finishing with their presence at the tavern.

"Then I owe my life to you," Hornsbuck said when Mika was finished. "I would not be here with Lotus Blossom now, were it not for you."

Mika said nothing, staring at the awful thumb. In truth, he hadn't even considered the fact that he had saved Hornsbuck's life. It just never occurred to him to leave Hornsbuck behind. RedTail had led them out of the confusing labyrinth of underground caverns, and the wolf would never have left Hornsbuck's side. And they could not have found their way out of the tunnels without the wolf, so Hornsbuck's presence had been mandatory. But it would have taken more energy than Mika had to explain matters, so he said nothing.

"I'm in your debt, Mika," Hornsbuck continued. "I'll never forget what you've done."

Depressed as Mika was, the huge warrior's words cut through the fog that gripped his mind. One could do worse than to have Hornsbuck in one's debt. Mika slipped the gauntlet back on his hand, then sat up and paid attention.

"I confess, I used to think you were all talk and little action," said Hornsbuck, "but this has proven me wrong. It will be hard to repay you, lad, but it's a matter of honor now.

"Mika, we're going to Exag, just like that demon told you to, and we're going to find the king and bring him his daughter," Hornsbuck continued. He leaned across the table to grip Mika's arm painfully and look into his eyes with an earnest expression. "And somehow, I don't care how dangerous it is, how perilous, or at what risk, we're going to face that demon and get your hand back! You can count on me, Mika. I promise you, I won't change my mind!"

Mika sat up straight in his seat at Hornsbuck's words, the very center of his being riveted to what the nomad was proposing. Although going to Exag might be unavoidable and finding the king might be necessary, Mika had absolutely no desire whatsoever to face down the demon—not even to get his hand back!

"No, Hornsbuck, I . . . I couldn't let you do that," he stammered. "This is my problem."

"No, Mika. It's *our* problem—yours and mine," Hornsbuck said firmly. "I'll not let you do this alone. After all, we're Wolf Nomads, comrades in arms, brothers in spirit. We're not afraid of anything. No demon can tell *us* what to do. No threat, no fight, no torture will ever stop us. Not even if they rip us limb from limb—not even then. Right, Mika?" Hornsbuck boomed, his eyes shining with excitement. He slammed Mika on the shoulder, nearly felling him with the force of his enthusiasm.

"Uh, I'm not so sure about the torture part and being ripped limb from limb. . . ." Mika ventured.

"Ha, ha, ha! There was a time that I might have believed you meant that, Mika. And I'd have despised you for it. Now I see that it's just a ruse to put people off your true nature. Clever lad! Well, it certainly worked. I never even suspected that you had it in you!" Hornsbuck thumped Mika again, a blow that knocked the turban down over his eyes and nearly threw him from his chair.

"You've left something out," said Lotus Blossom, who had been unusually silent. "I'll be going with you. Let you out of my sight for just a moment and you get all confused and strange. Had to work right hard to straighten you out again, I did. I'll go with this time to keep my eye on you and save myself some work in the long run."

"No, Lotus Blossom, I couldn't let you do that," Hornsbuck said solemnly. "This is man's work; it's no place for a woman!"

Mika gawked at Hornsbuck in total disbelief. Was he a lunatic? Lotus Blossom was twice the man Mika was! Mika wished he could let Lotus Blossom go in his stead, but he could think of no way to suggest it. When trouble starts, maybe I can just find a convenient hole and let the two of them take care of it, Mika thought to himself. In any event, Lotus Blossom would certainly be a fine addition to the party.

"Uh, Hornsbuck, I think that maybe you should let Lotus Blossom go with us," Mika said persuasively. "If there's any trouble, I'm sure that you and I can handle it, and this way we can enjoy the pleasure of the lady's company as well."

Hornsbuck glowered at Mika. But with Mika on her side, Lotus Blossom soon reduced Hornsbuck's arguments to feeble rumbles, and in the end, he acquiesced.

"Well, what did you do to earn this second finger?" asked Hornsbuck, anxious to change the subject. "And where's the princess? I haven't seen her around anywhere."

"I don't know what I did," answered Mika. "And I don't know where the princess is, either. She's probably lurking around here somewhere, thinking of ways to kill me."

As Mika sat there, ruminating over the proposed expedition, he slowly realized that it had been some time since he had seen the princess. When had he seen her last? Some time during the night. Right before that fellow shared his flask. The flask that left such an odd taste in his mouth. Right before he fell asleep . . . or was drugged! The thought leaped into his mind, and instantly he understood all.

"The princess has been stolen!" he gasped, quickly filling the massive pair in on the events of the evening and passing along his suspicions.

"The pig-dog was too much of a coward to find his own wolf, so he stole the princess instead," snarled Lotus Blossom. "We'll make him pay for it. We'll cut off his—"

"No time for that!" Mika interrupted. "We've got to find her before this finger business spreads any further!"

"Horse!" growled Hornsbuck. "Got to find another horse first. Then we'll find the princess."

"A horse!" wailed Mika. "No, we've got to find the princess, or I'll be covered with green scales from head to foot!"

"Mika, I can't do anything without a horse!" Hornsbuck explained patiently. "One just isn't enough for all of us. First we find another horse, then we find the princess, then we ride for Exag. Calm down, lad, no need to pretend you're afraid. You forget, I know the truth now. Come along with me. Lotus Blossom, pack!"

Rising from the table, Hornsbuck strode out of the tavern with RedTail and Mika trotting at his heels. Tam still slumbered beneath the table and as Mika hurried out of the establishment, he realized that Tam comprised the least of his worries; the tavern was scarcely likely to choose this late date to begin sweeping the floor.

"It has to be a big horse," muttered Hornsbuck as he strode through the streets. Mika hurried along behind him, dragging the roan by its reins.

"I'm sure we can find the right horse if you have the coins to buy it," he said, hoping that Hornsbuck would not notice that his purse was gone or that Mika was attired in new finery.

"I have coins," said Hornsbuck, hefting the purse that Mika had last seen given to Lotus Blossom.

They found the horse pens just as the sun was streaking the darkening sky with layers of crimson.

The pens were made of bronzewood, a strong and resilient hardwood found only in the Burneal Forest. Mika knew that the wood was all but unbreakable and judged its use costly but wise, for the pens were filled with a seething, swirling mass of wild-eyed horses.

"As nice a group of horses as you'll ever see," said a voice at his elbow.

Mika looked down and saw a small man standing beside him. The fellow barely came to the roan's stirrup. Twisted and bent, he looked as though he had been badly stepped on and had healed poorly. Given his profession, such a scenario did not seem unlikely. One arm was withered and emaciated, and the entire left side of his face, from temple to jaw, was sunken and misshapen and covered with a mass of ugly purple scar tissue. The eye—what remained of it—was milky-blue and unseeing.

"Ugly creatures, every one. Not good for anything but wolf meat," replied Mika as he turned and made as though to leave, thus officially opening the bargaining. "My friend here is interested in a horse, not carrion fodder."

The bent man quickly took himself off to Hornsbuck's side, having thus identified the buyer. He sized the big nomad up with a shrewd eye. Placing his hand on Hornsbuck's arm, he attempted to draw him closer to the pen.

"Look you, sir. I can tell that one such as yourself is a good and knowledgeable judge of horseflesh," the man said smoothly. "A rough and hardy fellow like you has no use for a soft city horse, pampered and petted by all who pass."

"True, true," said Hornsbuck, stroking his beard and standing firm.

"These horses may look a bit rough around the edges, I admit, but take another look, good sir. They are tough in nature, and wild and brave in spirit— fitting mounts for a warrior such as yourself."

"Uh, Hornsbuck . . ." muttered Mika, suddenly worried that the big nomad might actually fall for the glib talk of the merchant.

"Let the fellow speak, Mika," said Hornsbuck. "He seems a good judge of character."

Mika groaned inwardly as the merchant seized the opportunity and rushed in for the kill.

"These horses, these sturdy beasts are not ordinary horses. . . ."

"You can say that again," mumbled Mika as he leaned on the rails and looked at the sorry pack of horses wheeling within.

"They were captured deep in the Howling Hills, and their spirits are wild and untamed . . . fighters, every one, horses fit for a noble warrior such as yourself. Never could they be ridden by a city man."

"Or anyone else," muttered Mika. "Hornsbuck, what say we look further?"

"Let me show you the best of them," the man said hurriedly, placing his hand on the large man's elbow. Hornsbuck allowed himself to be drawn away.

Mika sighed and clucked to the roan, following after the horse-seller. The little man led them to a second pen; it held only one horse—the nastiest, meanest, ugliest stallion Mika had ever seen.

Standing at least seventeen hands high, the horse was a dull, mottled brown with a short, stiff, spikey black mane and brushlike tail. Its body, while massive and powerful, was covered with a variety of scars. Its eyes were black and ringed with white, a sign that Mika had learned to recognize as denoting madness in an animal. Its large, square, yellow teeth were bared over its gums as the men approached the pen. And even though it was securely snubbed to a thick post, it pawed the ground and strained to reach them.

"Now, this is not a horse I would show to just anyone," said the man. "It will take a very special sort to recognize this one's potential."

"Yes, a complete and total fool, that's the only sort who would be dumb enough to buy this horse. It's a killer, Hornsbuck!" said Mika.

To his horror he heard Hornsbuck say, "How much be you asking for this animal?"

Twilight fell as Mika sat with his head buried in his hands and Hornsbuck and the horse dealer finalized their bargain. Hornsbuck took possession of the horse and a complete set of heavy leather tack.

The stallion tensed as Hornsbuck untied the rope from the post. As soon as Hornsbuck flung the heavy saddle across the horse's back, it immediately sucked in air, inflating its abdomen to prevent the tightening of the girth. But Hornsbuck was familiar with that particular trick; a hard knee to the horse's stomach resulted in an explosive outburst of air and a quick cinch of the girth.

The ugly, hammer-headed creature gathered himself to buck as Hornsbuck stepped foot in the stirrup and swung into the saddle. But the nomad was no fool. As soon as he was seated, he clenched his knees together and squeezed.

Taken by surprise, the horse drew in a sharp breath. Immediately Hornsbuck tightened his massive thighs, compressing the horse's lungs still further, not allowing it to draw breath.

Unable to get air, the horse began to panic. It wheezed and sucked in vain, and every time it managed to take in a breath, Hornsbuck clamped down more tightly, the muscles in his massive thighs standing out like ridges of rock.

The horse was soon staggering about drunkenly, its legs trembling and shaking. Mika stared in pop-eyed fascination, certain the horse would soon fall to the ground and die. Even the dealer had stopped counting his grushniks and was gaping in stupified amazement.

Then, just as it seemed that the horse would surely

expire, its face contorted in an awful grimace of pain and its eyes nearly popping from its skull, Hornsbuck relaxed his hold on the animal's chest.

The horse lowered its head and took in great, wheezing, shuddering breaths. And when, after a time, Hornsbuck gently shook the reins, tapping them lightly on the stallion's neck, it broke into a trot instantly, with not a sign of trouble.

"Works every time," Hornsbuck said with a grin as he rode past the astounded pair. "And now, Mika, unless you have anything else to do, it's time to go after your wayward princess."

Chapter 10

"WHERE TO, NOW?" asked Mika, anxious to retrieve the princess and be on their way before the demon changed any more of him.

"Patience, patience," Hornsbuck cautioned with a wide grin.

They rode back to the tavern and found Lotus Blossom, mounted and waiting, with her gear packed efficiently on the back of her black- and white-speckled stallion. To Mika's surprise, Tam sat quietly at the horse's feet, looking almost normal. He wagged his tail happily at the sight of Mika, and his eyes grew bright as Mika approached.

"Ready, I see," rumbled Hornsbuck.

"Aye," replied Lotus Blossom, unable to meet Hornsbuck's gaze, as though she were embarrassed about something. "But there is a matter we needs discuss."

"Well, speak up, little woman," Hornsbuck said expansively. "What is it, some extra trinket you wish to take with us?"

"Nay, you ninny," growled Lotus Blossom, swinging around to glare at Hornsbuck. "And stow that 'little woman' business, or I'll shove your arm down your throat. The problem is bigger than a trinket. The stupid guard forbade me to leave town. I will go as I choose, but I do not wish harm to come to you and the boy, here."

Mika was stung at being called a boy, but not enough to challenge her.

"What did you do to deserve town quarantine?" asked Hornsbuck, seemingly no more than mildly curious.

"Oh, some little complaint about gambling with the caravans," said Lotus Blossom, waving her hand about vaguely. "Nothing of any importance."

"Cheating, no doubt," chuckled Hornsbuck. "Well, my plan will take care of that. Not to worry."

He would answer none of their questions, but bade them follow him. They rode toward the second gate, the one that led directly out onto the plains.

The gate had been built no larger than the largest of caravan wagons so as to prevent the entry of unwelcome visitors, as well as enabling it to be guarded by a minimum of two men. It was commonly known as Danger Gate, in reference to more wicked times when caravans had often been forced to race for the city, pursued by all sorts of dangerous armies of monsters and half-human villains. But those days were long past, and a tenuous peace of sorts now existed across the northern hemisphere of Greyhawk.

Hornsbuck led them to the gate, stopping just short of it in a corner of a building passed by the many groups of travelers who left the city each day.

Hornsbuck turned his back to the other travelers and thrust his thick hand into the leather pouch that hung from a thong around his neck and contained his most important personal possessions. His eyes twinkled mischievously as he withdrew his hand from the pouch and held up what appeared to be a slender, silver wand smaller than his smallest finger. Mika was even more confused when Hornsbuck climbed down from the saddle, stuffed RedTail's ears with bits of cloth, and told Mika to do the same to Tam. The wolves pawed at their ears, but a gruff snap on their muzzles halted their activities.

Satisfied, Hornsbuck climbed back into the saddle, lifted the silver wand to his lips, and blew into it so hard that his cheeks puffed out like a marmot's cheek pouches stuffed for winter. But strangely, even though Tam and RedTail's ears pricked, Mika heard no sound. None at all.

"What are you doing? What is that thing?" Mika asked, not liking the fact that he did not understand what was happening. Hornsbuck did not reply, but merely lifted the wand and prepared to blow again. Lotus Blossom began to laugh. It was obvious that somehow she understood. Mika sat atop his horse and felt stupid.

Suddenly, something very odd began to happen. All the wolves in the immediate vicinity started to howl. Then they began running in circles, and some sat down and pawed at their ears before sitting up and howling again.

Hornsbuck continued to blow the wand. With belated comprehension, Mika now recognized it as a whistle of the sort used to call in the wolves. Such a whistle was used but seldom—to signal the wolves after they had been loosed on some hapless prey, or at the great convocation of the clans when the wolves were likely to join in one vast pack and set off on a hunt of their own. Yet such whistles were rare, guarded closely by high chiefs who never allowed them to fall into other hands lest they be used irresponsibly. Such as now.

By some trick of his hand, Hornsbuck was directing the sound of the whistle so that it appeared to be coming from the gate itself. The two guards stationed beside the carved doors were totally unprepared for such a happening and didn't know what to do. They were ringed by at least twenty howling wolves whose numbers were increasing with each passing heartbeat.

The guards, staunch Wolf Nomads who had been selected for their important posts by dint of exemplary behavior, were overwhelmed by the sheer number of frantic wolves that answered the imperious, silent call as it continued to ring in their ears, asking, demanding, and finally, commanding their presence.

The owners of the wolves, townsmen and outlanders alike, were bewildered by the wolves' behavior, tugging and pulling and importuning the animals from the edges of the seething pack. But the wolves could hear nothing but the whistle and ignored the men who had been their soul companions from birth as though now they were unknown strangers.

Hornsbuck continued to blow the whistle, his fat cheeks turning bright red and the veins at his temples standing out prominently. Mika grinned widely as he realized the beauty of Hornsbuck's plan.

By now, wolves were pouring out doorways, leaping out of windows, cascading out of side streets, and filling the main road from wall to wall. Black wolves and red wolves, brown wolves and gray wolves, tan wolves and white wolves, large wolves and small wolves and every size in between, were all howling and baying madly, all headed in the direction of the gate.

Traffic came to a standstill, and people leaped for the safety of buildings as it quickly became obvious that anyone or anything that stood in the wolves' path was likely to be run down.

The torrent of wolves arrived at the gate, adding their mass to those already clustered around the beleaguered guards. One of the guards, realizing that it would be all too easy to die an ignominious death beneath the blanket of wolves, panicked and did exactly what Hornsbuck had hoped for—he lifted the bar, which had until now remained shut, and opened the gates.

As the river of wolves poured past them, following the elusive whistle, Mika caught sight of the Princess Julia running neck and neck with a large, white, male wolf. Mika signaled to Hornsbuck and Lotus Blossom, and the three of them, accompanied by their own wolves—no doubt the only ones in town able to resist the persistent call—pressed into the thick of the crazed animals and rode out of the city.

Outside the gates, wolves milled in an aimless mass. Some still howled, even though Hornsbuck had ceased blowing the whistle. Others bayed for the sheer enjoyment of it. Still others sat up, and noting that they were outside the gates, free of human constraint, began to look about with interest.

As Mika edged next to the princess and slipped a rawhide thong around her neck, some of the wolves began to run. They started to bay, a deep, wild sound of the hunt. Instantly, all of the other wolves formed into one vast pack and followed their lead. The last Mika saw of them, they were all heading out into the open prairie, every last wolf of Eru-Tovar. Their owners stood watching them go, helpless to stop them. The wolves would return, but only when the frenzy left them and they were good and ready.

Hornsbuck clucked in concern and shook his massive head in pity as they slowly trotted past the dumbfounded nomads. Sternly elbowing the chuckling Lotus Blossom in the ribs, he led his party out onto the prairie.

The princess seemed subdued and followed Mika, head held low without any indication of resistance. Mika noted with interest that the front of her creamy bib was stained with what appeared to be blood. He grinned to himself, more than a little certain that the blood was not hers; the man who had stolen her would think twice before daring such a deed again.

The day passed without incident. They rode due east until the sun at their backs burned red, an enormous globe at the edge of the horizon, tinting the entire sky a soft, glowing pink. Flocks of rooks tumbled and cawed in the twilight as they made their way toward their nightly roost. Swallows and tiny bats appeared, wheeling and spiraling as they dined on airborne insects. And the wind blew cool and steady from the north, carrying with it the faint scent of pine as the party stopped for the evening and made camp.

"We'll be back in the forest in two, maybe three, days, if the gods be with us," said Mika, wondering when Hornsbuck was going to turn north.

"Appease the gods, but put your faith in man," said Hornsbuck as he built a small circle of rocks and filled it with lumps of charcoal taken from one of his vast packs.

"Who said that?" asked Mika, not recognizing the saying.

"I did," said Hornsbuck. "Just now. Now stop your blathering, and go see if you can find us something to eat."

"But we have supplies," protested Mika, gesturing toward Lotus Blossom, who had just taken a strip of dried meat out of her pouch and was gnawing on it with her big, white teeth.

"A wise man lives off the land and saves his supplies for when he really needs them," Hornsbuck said, glowering at Mika, his back to Lotus Blossom.

"All right, all right," said Mika, holding up his hands and backing off. Taking his bow and arrows from the back of his roan, he whistled for Tam, who had traveled all day without complaint, and walked out onto the darkening plain.

The night closed around them as soon as they left the circle of the tiny fire. Mika stood for a moment and let his eyes adjust. Tam lifted his muzzle and inhaled deeply, allowing the cool, night air to linger on his tongue and nostrils, divining the messages that it carried. He turned briefly and gave Mika a look that said "follow," and then he was off.

Mika trotted effortlessly in Tam's footsteps, the

wolf always within sight, his tail held high and curved above his back. Tam followed the thread of scent on the air for a time and then put his nose to the ground. Snuffling loudly, he followed the invisible trail.

Must be a stag, thought Mika, who had seen no game that day other than a herd of antelope too far distant to chase, and numerous rabbits who were careful to stay out of bow range. His mouth watered at the thought of fresh meat sizzling over the fire.

Then he heard it, a soft call, endearing and yet plaintive, sweet and utterly melancholy. It was impossible to resist. Mika could not imagine what had made the sound; he had never heard anything like it in his life. He turned in the direction from which it had come, toward the stream.

Tam stood in his path, blocking the way and growling. His ears were pasted flat against his head, and his dewlaps were raised, exposing black gums. His incisors gleamed bright in the darkness, and his eyes were mere slits of reflective black light.

Mika took note of Tam's actions, and at any other time he would have been warned, fearful of some imminent danger. But somehow it didn't matter this time—the seductive beckoning drew him on. He was powerless to resist. Tam blocked his way, but Mika rebuked him sharply and pushed past him.

Before him, on the edge of the stream, stood an immense dead tree. Perched on one of the lower branches was a dark figure, its features impossible to determine in the dim light.

The thing uttered its mournful cry again. Mika put one foot in front of the other until he stood at the base of the tree. Tam barked and barked again, warning Mika, yet Mika paid him no heed.

Mika looked up into the branches of the tree. A foul stench filled his nostrils, and his bemused eyes saw a large figure squatting above him. The creature clung to the branch with four long, wicked talons. Its lower half was feathered, but its upper torso had the form of a woman. The creature's eyes gleamed down at Mika, filled with hatred and black, demonic evil.

A harpy! Mika's mind struggled to free itself from the hypnotic grip of the horrible creature, knowing that harpies lured men in with their song and then killed them, feasting on the flesh and feeding it to their young. Mika knew that he must fight or die, but the harpy sang on and he stood transfixed, unable to break the spell.

The harpy opened her broad wings and jumped down to the lowest branch, which swayed beneath her weight. The putrid smell of decayed carrion washed over Mika, gagging him, but still he did not move. The harpy leaned forward, her two human arms reaching for him, her milk-gorged, pendulous breasts swaying in front of his face.

Spittle drooled from the harpy's mouth, and her brittle, black hair stood up around her head in an awful aura, framing the hideous face and the long, sharp teeth that would soon be feasting on his flesh.

Mika stared upward, his fog-filled mind taking in each dreadful feature. Tam gave up barking; seizing the end of Mika's cloak in his teeth, the wolf pulled backward. But Mika was unmoving, and the cloak came free. Tam tumbled backward, caught in its folds.

The harpy's fingers caressed Mika's face as she

crooned her sad song. Even in his bemusement, Mika noticed that the harpy's cheeks were stained with tears and he realized that her grief-stricken song had not been for his benefit. But accident or not, it would not prevent him from being killed.

Mika was wondering if she would rip his face off or just throttle him, when suddenly, a great force slammed against the back of his knees and he plunged forward, striking his head on the tree.

"Great Mother!" he cursed as his head banged painfully into the dense wood. He covered his ears, shutting out the din that broke out beside him. He turned and saw the princess standing next to Tam, her blue and green eyes glittering in the dim light. Both of them were barking shrilly and flinging their front paws against the tree trunk as though they meant to climb it.

Mika looked up and saw the harpy. The life-threatening danger of his situation truly sank in for the first time; he quickly ripped off an edge of his tunic and stuffed it in his ears, preventing himself from hearing the hypnotic song. He glanced at the princess. She had saved him, and he wondered why.

He drew his sword, thinking to kill the harpy before she could attack. To his great surprise, she made no attempt to do so, but merely sat looking down at him with empty eyes, her arms hanging limp at her sides. Tears streamed down her cheeks and dripped slowly onto her swollen breasts.

Mika cocked his head to one side, wondering if this was some trick. But the harpy made no move, as though she did not care about her fate. Grief seemed to emanate from her in waves.

Almost without meaning to, Mika performed a mind-melding spell, adding a charm spell for good measure, and he merged his subconscious with the harpy, whom he knew could speak no language other than her own.

There was the familiar dizziness, and then his mind was filled with grief, a heavy, overwhelming sense of sadness and loss such as he had experienced upon the death of his family. He all but staggered beneath the weight of it.

What had caused this terrible feeling? he wondered . . . and then he knew. A picture formed in his mind's eye of a small, prickly creature, scarcely more than an infant, its feathers barely beginning to emerge. Naked and helpless. Warm waves of love bathed his mind and washed over the mental picture of the small one. But they were abruptly replaced by an aching sense of loss and desolation.

Mika saw an empty aerie, broken eggshells, and a trampled nest. He felt rage rise in his breast and hatred choke his breathing. He had the vague remembrance of a long, futile search which led to the emptiness and depression that now filled the harpy's mind.

Mika sensed that death was near and felt that the harpy welcomed it. With a shock, he realized that he had been chosen to end her pain.

Almost unbidden, another picture flashed into his mind of a small, almost featherless creature, though this one was in a cage in the marketplace of Eru-Tovar. A lightning bolt seared his mind, and conflicting emotions—rage, hope, hatred, joy, and a mindless desire to kill—beat back and forth in his skull. Mika put his hands to his head to still the rampaging thoughts. He staggered back, buffeted by powerful winds, and then slowly his mind cleared.

The wolves still clamored at his side, barking at the dark sky, almost ravening with frustration. Mika looked into the tree. The harpy was gone. He spotted her in the sky, her powerful wings bearing her to Eru-Tovar. He thought about the animal seller briefly, then erased the man from his mind, knowing without the slightest feeling of guilt, that he would soon be dead.

Harpies were universally hated and despised. Never had he heard a good word spoken in their behalf, but even now, as he trudged back to camp empty-handed, he found no need to apologize for his actions. The harpy's grief had touched him deeply, and he entertained the thought briefly that perhaps the harpy had as much right to life as he did. Mika glanced around him as though fearing that somehow, someone might have heard the thought. Seeing only Tam and the princess, he realized that he owed Julia his life.

More than a little uncomfortable, he dropped to one knee before her. "Thanks," he said in a low voice. She stared at him for a brief moment, her green and blue eyes glittering coldly, and then she strode past him, leaving him kneeling on the ground, feeling foolish. Cursing her, he rose and strode angrily back to camp.

"What luck?" asked Hornsbuck as Mika entered camp.

"None," said Mika, carefully putting his bow and arrows away, his gaze fixed on three stakes of skewered meat that were browning at the edge of the embers. "Nothing at all."

"No matter," grunted Hornsbuck. "Lotus Blossom shot two rabbits down at the stream when we went for water, and I flushed a partridge on my way back to camp. They'll be ready soon."

They shared the meat with the wolves as well as the flat disks of tough bread that Hornsbuck had laid out to bake on rocks scattered in the embers. Hornsbuck, Lotus Blossom, and Mika each drank a mug of hot honeyed-ale. Grunting good night, Hornsbuck and Lotus Blossom rolled themselves into Hornsbuck's voluminous cloak and fell asleep instantly, their whistling, groaning snores enough to bring a bear out of hibernation.

Mika carried his own bedroll away from camp, out of the immediate range of the snoring cacaphony, and then wrapping himself in his own cloak, he lay down on the cold, hard ground.

Tam circled several times and curled up at Mika's feet. The princess waited a few moments, as though deciding what to do, the rawhide thong dangling from her neck; she circled as well, finally settling apart from both Mika and Tam.

Mika stared up at the dark sky, arms locked beneath his head, searching out each of the bright pin-pricks of white light and wondering what mysteries they concealed.

He thought about his life and those he had loved. He thought about his strange encounter with the harpy, remembering her pain, wondering if all creatures shared the same emotions as humans.

He had always imagined humans to be the only truly feeling creatures on Oerth, but his limited experiments—polymorphing himself into a wolf and mind-melding with the harpy—had shaken that belief. What if it were true that all creatures were capable of such feelings? The mere thought was boggling. It would mean that humans had no clear rights of superiority or existence, no real right to subjugate everything else beneath their will. Mika's mind reeled, then steadied.

"It must be the drink," he said aloud, reassuring himself. Dismissing the bizarre thoughts from his mind, he shrugged deeper into the cloak, turned over, and was soon asleep.

The princess watched the sleeping human a little longer, her own thoughts a muddle of conflicting emotions. Why had she not allowed the harpy to kill the man whose death she sought? Unwilling to acknowledge the tiny flicker of liking for Mika that had begun to creep unbidden into her mind, she told herself that he would die, but at a time and in a manner of her own choosing—and only after he had returned her to her human form. After a time, Princess Julia closed her eyes and slept as well.

Chapter 11

THEY WERE OFF AT DAWN, munching hard disks of flat bread, twists of salty cheese, and a handful of galda seeds dug out of the leather saddlebags.

The horses, refreshed by the cold, clear water of the stream and the lush grass that grew on its banks, were filled with energy and strained at the reins, begging for speed.

Hornsbuck, his green eyes sparkling, looked at Mika and grinned. "Hheeaa!" he yelled, cutting his horse's flanks with the reins. The stallion lunged forward, his square, ugly head and neck stretched out before him, his forelegs reaching, grabbing, pounding the stony earth beneath them, sprinting away with great strides.

Lotus Blossom followed him instantly, her huge horse thundering into the lead within a few strides.

Mika's own steed twitched and trembled between his thighs. Suddenly, the roan bunched itself and sprang forward, seizing the bit between its teeth and taking control.

Taken by surprise, Mika was nearly jerked out of the saddle by the animal's burst of speed. He dropped the reins, now useless, and wrapped his arms around the roan's neck. The wind whipped around his head, bringing tears to his eyes. Tam and RedTail wheeled, thinking themselves pursued by some unsensed danger. Seeing nothing, they turned and raced after the horses; after a moment's hesitation, the princess followed.

Manes streaming, hair blowing, tails outstretched, horses, humans, and wolves streaked across the plains, hearts pounding, blood racing, muscles stretching in a glorious outburst of effort.

Hornsbuck roared exuberantly and beat on his stallion's flanks with the reins, urging him on to still greater speeds. Lotus Blossom screamed spiritedly, her pigtails flying, her horse still in the lead. Mika, entering into the spirit of the race, clucked into the roan's ear. The horse answered by plunging ahead, his great legs grabbing the earth and spitting it out beneath his hooves, leaving the rough gallop and entering the high, smooth, floating grace of the canter.

They drew up alongside Hornsbuck, paralleled him for a heartbeat, and then passed him by as though he were standing still. The stallion fought to overtake them but, burdened by Hornsbuck's greater weight, it proved an impossible task. Finally, the hooves of his horse beating a staccato rhythm, Mika drew abreast of Lotus Blossom and, despite her greatest efforts, passed her as well. Soon the pace slackened and then, with much blowing and snorting, the horses slowed and came to a halt.

"Cleared the cobwebs out of your skull, eh?" cried Hornsbuck. "Blew the stink of the city off us as well. By the Great She-Wolf, it's good to be back on the open plains!"

The sun was shining brightly, touching every plant, every blade of grass, every stone with warmth. The birds were twittering, celebrating the joys of life, and the wolves were prancing happily, even the princess. All were touched by the sheer glory of being alive. The only thing that bothered Mika, other than his hand and the ever-present misery of the curse over his head, was that they were still heading east into the morning sun, rather than north toward the forests of home. But Hornsbuck knew the prairies like the back of his hand and must know where they were heading, Mika reasoned.

They traveled for the rest of the day with only brief moments of rest. Mika could tell that the princess was having difficulty keeping up by the way she licked her footpads whenever they stopped. He knew that she still blamed him for her metamorphosis into a wolf, whether or not it was his fault; her cold, green and blue eyes fairly glittered with hatred.

In spite of that, Mika felt an odd respect for her. He wondered how he would react if someone were to turn him into a wolf. He felt the magic gem swing on its thin, gold chain beneath his doeskin tunic. Raising his hand to touch it, he wondered if it would be possible to change her back—it would be much more pleasant traveling with a beautiful woman than a wolf. He shook his head ruefully and lowered his hand, realizing that such a spell was beyond him and could only lead to a worse mess.

117

* * *

They speared a large land tortoise shortly before dark and roasted the succulent creature in its own shell with a handful of wild onions, salt, and cedar leaves to give it flavor.

The wolves hunted on their own. Mika heard the snarls and clash of snapping jaws, a terrified bleat followed by the high, thin shriek of a dying antelope, and then the crunch of bones. A short time later, all three wolves returned to the fire to groom themselves. The princess casually licked a splash of blood off her leg. Feeling Mika's gaze upon her, she looked up and stared directly into his eyes, licking blood off her muzzle the whole while. It seemed to him that she licked very slowly, using her long, pink tongue to savor each and every tiny drop of blood.

He stared at her, spellbound. There was something almost obscene in the way she seemed to be enjoying the blood, something almost sensual in her hatred. He shivered and looked away, unable to meet her gaze. Her dewlaps twitched and she smiled in a wolven way, curling up next to the fire.

"Yon lady has a thing for you, boy," smirked Lotus Blossom, who had observed the exchange of looks. "Best beware, or she'll have you one fine day. Gobble you up whole, she will, saving the best bits for last." She did not elaborate on what she considered to be the best bits, nor did Mika ask, taking himself off quickly, cheeks burning brightly. Lotus Blossom's bawdy laughter followed him.

Mika touched his peeling face, his blistered nose, and his scorched-bald scalp.

In his misery, he had wandered into the circle of staked horses. He leaned against the roan and buried his face in the horse's side. If only things were as they had been. If only things were back to normal.

Then an idea came to him. Maybe he could straighten out some of the problems, make some changes! He looked down at himself, touched the turban. There was nothing he could do about the clothes, but he could do something about the turban. Plucking the silk wrapping from his head, he cast it into the darkness, then pulled the spell book from his pouch and began leafing through the pages by the light of the moon.

"Bigby's interposing hand . . . glimmer . . . glow . . . grow! Here it is! . . . grow!" And in spite of his overwhelming depression, Mika began to get excited.

The roan swung its head toward Mika and nuzzled him affectionately. Mika patted the horse absent-mindedly as he memorized the words to the grow spell, repeating them over and over again to himself.

The necessary component for the spell was a bit of hair, and since Mika had none of his own, he tweaked some from the faithful roan. The horse switched its tail and stamped its hoof but remained at Mika's side, leaning against him slightly.

Mika snapped the book shut and, closing his eyes, recited the words to the spell.

It was working! Excitement coursed through Mika's body as he felt hair sprouting through his scalp! Then, he quirked his head to one side and looked down, puzzled. Something didn't feel right. In fact, something felt definitely wrong. Mika's entire body tingled. All over. Everywhere.

Mika looked at his hand, and his knees went weak. His hand was covered with hair! Dark, curly hair sprouted on the back of his hand, down each of his fingers, and even on his palm! He ripped the gauntlet off his other hand and there, too, even the demon digits were sprouting hair. It grew longer and longer as he watched in horror and disbelief.

He felt the hair pushing through the skin on his arms, his legs, stomach, chest, back, and feet. It spilled over the top of his tunic and curled around the arm holes. It curled around his eyes and explored the openings of his nose and mouth. Hysteria rose within him as he realized that the hair was continuing to grow, getting longer and longer with every passing heartbeat. Soon, he would look like a giant walking ball of hair! And when would it stop?

It had to be the gem, Mika thought hysterically. Ever since the gem had been in his possession, spells had been going awry, overcompensating, intensifying, when he did not intend them to. Evidently even the mere proximity of the gem boosted the natural effect of a spell.

A frightened snort from the roan broke Mika's gloomy thoughts. He looked up at the animal and reeled back in shock. The horse was covered with hair as well! Its frightened eyes rolled in terror, and it shook its head up and down violently as though thinking it could shed the strange new burden.

Mike laid a hairy hand on the roan's dense coat and patted it, speaking soothing words through furry lips, spitting curls of hair out of his mouth.

At last, the horse grew calm; Mika slumped to the

ground at its hairy hooves, wondering what to do.

Tam trotted up, having been off on business of his own, stopped short a few paces away, and began to growl.

"It's just me, Tam," Mika said with a sigh. "Just be glad you weren't here or you'd look like us, too."

Tam advanced warily, sniffing Mika and the roan carefully before being convinced that they were not monsters. Even then, he eyed them suspiciously and kept his distance, perhaps remembering his own strange experiences with Mika's spellcasting.

Mike continued to ponder solutions as his and his horse's hair grew and grew. Hair remover was his first thought, but then he would be no better off than before, and the horse would look damned funny. At last he decided on the only feasible solution, a heal spell.

Heal spells were cure-alls, capable of returning a person to health after the worst of wounds. But it was a higher-level spell than Mika was usually capable of performing. With his dubious record of late, he was most unwilling to attempt the spell. Only the Great She-Wolf knew what the result would be if he got it wrong, he thought. Still, it was the only solution he could think of . . . and with the aid of the gem, perhaps it would work.

Wrapping his arms around the horse's hairy neck, he pulled his dangling forelock out of his eyes, opened the spellbook, and studied the spell. It was a fairly short one, and to the point. Closing the book, he held onto the horse's neck with one hand and gripped the gem in the other. Closing his eyes, he began to chant.

The roan whickered and moved nervously beneath

his hand. Mika twitched his shoulders and stifled an impulse to scratch. It felt awful! Even worse than when the hair had been growing! The spell was working, though—the hair was reversing itself, drawing back through the same pores it had sprouted from. It itched. It tickled. It was almost unbearable. The roan looked as though it were being consumed by vast numbers of wriggling snakes.

The curls shrank back from Mika's nose, let loose their hold on his tunic, and shriveled back into his palms and the soles of his feet. All over his body he could feel the hair retreating, except on top of his head, where it remained at a decent Wolf Nomad length.

When all was done, he and the roan were returned to normal. The roan looked at Mika, blew hard, and pawed at the ground; Mika wondered if his horse would like him as well as it had before. He sighed deeply, relieved that it was all over. His hair had been restored, even if his hand hadn't, and the last signs of the terrible burns he sustained had disappeared as well.

Tam got to his feet and gave Mika an enigmatic look as the two of them walked back to camp. Mika wrapped himself in his cloak and sighed wearily, wondering if he wouldn't have been better off being a tree-cutter or a hunter. Then, relaxing on his bedroll, he fell into a deep and exhausted sleep.

The days following passed in much the same way as the first, except that Mika attempted to keep as much space as possible between himself and Lotus Blossom. It didn't always work; one night Lotus

Blossom pinched him on the bottom and winked at him suggestively as he knelt to serve himself some food. She did not pursue the matter, but Mika lost his appetite completely.

Several nights later, as they camped beside a low outcropping of gray rock, the only object of note on the vast empty prairie, Mika brought up the subject of their destination.

"Why, we're going to Exag, Mika. That's the plan. I know you're anxious to confront that demon again, so I'm plotting a course that will take us directly to him," answered Hornsbuck. "It can be dangerous, three alone riding open like this, but I knew that you would welcome the challenge should anyone be foolish enough to try us."

"Hornsbuck, I thought we were going home first," Mika said in near desperation. "Back to the clan. I— I'm out of everything. All my ungents and potions and healing herbs, they're all gone. I need more! We need to go back to the Far Fringe! What if something happened? What if one of us got hurt? I wouldn't be able to do anything. We could die!"

"Blossom, just listen to what the lad is saying," roared Hornsbuck. "Why, I didn't know you worried about us so. I'm touched, I really am. And for that reason alone, I won't take us home. I can't let you put our welfare above your own good. No, lad, we're heading straight for Exag, with no stops on the way!"

"Hornsbuck, what about the Phantom Forest?" Lotus Blossom asked slowly, twirling the end of her braid between thick fingers. "Be it not somewhere close? The boy could certainly refill his herb supply there. And I myself wouldn't mind hoisting a few flagons of their fine barberry wine, just to be polite, of course. Then we'll be on our way in no time."

Hornsbuck pondered the question while Mika strove to remember what little he knew about the Phantom Forest. As far as he knew, it was only a legend and not a real place.

"What's she talking about, Hornsbuck?" Mika asked as the big nomad combed his beard with his fingers, always a sign of deep thought.

"It be a place of much magic," Hornsbuck replied at length. "There are Wolf Nomads there, though of a different sort than us. But all things considered, they still be nomads and will be helpful to those in need. Aye, woman, it is a good thought. We'll head for the Phantom Forest, but then it's off to Exag."

Hornsbuck corrected their course slightly so that they were traveling southeasterly. Two days later they entered the forest.

At first, there was nothing to be seen but open prairie. Then, miragelike, the forest appeared, almost seeming to float above the ground like a vision induced by heat. It drifted before them, insubstantial and wraithlike, until the very moment that they entered the forest and actually rode between the massive trunks, inhaling the rich scent of the tall evergreens.

They trod upon the crackling roanwood leaves and breathed the spicy cinnamon aroma. Leaves cascaded down from high above, each leaf as large as Mika's head, twirling red and bronze and yellow torches of color as they spiraled down through the broad beams of dusty sunlight that broke between the branches.

And even though it was not his own forest, nor his clan, Mika's heart was light and he felt as though he were home.

Mika assumed that, phantom or not, this forest must be part of the larger Burneal Forest, which stretched for more than a thousand miles across the northern frontier, separating and creating a barrier between Greyhawk and the mysterious Lands of Black Ice.

"Have you ever been north of the forest?" Mika asked Hornsbuck the first night, as they lounged contentedly around the roaring fire, having eaten their fill of a plump roansbuck doe.

"You mean into the Black Lands?" asked Hornsbuck as he and Lotus Blossom guzzled their nightly allotment of ale. "Aye, we've been there, RedTail an' me. It was back a while, back before that last time I met up with you in the Howling Hills. Remember that time, Blossom?"

Lotus Blossom chuckled at the memory, uttering a deep belch in lieu of conversation.

"I don't imagine much has changed," Hornsbuck continued, not at all put off by his companion's behavior. "Strange place—the ice is black instead of white. Kind of blue-black actually. Gives you a real strange feeling."

"What were you doing there?" asked Mika.

"Oh, we were following someone. Nomad by the name of Klarg who stole the shaman's spell book and all his records and notes. Some sort of nonsense about thinking he could use the spells to work magic on the ice. Said he would raise an army of ice golems and come back and take over the village. All because of some woman the chief wouldn't let him marry. Woman! Pahh! They'll get you in trouble every time!"

Lotus Blossom elbowed Hornsbuck in the chest so hard that he lost his breath. He wheezed for a number of heartbeats until he was able to breath again. Lotus Blossom, ignoring his discomfort and the fact that she had caused it, emptied her horn without spilling a drop of the precious ale.

"Well, the whole clan was angry at him, all except the girl, and . . . and, well nobody listened to her," gasped Hornsbuck, holding his chest with one hand, his face still pale and pinched. "The clan council decided to have him brought back, make him an example for the young ones."

"Did you find him?" Mika asked casually, hoping that the poor fellow had escaped.

"Aye," said Hornsbuck. "But an ice dragon ate him afore we could lay hands on him. Never saw a dragon so big. The thing must have been ten or even twelve times my height. And big! Why, I bet it was as big as Jayne's! All blackish blue it was, not white like most ice dragons. Its teeth were jagged and splintered like ice shards, and its scales sparkled like oil on a pond.

"Saw it get him, I did," continued Hornsbuck. "Sort of played with him, batted him around like a cat with a mouse. You know how they do it; almost let him get away, then caught him again. It ate him one limb at a time. The poor fellow was still screaming when it bit his head off. I thought about shooting him, putting him out of his misery, but I was out of bow range."

"Oh," said Mika in a small voice, unable to rid himself of the awful vision.

"Serves him right," Lotus Blossom said sanctimoniously, belching a second time. Hornsbuck laughed as though she had told an amusing tale, and they soon lapsed into a conversation of their own, punctuated with giggles and furtive snickerings. Mika stared at his gauntleted hand and wondered if there were any hope for him at all.

Chapter 12

THEY TRAVELED FOR EIGHT DAYS through the strange forest, growing accustomed to the peculiar changes that occurred without warning. They would be riding on firm ground, the forest all around them, when suddenly things shifted imperceptibly so that the forest seemed to waver in and out of their vision and they would find themselves riding on the prairie, the forest gone completely. And then, just as mysteriously, the forest reappeared as solid rock.

Sometimes both dimensions were present at the same time and Mika was uncertain where they really were. It was disconcerting, but there seemed to be no real harm in it, and he soon learned to carry on as though nothing out of the ordinary had happened.

On the evening of the eighth day, they set up camp at the base of an enormous oak tree in a strange, circular depression. A number of large trees had fallen to the north of the oak, victims of blight and windstorm. Their piled trunks created an effective wind-

break against the cold night wind.

The land rose slightly on all sides of them, cupping their campsite in the center of the depression. Tall ferns grew thickly on the perimeters and spilled down the slopes. A small pool of water welled between the massive, gnarled roots of the oak.

One thing, however, was very unusual. A large number of enormous boulders were scattered about the edges of the circular depression on the high ground, their presence totally inexplicable. Each was taller than either Mika or Hornsbuck and could not be encircled by both men together. Marks found in the center of the depression suggested that they had once rested in the circle. But no amount of thinking told them how or why the boulders had been moved, or by whom.

Finally giving the problem up as unsolvable, they set about making camp. Several times during the night, Mika had had the eerie feeling of being watched, yet there was nothing to be seen. Even the wolves seemed nervous, whining and looking up abruptly.

After dinner, Mika, Lotus Blossom, and Hornsbuck scouted the area, the wolves running before them, sniffing the thick ferns and whining through their muzzles, a shrill, high-pitched sound that Mika knew meant they were nervous and uneasy. Yet despite their thorough search, they found nothing to warrant further suspicion. Looking at the boulders, Mika had the nagging feeling that there was something obvious that he was missing.

They returned to camp and got ready to sleep. Mika's sense of being watched grew stronger as he unbraided his hair for the night, shaking it loose

around his shoulders and combing it out with his fingers. He thought he caught a glimpse of a small, blue face looking at him through the ferns. He blinked, and when he opened his eyes the face was gone. The fern did not move. It must be my imagination, he thought. But then he noticed the princess staring at the spot and he wondered. Shrugging, he rolled himself up in his cloak and slept.

Sometime later, deep in sleep, long after the last coal had crumbled to ash, he heard a wolf barking. All of the wolves. It was the sound of danger, but he could not seem to rouse himself. He snuggled deeper in the warmth of the cloak, thinking that it was a dream. Then he felt the earth tremble beneath him, and he heard soft whispers. He wakened, but before he could even leap to his feet, he felt teeth grab hold of the tunic at the nape of his neck and jerk him backward. He came fully awake and jumped to his feet just as something large rushed past him, displacing the air with a great rush.

Mika stumbled; tripping over Tam, he fell to the ground heavily, an accident that saved his life. A club crashed through the space where he had momentarily stood and thunked into the soft ground. Mika leaped at the shadowy figure who wielded the club and wrestled it to the ground, struggling to reach his knife without losing the unknown assailant.

All around him, small blue figures flitted through the camp and, silhouetted against the grayness of the sky, Mika saw a multitude of bodies darting through the ferns.

"Hornsbuck! Blossom!" he yelled at the top of his voice as he struggled with the small, strong body. All chaos erupted: strange, high-pitched shrieks, gut-teral voices speaking an unknown language, snarl-ing, snapping wolf sounds, Hornsbuck's roars, and the alarmed whickers of the tethered horses.

Mika wrestled with his assailant, rolling over and over, each struggling to overwhelm the other. Then it was over. Rolling up against an oak, Mika pounded his opponent's head against a hard root, and the man lay still. Blue paint and blood stained Mika's hand, and from the limpness of the body, Mika sensed that the man would never rise again.

Then, with a rush, they were gone. Mika, Hornsbuck, and Lotus Blossom were left standing back to back, heaving great gasps of air. A wolf barked in alarm. Mika turned and saw a dark movement, barely leaping aside before one of the huge boulders came crashing down the eastern slope and rolled over the spot where he had stood. An enraged yell told him that Hornsbuck and Lotus had also jumped clear.

"Here comes another one!" yelled Lotus Blossom. Mika looked up in time to see a second boulder pick-ing up speed as it rolled down the western slope.

"Look out, the first one's coming back!" screamed Mika, seeing that the boulder had come to a halt high on the opposite bank and was now rolling back toward them.

"Make for the high ground," shouted Hornsbuck, pushing Lotus Blossom before him. Mika dashed for-ward, clawing at the ferns, attempting to reach safety before another boulder crashed down on them.

Just as he reached the top, a swarm of tiny men, barely as tall as Mika's chest, darted toward him, brandishing small spears and swinging heavy, thorn-tipped clubs. Any one of the blows would have been painful, if not fatal, and Mika tumbled backward, rolling head over heels to the foot of the incline.

"Mika! Flannae! Aborigines! The spears and clubs are tipped with poison. We're surrounded. Get us out of here—use the gem!" Hornsbuck cried in alarm. Mika dove to one side as another boulder barreled down the slope, barely missing him and filling the air with the sharp scent of crushed ferns.

Wolves yelped and the horses plunged and neighed in fear all around him; giant boulders hovered on the edges of the deadly depression. The black night rang with the excited cries of the tiny aborigines who shouted out their hatred in an unfamiliar tongue.

Mika's party was in great danger, that much was obvious. They could not continue to avoid the boulders forever. Sooner or later, one of them would be struck and killed, crushed beneath the great weight, ground into the earth. And there was little that they could do about it. They were sitting ducks, fools for not having seen the trap they'd ventured into of their own accord.

"Damn you, Mika! Where are you?" cursed Hornsbuck as yet another boulder rushed down the slope, almost pinning RedTail between it and another stationary stone. "Stop fooling around and use the gem!"

But Mika did not want to use the gem, nor had he told Hornsbuck about the dreadful ramifications. A spear thunked into the ground next to him, slicing open the edge of his tunic. Another landed between his feet. A boulder appeared above him and wavered on the edge of the incline.

Mika turned and ran, dodging another boulder, larger than most of the others as it rampaged down the southern face of the depression.

He did not want to use the gem, but it was obvious that he would have to do something. Fumbling in his leather pouch he pulled the spell book free and quickly flipped through the pages as he searched for the first-level shield spell he had learned as a youngster. In the darkness it was hard to see the words, and Hornsbuck kept pulling him from one side to the next as boulders continued to crash down the slopes. He found the spell and tried to read the words in the dim light.

"Mika, hurry up!" bellowed Hornsbuck as another boulder passed close enough to nearly brush his eyelashes. Squeezing his eyes shut, Mika quickly recited the words of the spell and prayed that he had gotten it right. Suddenly he heard a low hum, and he sighed with relief, knowing that the invisible shield was in place.

"Hornsbuck, you and Lotus Blossom get behind me!" he whispered hoarsely, then called the wolves to him, hoping that the horses would be all right. The shield would not be big enough to protect them as well.

"I've put up a shield," Mika told Hornsbuck and Lotus Blossom softly after they'd followed his directions. The trio of wolves followed immediately, milling about, their harsh panting betraying their nervousness.

"Took you long enough," growled Hornsbuck.

"Damned aborigines! Always trying to kill you."

Mika was about to ask why, when Lotus Blossom was knocked off her feet and thrown into Hornsbuck, who in turn landed on top of Mika, pushing him to the ground and burying him beneath his bulk.

"Damn it, Mika, I thought you said you put up a shield!" cursed Hornsbuck as he spat out a mouthful of leaves and dirt.

Mika blinked the dirt out of his eyes and tested his ribs to see if any were broken. He got to his feet and stared around as he picked the twigs out of his hair and realized what had happened.

A boulder had struck the rock behind them and shoved it forward. Fortunately, it had been at the very end of its momentum and had exhausted most of its velocity, or Mika and the others might have been fatally injured. As it was, they were merely jostled and frightened.

"Um, a shield spell only protects us from frontal attacks. Improves the odds a bit, but it's not perfect," mumbled Mika, knowing that it was only a matter of time before the shield was breached. He would have to do something else. But what?

As Hornsbuck cursed, Mika searched his memory. He had it! A web spell! Webs would keep out the boulders and would protect them from all sides! And best of all, he wouldn't have to use the gem!

Once again he hurriedly leafed through the book until he found the right page, closed his eyes amid a cacophony of clashing rocks, wolf whines, and foul curses, and spoke the words of the spell.

Instantly, great, gobby, gray webs dropped down from the branches above and circled them in a small space no wider than six feet across in any direction. They could see through the gray, gauzy webs, yet Mika knew that his party was almost completely concealed.

"Hope this works, Mika," rumbled Hornsbuck. "Here comes another one of those damned rocks. How many more can there be?"

Remembering the large number of stones scattered about the area, Mika doubted that the aborigines would run out of boulders any time soon.

The boulder paused on the lip of the crater and then, urged on by a chorus of high-pitched cries, sped down the bank, picking up speed until it seemed to fly above the ground. It struck a small incline, giving it enough impetus to leave the ground and sail through the air, striking the web from above.

Though Mika, Hornsbuck, and Lotus Blossom had ducked and were not struck by the rock, the force of the impact dislodged the web from the tree limb, causing it to collapse on top of the group, burying them in its glutinous folds.

"Mika!" bellowed Hornsbuck as he tried to fight his way out of the enveloping, sticky, gray mass. But all the big man succeeded in doing was to pull the web down from the other branches until all of them, wolves and humans alike, were completely covered with the clinging material.

The web wrapped itself around Mika's head and nose, effectively blinding and all but smothering him. Unfortunately, he could still hear Hornsbuck cursing him for a blundering fool, and feel, as well as hear, the rumbling passage of another boulder which seemed to be coming directly toward them. Loud cheers broke out around the perimeter, and Mika knew that this boulder would be the last.

In desperation Mika gripped the magic gem, closed his eyes, and with a sense of awful inevitability, he calmly spoke the words to the third-level protection from missiles spell, one he was very familiar with, having used it many times to protect himself in battle. No sooner had he finished speaking than he heard a loud crash a short distance away and saw a hint of shimmering, blue light through the web, similar to that caused by massive storms. The rumbling movement ceased instantly.

Mika pulled the last of the webs from his head and saw that the immense boulder had stopped a hand's width away from the wriggling, web-covered mass still caught beneath the sticky shroud.

Still enveloped by a peculiar sense of fate, Mika slowly looked through the book until he found another spell, one he had never used before. Somehow he knew that the magical stone would enable him to use the spell.

Clutching the stone in one hand, Mika recited the words; slowly the entire group of them rose above the ground. All three wolves shrieked with fear; Hornsbuck was still shouting and struggling with the clinging mantle of webs; Lotus Blossom clutched at him as though she were drowning; and with Mika pointing the way like some strange figurehead draped in amorphous folds, they floated out of the depression and drifted above the ground until they were level with the treetops.

Below them, Mika could see a scattering of aborigines waving their spears and crying aloud with what he fervently hoped was fear. Unfortunately, it did not seem so, for even now he could see several of the small, blue men reaching for their bows and arrows while others made ready to throw their poison-tipped spears. Hovering as they were, Mika's group made excellent targets. Mika sighed and closed his eyes once more.

New words rolled off his tongue with ease, even though he had never used the spell before and had read it only once or twice. Holding the stone in his hand, he reflected that the gem did indeed heighten one's abilities, for he could picture the words of the spell as clearly as though they had been written on the inside of his eyelids. The gem made it almost too easy. And it exacted a terrible price for its power, as well.

Alarmed cries broke out beneath him. Opening his eyes, Mika looked down and saw billowing smoke pouring from his fingertips and drifting toward the ground in great clouds of noxious, yellow fumes. He moved his hand, gesturing in a broad, sweeping arc, and the bilious vapors spread out over the entire area, excluding only the northern portion of the crater where the horses were tethered.

The aborigines pointed up at the descending cloud and gestured wildly, conferring with each other, no doubt in an attempt to figure out what the mysterious manifestation was. They soon found out.

No sooner had the cloud reached them than did the blue men begin to cough and clutch their throats.

A few—very, very, few—managed to stagger out of the affected area and stumble away. The others crumpled to the ground instantaneously and did not move again.

Holding the gem, Mika pointed his hand and spoke again, causing a great wind to rise and sweep the area clean, ridding it of the last of the poisonous fumes. Then, and only then, did he cause the three adventurers to be lowered to the ground.

"Well, Mika, when you do something, you do it up right," said Hornsbuck. "But I don't understand why you waited so long in the first place. Why didn't you just use the gem right off, instead of messing around with those other spells that didn't work?"

"Uh, well, uh . . ." stammered Mika, feeling sick inside and wondering how soon the feminine changes he anticipated would make themselves apparent.

"Never mind," said Hornsbuck. "Let's go and take a look at them and see what we've got here."

Mika hung back as Hornsbuck and Lotus Blossom strode up the bank. He had no real interest in looking at the corpses of his victims. He did not really care that they were dead. After all, they had attacked him first and tried their best to kill him, hadn't they? Better they were dead than him! But he did care that he'd been forced to use the stone not once, not twice, but three times in order to save their lives.

Had he not acted when he did, every one of them—he, Hornsbuck, Lotus Blossom, TamTur, RedTail, and Princess Julia—would be dead, smashed like bugs beneath a stone. He grew ill at the thought and leaned his head back, drawing in deep breaths of air to clear his mind.

Slowly, things steadied around him and he grew almost calm. Maybe the Great She-Wolf had some special plan for him. He could but put his faith in her and hope that this was not all a vast cosmic joke, with him as the final punch line.

As he raised his head, he saw the princess staring at him speculatively. He met her gaze squarely, and they looked into each other's eyes. Hers glinted in the pale starlight, with no hint of the usual hatred and cynicism. Instead, she bobbed her head in what might have been a nod of approval or thanks. Mika nodded in return, confused by her response, and they stared at each other a minute longer.

"Mika!" bawled Hornsbuck suddenly. Mika hurried up the bank, Tam at his side, breaking the tenuous bond with the princess. But his heart felt strangely light.

"Here they be in person, the little blue buggers," growled Hornsbuck, gesturing at a pair of bodies that lay sprawled on the ground at their feet. "Ever seen anything like them before?"

"No," Mika said slowly, looking down on the result of his handiwork. The men were small, no more than four feet tall. They were all but naked, wearing only the merest of fur loincloths and nothing else but a thick layer of blue paint from head to toe. Their hair was thick, wiry, and daubed with the paint as well, then twisted into a myriad of snaky locks that hung down to their shoulders, forming a wild and barbaric headdress. Their brows were thick and straight, nearly meeting over the bridge of the nose, which was short and flat and wide of nostril. Their eyes, which were unfortunately still open, were a surprisingly soft shade of blue. Their teeth had been filed to sharp points.

The two blue men at Mika's feet still gripped their spears; one had strung his bow and appeared to have been ready to loose the arrow when the fumes struck him down. Their weapons were made of sablewood and were beautifully crafted.

The dead men were wiry, and their musculature was well-defined. On their chests, biceps, and thighs were rows of geometric cuts that had been limned with a darker shade of blue. The men appeared to be in excellent physical condition, albeit rather thin and dead.

"Flannae, you say?" asked Mika.

"Aye," said Hornsbuck. "Aborigines. Savages. Some say they were the very first to settle the Burneal Forest. You seldom see them any more and never in great numbers. I used to run into them often farther north, years ago. Wonder what they're doing this far south?"

The question seemed moot to Mika. They were a warrior party and, from the look of the now obvious setup, it was apparent that they had played out this same scenario often and with probable success.

They found this theory borne out on further examination of the remainder of the bodies. Many of them carried weapons of nomad design and wore bits of jewelry that spoke of travelers from other climates. Mika excused himself to tend the horses, leaving Lotus Blossom and Hornsbuck to accumulate the evidence, stripping the incriminating ornaments and weapons from the dead so that they might present them to the clan council.

In truth, while he enjoyed sparring with friends, he

had no stomach for real fighting in which he might actually be injured, and he truly disliked killing, doing so only when all other avenues of escape had been closed to him. But Hornsbuck, grizzled veteran that he was, had no such objections and would regard Mika's qualms as cowardice, which, in fact, they were.

Mika patted and soothed the horses, calming their jangled nerves with soft-spoken words until they stood quiet with their heads bowed low.

With the horses tended to, Mika quickly broke camp, packing what little remained of the adventurers' supplies, viewing, with a shudder, his broken and splintered spear. Had Tam not wakened him when he did, Mika would now be lying alongside that spear, equally broken and splintered.

A sudden thought struck him, and he looked up to see the princess watching him. She turned aside, but not before Mika wondered whether it had been she, not Tam, who had wakened him . . . and saved his life.

The group packed their booty and mounted their horses, riding out even though it was still long before dawn, unwilling to spend another heartbeat in the pit that had almost become their grave.

They rode steadily, keeping watch in case those at the pit had been part of a larger whole, but they neither saw nor sensed any others. By first light, they had left the area far behind.

Hornsbuck dozed in the saddle, trusting to Red-Tail and Mika to warn him of danger. For once, Lotus Blossom was silent, wrapped in her cloak against the morning chill. But Mika's mind was on other thoughts. He found himself watching the slim flanks of the princess as she trotted ahead of the horses and wondering what she really felt . . . and for that matter, what it was he really felt, as well.

Chapter 13

HORNSBUCK AWAKENED with a number of snorts and loud sneezes. He glowered about him suspiciously as though suspecting that someone else was responsible for the noise. He scowled at Mika.

"What's the matter with your hair?" he asked, frowning angrily like a bear wakened from its winter sleep.

"My hair? Nothing. Why?" asked Mika, putting his hand to his head in confusion.

"It's all loose. Hanging down on your shoulders like a harridan's," growled Hornsbuck, looking away as though he had seen something indecent. "Fix yourself."

It's happening! thought Mika, horrified that Hornsbuck had compared him to a woman. He hurriedly scraped his hair together and, brushing it thoroughly, worked it into the intricate braid that ran from the center of his forehead, down the middle of his skull, and ended at the nape of his neck; he tied it off with a strip of leather. The complicated procedure was made more difficult by the metal gauntlet, which caught on the hair itself and caused his motions to be awkward and clumsy. Mika was forced to work carefully, and it took him twice as long as usual to finish the braid.

It was nomad tradition for men to wear their hair in this fashion; the high, thick braid cushioned the skull from all but the hardest of blows. Men often wore their hair loose when in camp or in the safety of the clan, but Hornsbuck seemed to view it as a sign of personal laxity and would not permit it in his presence. Mika had never once seen Hornsbuck unbraid, or even comb or wash his hair, in all the time he had known him. He tried to avoid thinking about it.

"Quit yer fooling, Mika. You be worse than a woman with all this hair business!" grumbled Hornsbuck.

Mika was mortified and confused as well. What was he to do? He tried to finish the job, braiding his hair as quickly as possible, ignoring the painful catches as he drew the hair far tighter than normal, pulling it so hard that his eyes watered. But even the pain was a welcome antidote to the lurking curse.

The princess had listened to the exchange with interest and watched Mika with a look of cool amusement in her strange blue and green eyes.

Tam watched the interplay between Mika and the princess, and a strange, hostile look appeared in his eyes. What exactly was the relationship between the man he had followed since his earliest memories and this wolf who was no wolf? Tam did not know, but it seemed to him that Mika thought less and less of him and more and more of the princess. He had not even commended Tam for saving his life the night before. Tam looked away with obvious hurt in his eyes.

Mika took special care to watch his actions all that day, speaking in an extra deep voice and making decisions in a firm, masculine manner. When they made camp that evening, he strode about brusquely and hawked and spat many times. He even leered at Lotus Blossom as she shrugged out of her heavy-leather tunic before dinner and walked around camp, scratching her ample belly and heavy breasts before she changed into a loose shift that thankfully covered her from neck to knees.

He leered, but in truth the sight of all that pink flesh made him quite ill, and he worried more than ever over the fact that it did nothing to excite him. This stirred him to greater eccentricities, capped by his pinching Lotus Blossom's enormous backside, earning him nothing but angry glowers from Hornsbuck.

Even this did not curb his activities, and Hornsbuck and Lotus Blossom were both staring at him openly before the evening was out. Unable to stand the strain any longer, Mika went to sleep early . . . without unbraiding his hair.

"Don't know why you bother, you haven't enough of a beard to matter," Hornsbuck commented casually the next morning as Mika prepared to shave as he did every day, scraping his face with the edge of his knife.

"Yes, I do! Why I . . . I could shave twice a day and still have bristles!" Mika exclaimed as he leaped to his feet and faced Hornsbuck, his face dripping with

147

lather, the blade trembling between his fingers.

"Well, all right. If you say so!" said an astonished Hornsbuck. "It's no matter to me. I just don't see why you bother. Growing a beard's much easier than cutting your face to ribbons every day. Never could see the sense of it myself."

Mika blinked and backed away. Got to get a grip on myself, he thought, his hand rising to his lathered chin. This is getting out of control. He saw the princess grinning at him, her tongue lolling out the side of her mouth. Suddenly enraged, he flicked a gob of foam at her.

His aim was good, but she was faster; she scampered away, her upturned tail spattered with foam and her eyes crinkled into slits of wolvish laughter as she looked back at him over her shoulder.

They went on like that for the next ten days. Mika stopped shaving and grew a beard which he was forever stroking and pulling and examining in pools of water to check its growth.

He spoke in deeper and deeper tones, causing Hornsbuck to ask him whether or not he was ill. Lotus Blossom stopped pinching him, even when he grew worried enough to make it easy for her. He strode and hawked and spat and gestured with masculine vigor and took to going about with the top half of his tunic unlaced, baring his chest to the coldest of breezes. "Ah! Invigorating!" he would roar with appreciation and inhale deeply, while trying to hide the fact that he was covered with goose bumps, splotched and trembling from the cold.

Hornsbuck began to look at him strangely, eyeing

him from beneath his shaggy eyebrows and studying him when he thought Mika would not notice. But of course he did, and immediately thought that Hornsbuck was seeing through his charade and so increased his virile mannerisms even further, until he became a ludicrous caricature of himself.

One night, as they sat in front of the fire after the evening meal, Mika began relating a fanciful tale that involved himself and seven nubile beauties performing a variety of incredible and totally unbelievable sexual acts. Hornsbuck interrupted the story and took the mug of ale from Mika's tightly clenched fist.

"Mika, are you going strange on me?" he asked. "I know you be worried about this demon business, but you be acting exceptional strange lately. You even look different. Now we be friends, and I owe you my life, but if you be going crazy, tell me now. I don't want to get into a tight spot in Exag and find myself with a loon on my hands."

Mika stopped cold, wondering what it was that had given him away. Some small gesture? An accidental high note in his voice, perhaps?

He stared at Hornsbuck, wondering how the old nomad would react if he told him the truth. He who was so particular and so offended if a man even left his hair unbraided! No, it would never do. He could not tell.

"I don't know what you mean," he said in his deepest baritone and then looked away, unable to meet Hornsbuck's steady gaze.

There was a moment's silence, and then Hornsbuck lowered his eyes and turned away.

"Well, lad, tell me if you ever feel yourself slipping over the edge. I have a stake in this, too, you know." And then they sat in awkward silence until Mika hawked and spat and took up the thread of the lapsed conversation once more.

It went on like that for the remainder of the journey, Mika acting more and more strangely and watching Hornsbuck and Lotus Blossom covertly to gauge the success of his performance.

Hornsbuck in turn, tried to act normal, laughing and joking, but secretly he watched Mika to try and discover what was causing his friend's strange behavior.

Chapter 14

THEY RODE INTO THE NOMAD CAMP on the morning of the twelfth day of Patchwall. The forest was a fiery, autumnal kaleidoscope of brilliant oranges, flame reds, and golden browns as alder and oak, balsam and birch, sablewood, yarpick, and the majestic roanwood burst into their final transcendent displays of color.

The cold breath of winter would soon be upon them, and Mika rejoiced in the beauty of the forest as they entered the clanlands. Throwing back their heads, Mika and Hornsbuck each howled out their own individual wolf cry, announcing their arrival to all within hearing, as was demanded and expected by proper Wolf Nomad etiquette.

There was a moment's silence, and then the air was shattered by a cacaphony of wolf cries that rose and fell and shivered along the nerves. Each nomad developed his own cry, his own special voice that was as distinctive and as easily identifiable to his clansmen as was his face.

Soon, there was the first glimpse of movement and then the woods were full of them, wolves and nomads as they raced to meet the newcomers.

The wolves appeared first. All sizes and colors. They leaped and bounded and sniffed the new wolves from head to tail, each in turn going through the ancient ritual.

Tam and RedTail were both dominant males. Normally there could only be one dominant male in each pack who ruled completely and bred with the dominant female. It was extremely unusual for two such males to occupy the same territory. Never would such a thing occur in the wild, where they would have been required to fight for dominance, leaving only one of them the clear victor.

But Tam and RedTail were both dominant males who had been brought together by the association of their humans, and they adjusted their behavior to fit the needs of the situation, respecting each other, living in harmony, and fighting shoulder to shoulder when the situation demanded it.

But they were still interlopers in foreign territory. They found themselves confronted by a tall, rangy, white wolf whose tattered ears and scarred neck and shoulders told of many battles. His mere presence told of his victories. He sniffed them carefully, and only when he stepped aside and urinated on a nearby tree, slating his ownership of the territory, did they know that they had been accepted without challenge.

The princess faced a gauntlet of a different sort. Although posing no threat to the males, she was of great interest to them sexually, and she was sniffed from head to tail, over and over and over. One inexperienced young male, whose enthusiasm was larger than his propriety, tried to mount her. But her patience was frayed beyond its limits, and she turned and snapped at the youngster, nipping him painfully on the ear. He leaped away, bright dots of blood beading on his velvety, gray ear, and slunk off into the brush, tail tucked between his legs amid a chorus of yips that sounded suspiciously like laughter.

Then the females crowded in, sizing the princess up with hot eyes, sniffing, prodding, poking, shoving her with their noses, searching for a sign of weakness. But while she had endured the inspection of the males—had almost seemed to enjoy it, even—she had no patience with the females. Baring her teeth, she growled at them. They drew back and averted their eyes, yet they did not leave her side. She felt a sudden flash of fear and looked to Mika for some small guidance, some hint of assistance.

Mika rode into the throng, nudging the wolves aside with the big roan, scattering them like dried leaves. The princess trotted alongside the horse, grateful in spite of herself for his intercession as they approached the clansmen.

The youngsters were first, as usual. Boys only, as was seemly, ran forward on hard, calloused feet, yipping and hooting out their juvenile cries, throwing up their arms and cavorting with the exuberance of youth. They wore tunics of roanskin and necklets and armbands of horn and bone. Few of them wore wolfskins or tails, and none had wolves of their own, for they were still too young.

The women followed close on their heels, always

glad to see newcomers, interested in anything and everything, their dark eyes flashing with excitement.

They were dressed in a wide variety of styles. Some wore full overblouses, bare of ornamentation, that hung in shapeless folds to the waist, and long, full skirts that swept the ground, giving each the charm of a fat bear. Others wore softly tanned tunics that clung to the body and gave more than a hint of the charms contained within. But despite their appearance, their behavior was circumspect, for the Wolf Nomads would not tolerate licentious behavior from their women. At least not in public.

The men came last, strolling leisurely, unwilling to sacrifice their dignity by increasing their stride. The men, all those old enough to have passed through the initiation, wore the usual male nomad attire: sleeveless leather tunics that reached from throat to mid-thigh, tall, knee-high leather boots, and little else.

Many wore wolfskin cloaks, for the season was well advanced and the days were becoming chill. A few wore leather helms, adorned with wolf ears. Others wore full wolf skulls perched atop their heads. Most wore wolf tails in some manner, dangling from the sides of their braid, hanging from the earlobes or simply attached to the edges of their helms.

The men wore jewelry more often than the women, ornaments of bone, horn and fangs fashioned with great skill, and using copper, gold, and silver inlaid with precious and semi-precious gems. This ornamentation was outward evidence of their bravery and courage, prizes taken in battle or won through adventure, for bravery and courage were much admired among the Wolf Nomads.

Clustered at the fore of the men were the chief of the clan, and the senior shaman and magic-user.

Behind these two titular heads of the clan were a gaggle of lesser chiefs, all of whom were to be accorded the proper note of respect, and none of whom mattered to Mika, for his attention was taken by a lissome beauty with dark, curling hair and a lascivious smile. She looked directly at Mika with a promise in her eyes.

To Mika's delight and absolute confusion, he felt definite stirrings of interest! It was suddenly obvious that the curse had not yet ruined him completely. He threw his shoulders back and grinned at the girl, anxious to hold her to her promise, whatever it might be!

But first there were all the boring rituals to be gotten through. He sighed and turned his attention back to the far less-attractive men and, following Hornsbuck's lead, he raised his hand in greeting.

"Welcome, brothers," said the chief, a tall, thin man with a beaked nose and sharp eyes; a fur cloak comprised of the pelts of winter weasels hung around his shoulders. The fur was thick and luxurious, and white like drifting snow, but all of the heads, tails, feet, and claws had been left on when the cloak was stitched so that it seemed like the man was covered with scores of little, dead bodies. Their empty eyes stared out at Mika, and the little feet that had once sped through the forest so lightly dangled lifelessly against the man's chest.

"We do not see many visitors here in the Phantom Forest, and we welcome you to our humble camp. You honor us with your presence. Refresh yourselves, and when you are rested I would be honored to welcome you properly at my fire."

"It would be our honor, noble one," replied Hornsbuck, bowing low in the saddle before the chief. Mika mimicked the older man, knowing that tradition demanded complete and utter respect be shown a chief.

The chief nodded and withdrew, leaving Hornsbuck, Lotus Blossom, and Mika to go with any one of the many women who volunteered their dwellings for rest and refreshment. A woman so chosen would achieve great esteem, and Mika and his companions were besieged by those clamoring for the honor. Mika had no difficulty making his choice. Leaving Lotus Blossom and Hornsbuck surrounded by matrons of dubious charms, he dismounted and started toward the dark-haired beauty who hovered silently at the edge of the crowd.

"Mika," hissed Hornsbuck, laying a cautioning hand on Mika's arm. "Do nothing foolish," he warned. "Clean up. Eat. Be polite, stay out of trouble, and meet me back here no later than sundown."

"Fear not, Hornsbuck," Mika boomed in his new, deep voice. "I shall do nothing wrong."

Hornsbuck stared at him a minute longer, then shaking his head and sighing deeply, he allowed himself to be drawn into a conversation with Lotus Blossom and another woman of similar girth.

"Come, Tam," boomed Mika. Smiling at the woman, he set out to discover just how much damage the curse had exacted.

Chapter 15

THE WOMAN WAS WAITING. Without speaking, she held out her hand to Mika.

Mika took the small, soft hand and drank in the sight of her as happily as a drowning man views the sight of land.

She was tall, rising nearly to his chin, her hair a mass of tumbled curls the color of ebony and shining with blue highlights. Her eyes were dark brown flecked with gold and her wide, generous mouth a delicate shade of rose. A sultry smile lifted the corners of her mouth and there was little or no need for conversation, so implicit was their unspoken understanding.

Her name was Starr, and she wore a tunic of some dark blue material, shot through with a sparkling, silver weft. Although it covered her modestly from throat to knee, it was impossible to disguise her more than ample physical endowments. She was shod with tall, roanskin boots trimmed with long fringe dyed blue to match the dress. A silvery blue shawl completed the outfit.

Mika cleared his throat several times, feeling himself fill with lust just looking at her, wanting more than anything in the world to wrap his arms around her and hold her tight, to lose himself in her and never return.

But of course that was impossible, for he could feel the eyes on him, watching from all directions. As always, there was the game to be played and others' needs to be satisfied before his own.

Behaving most circumspectly, they walked hand in hand through the village, trailing the roan behind, talking politely of things that did not matter and did not interest them until none but children watched them; then they silently stole into the forest that surrounded them on all sides.

They tied the horse to a tree and left it to graze. Tam and the princess were left to their own devices as Starr led Mika deep into the heart of the forest to a small, mossy clearing obscured from sight by tall ferns and dense bushes.

Overcome by his feelings, an equal mixture of joy and lust, Mika completely forgot his fear of the curse, or rather, the condition of his body assured him that if he were going to be stricken, it had not happened fully, yet.

He detached the beautiful, blue cloak from the shoulders of his tunic and laid it down on the thick carpet of moss. His tunic quickly followed, and then his soft boots, leaving only the magic gem on its thin, gold chain and his cumbersome metal gauntlet. Thankfully, she took no notice of his deformity.

Starr gazed at him openly. Her eyes widened with appreciation, and her breathing became more rapid.

She reached for him, her desire as open as his own.

He put out his hand and stayed her gently, smoothing her silky hair with his gloveless hand. She obeyed him, standing proud and still, allowing him to slowly undress her with fingers that shook with longing.

The dress dropped from her shoulders, and Mika gasped with pleasure at the sight of her beautiful, proud body. She held her arms gracefully at her sides, allowing him to caress her with his eyes, even though she shivered as the cold air stroked her naked body.

Mika smiled down at her, stepped forward, fitting his body against hers, and wrapped him arms around her. He felt her warm breath on his shoulder as the soft points of her breasts pressed against his chest.

His mind was enflamed, and his knees buckled as he sagged down onto the cloak, bringing her with him. The dread curse was forgotten, mind and body enflamed with the need for gratification.

Then his body began to move on its own, ignoring his frenzied mind, following age-old commands that needed no thought or direction. His soul sang with joy, and he was but a heartbeat away from the final moment of ecstasy when something . . . some great, heavy, oppressive, black force intruded, thrusting its way into his concentration and shattering it completely, like plunging a red hot sword into freezing water.

He felt the prickle of unfriendly eyes on his back. The short hairs on the nape of his neck were electric with danger.

Still locked in position, Mika turned his head and looked over his shoulder, wondering what enemy he would see, and there . . . there looking back at him, was the princess!

Glaring was a better work. Hatred blazed out of her blue and green eyes, and Mika felt his lust for Starr dwindle away as though it had never existed.

Starr moaned as she ground her hips up to meet Mika's and circled his neck with her arm, trying to pull his head down to hers.

"Mmmmmm," he muttered, kissing her perfunctorily, but quickly twisting his head around to glare back at the wolf who was still staring at him.

"Oh," cried Starr as she raked his back with her nails.

"Owww!" yelped Mika.

"Ummmm," murmured Starr.

Mika cast one last furious glance at the princess, then turned back to Starr, hoping to recapture the wonderous feeling he had lost.

Starr moaned and wriggled in response to Mika's kisses and caresses, but try as he did, he could not free himself of the princess's ominous scrutiny. No matter which way he moved, he continued to feel the force of the princess's gaze on his unprotected body; the moment slipped away and was not regained.

Filled with rage, he rose to his feet and threw a rock at the princess; but she merely ducked and took shelter between two boulders where he could not reach her easily and contined to watch him, a sullen expression in her odd-colored eyes.

"Is something wrong?" Starr asked, arching her eyebrows as he returned to the cloak. She snuggled into his embrace, her head cradled on his arm. "Do I not please you?"

"I like you just fine," muttered Mika. "It's not that at all."

"Oh, what is it then?" she asked, curling a tendril of chest fur around her finger.

"Uh, nothing," Mika said glumly, now knowing with certainty that the curse had begun to take effect. What a time to happen! It could not be simply that the princess was watching, a thought he dismissed as unlikely. Tam had often watched him cavort with other women with merely an amused expression at the foibles of humans, and it had never had this dwindling effect on him.

Mika sighed, nearly consumed with despair. He sat up and grabbed his tunic, Starr all but forgotten. Now more than ever he realized how important it was for him to get to Dramidja and find the red stone.

As he bent over to put on his tunic, the stone dangled from his neck, spattering intense blue prisms of light across Starr's body. Perhaps curious, or perhaps merely annoyed at the interlude which had not developed as expected, she reached up and, before Mika realized what she was doing, grasped the magic gem and pulled the thin chain over his head.

"It's beautiful," Starr said as she slipped the chain around her neck, allowing the glittering, blue-green stone to drop between her breasts. "You don't mind if I keep it, do you?" she asked playfully.

Seemingly out of nowhere came a streak of black and the stone was seized, snapped shut between strong jaws that pulled the chain tight.

"Urrk!" gasped Starr as the chain cut deep into her throat, threatening to cut off her air.

"Help! Do something!" she gurgled in a peculiar, high-pitched voice. But Mika could do nothing, for he had fallen to the ground, his hand gripped by the terrible, red flame of pain that burned its way into his flesh and left him crying out in agony. He did not have to remove the metal gauntlet to know that somehow he had angered the demon and now possessed a third horrible demon digit.

Mika was never certain how long he lay naked on the cloak, wrapped in pain and misery, but it could not have been long, for when he regained his senses, things were much as they had been when the pain began.

Starr was still on her back, her hands wrapped around the chain as she tried to prevent it from biting further into her throat.

At the opposite end of the chain, the gem clutched firmly in her teeth, was the princess. Her feet dug into the ground as she jerked on the chain with all her might. Each tug elicited some further gasp from Starr, her face darkening perceptively and her eyes and tongue protruding in an ugly manner.

Disregarding his own pain, Mika leaped to his feet and ran toward the princess, who swung around in the opposite direction, avoiding him. The change of direction caused the chain to pull against the mass of Starr's hair, thus easing the pressure on her throat. Unfortunately, this change of direction also jerked her forward on her hands and knees and brought her face to face with the snarling wolf.

The princess gave a sharp tug, and Starr fell forward, breaking her fall at the last moment by planting her palms against the ground, bracing herself against the wolf's strength.

"Help!" shrieked Starr, her voice nearly drowned out by the princess's growls.

Mika grasped his sword, and with one swift blow, severed the chain that connected the two women. The princess gave Starr one last malevolent look and then dashed up the bank and was gone, the remains of the chain dangling between her teeth, the gem still in her possession.

"Oh," sniveled Starr as she dropped to the cloak and wailed. Mika sank down beside her and cradled her in his arms, smoothing her hair tenderly and murmuring soft words of comfort.

"Why did she do that?" Starr asked shakily, her eyes magnified by tears as Mika daubed gently at the cuts on her neck with damp moss, grateful that she had not been killed.

"Uh, it's a long story. The necklace actually belongs to her," said Mika.

"That's silly," Starr sniffed. "How can a necklace belong to a wolf? And how come you have two wolves? I didn't think that was allowed."

"It really *is* a long story," said Mika. "And I don't really *have* her, she's just sort of traveling with me."

"Well, I don't like her. She hurt me," Starr cried. "She's dangerous. You should get rid of her before she kills someone."

Mika sighed. Drenched in his own misery, he stared at the gauntlet, all the while doubting that Starr was very high on the princess's list either, and wondering how on Oerth he would ever get the magic stone back.

They dressed in silence, and Starr wrapped the shawl around her neck to cover the ugly red bruises. Walking apart with no sign of their earlier warmth and affection, they made their way back to the village.

Chapter 16

THE DRUMS WERE BEATING softly yet insistently, announcing the gathering of the full council of the clan. Mika had refused Starr's offer of her home to make himself ready, knowing that she would be far happier if she never saw him or his wolves again.

In fact, at the last minute he had decided to not ready himself at all, to appear before the council just as he was, unwashed and ungroomed, so as to present an image of himself as a rough, tough warrior, to offset any and all doubts that might arise over his manliness.

He knew from years of watching his father prepare for meetings that such was not the norm, but Hornsbuck would surely arrive looking his usual untidy self. The two of them would look as though cut from the same mold.

Feeling reassured, he examined himself in a pool of still water for any external evidence of change. Nothing appeared different except his manhood, which drooped sadly, huddling into itself as though knowing that it had failed and wished to hide; and, of course, the metal gauntlet concealing the demonic monstrosity that had once been his hand and now tingled with three demon digits.

Mika condescended to retie his hair, which was coming loose from its braid and sagging about his ears. He knotted a thong of leather around the end of the braid and jerked it tight, wishing that it were the princess's neck.

He brushed bits of moss and dirt off the beautiful, blue cloak, admiring it once again, then straightened the soft, gray doeskin on his hips. His fingers lingering on the buttery softness; he wondered why he had never purchased such a garment before and had made do with hot, bulky, ugly, leather tunics for so many years.

Suddenly, lightning shot through his mind and he withdrew his hand as though burned, frightened by the emotions that had coursed through him. It must be the curse! Never before had he worried about clothes and appearances. He had always taken such things for granted. Now he was fussing over what he wore, like . . . like a woman!

Angrily, he pulled the tattered, old, gray, wolfskin cloak that had belonged to his father out of his shoulder pouch and exchanged it for the beautiful blue cape. He tried to ignore the fact that moths had been at it and it appeared slightly bald.

He settled the grinning skull on top of his head and crossed the paws over his chest, knotting them securely, feeling the all but hairless tail flop against the back of his calves as he stomped out of the forest, a terrible scowl on his face.

He would fight it! He wouldn't give in. He would fight the female curse every step of the way. He would find a red stone and reverse the process, and none would ever know that there had been a problem.

By the time Mika arrived, all of the chiefs had gathered and were seated in the high chiefs' dwelling, which also served as a council house. It was quite large, with many rooms built around the central core, sizeable enough to accommodate a full assembly.

Trabec, the chief, sat before the fire in the place of honor. Oban, the head shaman and magic-user, from whom Mika hoped to obtain a new supply of herbs and potions, was there as well, grasping the carved staff of his profession.

Two score of lesser chiefs were also seated around the fire, representing each of the major families that comprised this clan.

As Mika entered, he noticed immediately that all of them—every last man—was dressed in his finest clothing, the softest and most carefully tanned skins worn only for ceremonies, then folded away with leaves of aromatic cedar until the next gathering.

Full wolfskin headdresses and cloaks sat atop those fortunate enough to possess them, tokens of the bravery and remembrances of wolves long gone to the spiritworld. Also worn were the pelts of wolves that had been their bond brothers or those of their ancestors.

Young members of the council, those too young for such badges of merit, wore only ears and single tails upon their helms which were given them on their initiation day by the elders. These less-privileged young men sat on the outskirts of the farthest circle.

Mika was startled to see Hornsbuck seated next to Trabec. It was not his presence that surprised him, but rather his appearance.

For a moment, Mika nearly mistook him for someone else, for Hornsbuck was scrubbed so clean that Mika was certain he would squeak if touched. Hornsbuck's skin fairly glowed with a rosy sheen. His hair gleamed white-blond in the firelight and was neatly combed and braided, not a single strand out of place. Even the monstrous brush that was his beard and mustache had been meticulously trimmed and groomed.

He wore a magnificent tunic of roanskin, the fur still on, thickly pelted, a rich, dark shade of auburn. He wore a belt of hammered silver around his waist, inlaid with turquoise and gold. A necklet fashioned of massive silver links hung from his thick neck, and at its end, in the very center of his chest, hung a huge, fist-sized chunk of unworked turquoise.

On his feet were boots that rose to his knees. The soles were made of thick, bison leather, but the sides were cut from the same pelt as the tunic. They, too, were ornamented, little turquoise beads and tiny silver bells dangled from the fringe that edged the top of the boots.

His head was too broad to fit into any wolfskull, but he had thrown a cloak made of three wolf pelts across his shoulders. RedTail sat at his side, and even he wore a collar of fingers, human and otherwise, his own grisly tokens of past victories. Lotus Blossom, being a woman, was absent, for women were not permitted to participate in such weighty matters as council meetings.

Mika paused in the doorway, feeling all eyes upon him, critical eyes that took in his dirty, ungroomed hair, his sweat-stained body, and his strangely colored garments.

He saw them stiffen and felt the disapproval and shock in their eyes, realizing that he had insulted them by appearing in such a condition. He started to withdraw, thinking that perhaps he might yet have time to bathe and groom himself properly, but it was not to be.

"Come, Mika, we have been waiting for you," said Trabec. "You are the last to arrive."

"Please pardon my appearance," said Mika, feeling the hostility rolling toward him in all but visible waves. "I do not own any other garments, having lost all in our recent ventures." That did not excuse his ungroomed state, but it was the best he could think of on such short notice.

The tension eased somewhat as the members of the council prepared themselves for the telling of the adventure. Unfortunately Starr, the woman with whom he had spent his time instead of making ready for the meeting was, by some nasty quirk of fate, moving among the council, pouring mulled mandrake wine into waiting mugs. She turned and shot Mika a look of pure disgust.

"Sit beside me," said Trabec, patting the ground to his right, forcing Oban to give way reluctantly. Mika did not wish to usurp the shaman's place or offend him in any way, as he would soon be asking for favors, but short of affronting the chief, there did not seem to be any way to avoid the invitation.

Mika and Tam squeezed into the narrow space, and Tam managed to sit on Oban's wolf's tail, causing her to yip as though she had been seriously injured. Oban lifted his wolf up and all but tossed her into the wolf belonging to the man seated on the other side of him, causing still further commotion.

Trabec ignored the furor. When the last of the snapping, growling, and muttering had faded away, he began to speak.

"We are gathered here tonight around the sacred council fire for the telling of the adventure of our brothers, Mika and Hornsbuck, born of the Far Fringe wolf clan, full brothers of the Phantom Forest wolf clan. This is their story. I will allow them to speak."

"Ow! Ow! Ow!" howled each member of the council, thumping their cups on the ground. All eyes turned to Mika and Hornsbuck.

Hornsbuck cleared his throat. Everyone stared at him expectantly.

"I was but second in command," said Hornsbuck. "Mika was in charge of the expedition. It would be improper for me to speak first. But here is my contribution to the clan." He took a pouch from inside his tunic and handed it to Trabec. The chief opened the pouch and poured out a handful of rings, necklets, and earpieces that Mika recognized as the booty taken from the Flannae aborigines.

Mika felt his heart sink within his breast at the outpouring of wealth and the collective gasp of breath. What on Oerth was he to do? He had not a single grushnik to contribute on his own behalf.

Hornsbuck fell silent, and all eyes turned to Mika.

He sat staring at the ground, eyes and cheeks burning. The silence grew painful.

"Mika? We would hear your tale," urged Trabec. "How came you to be here among us, and what report you of your clan, many of whom are closely related to us?"

This was news to Mika, and his heart sank still further. He had dreaded telling his own clan what had happened on the mission to Eru-Tovar, and now it seemed that he would have to tell the terrible news twice.

Mika knew that his quest had not failed through any fault of his own. But now, with everyone looking at him expectantly, waiting for him to speak, he did not feel so confident that they would understand.

"Mika?" prompted Trabec again.

And with faltering voice, Mika told of the adventure that had begun so confidently with himself in charge of two score Wolf Nomads and ended with the death of all except himself and Hornsbuck.

Gasps of shock and grunts of pain echoed around him as he recited the names of those who had ridden with him and not returned—names obviously related to those around him.

"We were doomed from the start. . . ." said Mika as he continued the awful tale.

Whispers of anger buzzed around him like maddened wasps, slowly diminishing as he spoke of the treachery and witchcraft that had stalked them from the start and of the mysterious, sleeping beauty who was the Princess Julia. The room was silent as he told of the final battle with the demigod of evil, Iuz, and the subsequent encounter with the demon, leaving out all mention of the curse.

The mutterings turned to startled exclamations as he spoke of the magic gem which turned the princess into a wolf. Mika felt Starr's eyes on him. He risked a glance, only to find her staring at him with lips compressed into a thin, tight line, her hands on her hips, and angry realization in her eyes.

Mika could not help but notice that the shaman started back at the mention of the demon. "Oban, do you know of this demon?" he asked.

The shaman looked away.

"Tell us what you know, please!" Mika begged.

The shaman turned his head back toward Mika. His eyes glittered brightly as though he were feverish, and his thin lips curved in an unpleasant smile.

"I do not *know* him, but I know *of* him," he said. "Few make his acquaintance and live. He is all that is evil in the world, all that is foul and corrupt, all that is wicked on Oerth and . . . his name is Maelfesh!"

At the mention of the name there was a gasp, and those gathered in the building huddled together, pulling away, putting distance between themselves and Mika.

Mika felt as though his soul had been turned to ice. Maelfesh! The most evil and demonic of all demons. He had not even suspected that it was Maelfesh. Why would such a high-level demon bother with a lowly human? It just didn't make sense! Why! Why! Why! Feeling more lost than ever before, squeezed in the grip of something beyond his comprehension or capabilities, Mika was ready to give up. Hornsbuck read the surrender in his eyes.

"All the more reason to go on!" boomed the large

174

nomad's voice.

Mika looked up and saw Hornsbuck lighting his pipe casually with a steady hand.

"You dare not do that, brother," said Trabec.

"It would be suicide." He expressed Mika's feelings exactly.

"We are Wolf Nomads, not mouse-tailed cowards," said Hornsbuck. "Wolf Nomads laugh in the face of death. We tempt fate to the limits, and welcome danger with open arms. We do not run from demons!"

Why not just this once? thought Mika, groaning inwardly. That damned code of the Wolf Nomads was going to get him killed yet. But once the code was invoked, there was no going back—certainly not after it was invoked in front of an entire clan council. Now Mika was committed to complete the journey to its all but inevitable conclusion.

"Ow! Ow! Ow!" howled the council, each of them raising their horn mugs and toasting the courage of their brothers.

"Oh! Oh! Oh!" screamed Mika, but no one save the shaman heard him.

"What is to become of the princess?" asked Trabec in a somber tone.

"I am taking her to Exag and returning her to her father," said Mika, glad to discuss something other than the death of his men.

"I had hoped to refill my potions and healing ungents and consult with your shaman on a matter of importance before we set out to finish our mission," said Mika. "Only this has prevented us from making directly for Exag."

Trabec looked at Mika without speaking for long heartbeats, his dark eyes hard as flint. Finally, he spoke.

"I am not sure you should be allowed to continue," Trabec said sternly. "I am uncertain that you deserve the honor. Enor, your chief and my blood relative, would have strong words to say. In his absence, I must speak for him. How many more men will you kill in the doing? We would not care to lose our brother, Hornsbuck. Nor would we be able to dissuade him from what he considers to be a mission of honor and I consider to be a mission of death."

A cold chill flowed over Mika, and it seemed that he could already feel the pain starting in his next to last finger. It had never occurred to him that he might not be allowed to finish the mission, to take the princess to Exag, find her father, and appease the demon. If that were to happen, he would be well and truly cursed! If the demon didn't kill him outright, the curse would finish him off for sure.

"No!" he boomed in a desperate tone. "I do not ask for any men to accompany me. I will accomplish the mission on my own. No one will be at risk but myself. I beg you to allow me to complete this task!"

"You hardly seem to be the proper choice for such an important mission," Oban said nastily. "The princess herself dislikes you so much that even you admit that she has tried to kill you.

"I say that you cannot return a princess to her father in the form of a wolf," Oban continued. "Important diplomatic relations could be established that would work to our benefit if we changed her back to human form.

"Meanwhile we must not allow Mika to go anywhere near this girl, uh, wolf, again," said Oban. "Send someone else who can do the job correctly. I myself would be willing to volunteer under the circumstances."

I bet you would, you sanctimonious old frog, thought Mika. I wonder what else you'd volunteer to do while you were at it.

"I agree with Oban," said the shaman's assistant, a whey-faced, hollow-chested, scrawny fellow who bore a strong family resemblance to the shaman. "I think Mika's done enough harm."

There was a murmur of agreement around the circle as the various chiefs conferred. Mika could feel the tide swinging solidly against him. He jumped to his feet and opened his mouth to speak, desperate to try to explain what had happened, to tell them that there had been nothing else he could have done.

"I didn't—I couldn't—I, uh, tried, uh . . ." he stammered. But the voices only muttered louder now, expressions growing blacker. With a sinking heart, Mika looked into eyes that were dark with grief and anger.

Then, just as it seemed that all was lost, a single voice roared out. "Wait!" it said with such force that it drowned out the rising clamor of voices, causing them to trail away into silence.

"Although it is true that our brother has a . . . a somewhat unique manner of doing things at times," said Hornsbuck, still seated, "I cannot fault him for anything that happened. And neither can any of you since, may I remind you, none of you were there to say otherwise."

"But . . ." stammered Oban. "But so many were lost and . . ."

"Through no fault of Mika's," interrupted Hornsbuck. "I was there, and I know. We did the best we could, and Mika deserves the opportunity to finish the mission. We have discussed the matter between ourselves, and I, for one, feel that he is capable of finishing it rightly. I say that you should give him the chance."

So saying, Hornsbuck detached a wolf tail from the end of his braid and tossed it into the center of the circle, to the right of the fire at Mika's feet. "I say yea." He looked around the circle, gazing at each and every man in turn.

There was an undercurrent of muttering and then Oban, flushed of face, dark eyes glittering, scuttled to his feet and faced Mika. He ripped the single wolf tail from his own thin braid and cast it down to the ground, to the left of the fire at Mika's feet.

"I say nay," he said in a cold voice.

"I say nay, also," echoed his assistant, who threw his own tiny tail down beside Oban's.

There was a moment of silence; no man was willing to make the next move.

"I say yea," said a soft, calm voice, and Trabec slowly detached his own full tail and placed it deliberately beside Hornsbuck's. There was a sharp, gasped intake of air and after that, there was no question of the final outcome. When the tails were counted, all but two had voted in Mika's favor.

"Where is this fabled gemstone?" asked Oban pointedly when the commotion had died down. "I would see it."

"Uh, the princess has it," said Mika.

"What! How can a wolf carry a gemstone?" asked Oban. "Why do you permit it? It could easily be lost!"

"It . . . it was sort of an accident," said Mika. "She seized it this afternoon, and I was unable to retrieve it. That is why I appeared before you in such an unkempt state," he added in a moment of brilliance. "I have been trying to get it back all afternoon."

"You must retrieve it immediately!" directed Oban.

"I shall," promised Mika, wondering how on Oerth he would manage to get the gem away from the princess.

Chapter 17

IN THE END it was Starr who helped him obtain the gem, though not out of any thoughts of kindness toward him.

"Klaren was my cousin," she said in a cold tone, naming one of the nomads who had been lost on the expedition. "We were very close when we were young," she added as they stood outside the council building while the men began their serious drinking.

"I did not cause him to be killed," protested Mika. "We all took our chances. He was just less lucky than I."

"I'd be willing to bet it always works out that way," Starr said, eyeing him in a calculating manner. "I'll bet you always manage to come through lucky, as you put it, without a scratch, while others get killed."

"So what do you want me to do, get myself killed next time?" asked Mika.

"Try it, I might like it," Starr said coolly, brushing past him.

"Starr, you're not being reasonable," groaned

Mika as he caught her arm.

"Reasonable? You expect me to be reasonable?" asked Starr. She shook his hand off and turned to face him, fixing him with a cold stare.

"I know your type, Mika. I've seen lots of men like you, draped in gems and chain mail, boasting of your prowess with dragons and damsels. You don't want your women reasonable. Cute, maybe. Sexy. Even agreeable, but never reasonable unless you're asking something unreasonable. Sorry. I don't feel reasonable.

"But I do feel sorry for that poor princess. You've certainly fixed her good. What will you do to me if I don't please you, turn me into a worm?"

"Starr," groaned Mika.

"Oh, Starr yourself," fumed Starr as she turned and stormed off into the forest. "I'm going to help the princess."

"Starr, wait!" cried Mika. "You can't do that! She's dangerous. She tried to kill me, and she certainly doesn't seem to like you!"

"That was before I knew what had happened," said Starr, her back rigid with anger. "It's different now."

Mika started to call out to her, to grab her and force her to listen, when a sudden thought hit him. Maybe, just maybe, Starr could do it. Maybe she could talk to the princess and smooth things over; women were good at that sort of thing. Perhaps she could even persuade the princess to give him back the gem!

He missed the gem, missed the heaviness of it hanging from his neck. Somehow it had become very important to him in the short time he had possessed it, and it bothered him that it was gone.

"All right, Starr," he said, making his voice as humble and contrite as possible. "Do it your way. I guess you could be right after all. I suppose I have been pretty unfeeling about the whole thing. I was only trying to do what I thought was right, but I can see how it might not appear that way. I'll do whatever you want, if it will help that poor girl out there."

"*What?* I don't believe you!" Starr said as she turned around and stared at him suspiciously. "Is this some kind of trick? What are you up to?"

"Starr," Mika said quietly in a pained tone, doing his best to look innocent. "You're not being fair. First you accuse me of being unfeeling, then when I agree and offer to help, you accuse me of being up to no good. What do you want of me?"

Starr looked at him uncertainly. "Do you really mean it?" she said. "No tricks?"

"No tricks. And yes, I really mean it," said Mika, opening his eyes wide in what he hoped was an innocent expression. "What do you want me to do?"

"Well, it seems as though she's run away," Starr said, tapping her chin with her finger "But she can't know very much about hunting, or even how to hide. I'll go get something for her to eat, and you bring this other wolf here, Tam is it? And we'll go look for her. Tam will find her. Won't you, Tam?"

Tam yawned broadly and looked away, clearly uninterested. The wolf lay down on the ground and closed his eyes.

Starr returned more quickly than Mika would have expected, struggling with an armload of edibles.

"What did you get?" asked Mika.

"Roansbuck steak, done on the rare side, with lots of pepper, mushrooms, onions, watercress, plantain greens with garlic, and a lovely pudding with ground yarpick nuts sprinkled on top. I made it myself this afternoon," said Starr, showing Mika the wooden platter filled with numerous plates and bowls.

"Starr, this is a wolf we're talking about," cried Mika. "Wolves don't eat pudding and salad. A slice of raw meat would be more appropriate."

"Don't be stupid, Mika," said Starr. "She's a princess, isn't she? I would never eat a piece of raw meat—ughh! Even if some horrible person were mean enough to turn me into a wolf, I'd still be me inside."

"You could be right," said Mika.

"Of course I am," said Starr with a little sniff. "I'm always right." Turning away from him, she walked into the forest and began to call.

"Here, princess! Here, princess! It's Starr. Please come out! I've brought you something to eat."

Starr and Mika wandered back and forth in the dark forest, Star calling out to the princess, Mika trailing behind as he tried to get Tam to search for Princess Julia.

But Tam had had his fill of the arrogant bitch. He didn't like her as a wolf any better than he had when she was human. Every time he had even tried to sniff her tail, perfectly proper wolf etiquette, she had snapped at him and growled.

No, Tam wasn't interested in searching for the princess. She could stay lost forever, for all he cared. Showing disinterest, Tam sat down on the ground and nibbled at a flea on his flank.

They had been wandering for some time without any sign of the princess, when suddenly Starr gave a sharp cry. Huddled atop a tall boulder was the dark form of the princess. She stared down at them without expression, her eyes mere slits in the darkness. The gem sat on the moss-covered surface of the rock, directly in front of her muzzle.

A painful aching filled Mika at the nearness of the gem. Yet he held back, making no effort to seize it, knowing that if he made one false move, the princess would grab it and be gone before he could reach her.

"Princess?" Starr called in a soft low tone. "Princess, I know what's happened to you. Mika told us. I don't know what I can do to help, but I'd like to be your friend . . . if you'd let me."

The princess looked at Starr, and Mika held his breath, waiting for the first hint of movement, never really believing that the princess would allow Starr near her.

The moment stretched further, drawing more and more tense with every passing heartbeat. The princess and the woman continued to stare at each other. Then, just as Mika began to think he'd have to do or say something to break the tension, the princess whined and lay her head down atop of the rock.

"Go away, Mika," said Starr without even looking at him.

"What?" asked Mika, thinking he'd heard wrong.

"Go away!" Starr said quite clearly. "The princess and I have things to talk about."

Mika wasn't at all sure he liked the sound of that. As a matter of fact, he was quite sure that he didn't like it at all, but there was nothing to be done, for Starr and the princess were both giving him the same imperious look, waiting for him to leave.

"Uh, all right, I guess," Mika said unhappily. "I'll be back at the council lodge if you want me."

He could still feel their eyes on his back long after he had passed out of sight. He had the uncomfortable feeling that they would soon be talking about him. It didn't help in the least, knowing that the princess couldn't talk. Somehow they would manage. Women always did.

Tam yawned, got to his feet slowly, stretched leisurely, and then padded after Mika. So the sharp-toothed vixen had been found. Well, maybe she'd get lost again, Tam thought to himself.

Mika and Tam made their way back to Trabec's dwelling. The ceremony was well advanced. Many cups of mandrake wine had flowed since they had left to find the princess. The pipes were being lit now, tamped full with wolfsbane, a narcotic weed used in sacred nomad rituals. Mika settled himself in the thick of things, determined to forget his problems for the rest of the night.

They smoked their pipes and drank their wine and spoke of the dead, remembering them, honoring their passing. Those who had been blood-tied were accorded central seats and granted extra portions of wine and weed. Soon, the dark night air was filled with a cacophony of howls, some sounding a little strange because the howlers, both wolf and human, were no longer seated upright; some were on their backs, others on their sides, and still more on their faces. Howling was very difficult when lying on one's face. But Wolf Nomad ritual demanded that the dead be honored with a chorus of howls and so, wine and weed notwithstanding, the celebrants did their best.

Mika wakened early the next morning clutched in Hornsbuck's massive arms. For one horrified moment, he wondered if the curse had advanced to the full extreme without his knowledge.

He separated himself from Hornsbuck, scrambling backward on the hard, dirt floor. Wolves and nomads were everywhere, lying where they had fallen, overcome by their unswerving devotion to nomad custom.

Mika felt less terrible than he might have expected, but he realized that he had missed much of the ritual by looking for the princess.

The princess! Mika reeled out of the dwelling and staggered off in the direction of the forest. He had to find Starr and the princess. He should never have left them alone together for such a long period of time. What if their initial truce had not lasted? What if the princess had hurt Starr? He'd be in even worse trouble!

Berating himself for leaving, he rushed into the woods, with Tam following on equally unsteady legs. He remembered the direction from the night before and fought his way between the dense growth of trees.

"Damn trees," he cursed. "Why can't they grow in straight rows!"

He heard them before he saw them—the giggling gave them away. He slowed, and then for some unknown reason, he crept forward and hid behind

187

the base of an immense roanwood tree instead of announcing himself in a straightforward manner, straining to hear what was being said.

". . . and then, you won't believe this, but I swear it's true. He said, 'Starr, I could learn to love a girl like you.' " Starr deepened her voice, and Mika realized with a terrible shock that she was parodying him! He peeked out from behind the tree and saw Starr strutting back and forth in front of the rock where the princess still perched, watching Starr with laughing eyes.

Mika stumbled away, his face and ears burning. Was it possible that women talked to each other like this often? What else had Starr told the princess? His mind reeled. Suddenly, he felt positively ill. He sat down on the ground and held his head.

"Oh, there you are, Mika dear," said a sweet voice. Mika could barely manage to raise his head. He looked at Starr through bloodshot eyes, feeling the birth of a monstrous headache beginning to throb behind his eyes.

"Is something the matter?" Starr asked sweetly, her big, brown eyes gazing down at him with the utmost innocence.

"I . . . I don't think I feel very good," he whispered.

"Poor dear," said Starr, her voice trembling with solicitude. "I was just telling the princess that we should come to see how you were. I was sure you would devote yourself to drinking in a serious manner—only to show your respect for your men, of course," she added hastily. "Come along with us, Mika. The princess and I will take care of you!"

Mika looked from one set of female eyes to the other and put his head down on his knees and groaned, for that was precisely what he was afraid of.

Chapter 18

MIKA ALLOWED STARR TO LEAD HIM back to the village and tuck him into bed. He fell asleep instantly and did not waken until the following morning, his exhausted body doing its best to catch up on lost sleep.

When he wakened, he jumped out of bed, thunderstruck that he had slept so long. There was still much to be done! He dressed hastily, glad to see that his gauntlet had not been removed, unable to remember undressing—or anything else for that matter. Much to his surprise, the magic gem had been returned to him as he slept, the gold circlet atop the gem affixed to a brand-new chain of finely forged links. The gem felt warm against his chest, and Mika felt better than he had in days, even though his head still ached with the remnants of a headache.

Starr watched him from the low doorway as he struggled to cram his foot into his boot.

"The princess and I decided that you should keep the stone for safekeeping, Mika. But remember that it's hers, and you must give it back once she is safely home."

Mika sat down on the bed, waiting for the catch, wondering what additional price they were going to extract from him. Getting the stone back couldn't be that simple! Tam snoozed at the end of the bed, and even he opened one eye and twitched an ear.

"What else?" Mika growled suspiciously when nothing else seemed forthcoming.

"Nothing else," Starr said with a gentle smile. "Just keep your word, or you'll be sorry."

"Of course I'll keep my word," muttered Mika as he slipped past Starr and hurried out the door, unwilling to meet her steady gaze. "What do you think I am, untrustworthy?" Fortunately, he was halfway down the path before she answered. He barked a command to Tam and somehow managed to miss her reply.

Mika stopped long enough to pull on his second boot before wandering through the village to look for the shaman's dwelling. Like it or not, he still had to refill his supply of healing herbs and hopefully pick the man's mind for a cure for the awful demon fingers. His task would be complicated by the fact that the shaman did not seem to like him and had voted against him in the council, although Mika did not understand why he had done so.

He found the shaman's dwelling by following the directions of a small child. Like all nomad dwellings, it was constructed of roanwood posts driven deep into the ground and then interwoven with smaller branches and plastered over with moss and mud. He called out, and when there was no answer, he stepped over the broad sill and entered with Tam at his heels.

Considering the sour nature of the shaman, it was a most pleasant dwelling. He found himself in an unusually large room, with windows the length of one wall. Under the windows was a broad, wood slab, half of a roanwood trunk that served as work space for the preparation of ungents, tinctures, potions, and possets, many of which were placed neatly on the shelves that lined the walls in a wide variety of tiny bottles, horns, vials, and tubes.

Strange plants, only a few of which Mika recognized, grew in moss-lined niches carved in the wooden pillars that supported the roof. Large bunches of dried herbs and medicinal weeds were suspended from the beams. Sacks labeled bat's wings, spider's legs, salamander eyes, and other ingredients necessary for the working of spells were stacked in an orderly fashion under the bench.

A small, gold and silver pseudodragon was perched on the window sill, preening itself in the warm sunlight. The creature hissed at Mika, its long, forked tongue flicking in and out as though tasting his blood, and its poisoned tail quivered nastily above its head. Mika gave it wide berth.

Oban's workshop also featured a large, stone hearth in the center of the room, raised to waist level, bringing it within easy reach. Even now, an immense cauldron hung over the coals, emitting a dank, sulfurous stink. Tam backed away, pawing at his nose as a yellow cloud belched out of the pot and rolled over them.

Mika was bending over the cauldron, trying to figure out what was being brewed, when a voice spoke out behind him, calling his name. He turned, wondering why Tam had not warned him of the shaman's approach, but he saw no one.

The voice called his name again. Searching the room, he saw the pseudodragon hovering in mid-air, scarcely a hand's width away from his face, the dangerous, barbed tail ominously close. He flinched back and tried to speak in a level tone.

"Your pardon, honored shaman. I called before I entered, but no one answered. I have come to consult with you on business. Your helper is most impressive, but may I beg your presence in person?"

The pseudodragon darted forward, its little, brightly colored wings vibrating so swiftly that they could barely be seen, its deadly tail positioned to deliver a fatal sting. Mika shielded his face with his gauntlet, knowing that to be stung on any portion of his body was to die. Tam snarled and lunged for the effervescent creature, his teeth snapping on empty air.

"No, Tam, down!" cried Mika as he batted at the creature, trying to knock it out of the air, alarmed that Tam might actually catch the dangerous thing.

"Mika," it said just as Mika's hand struck it full on the body. Abruptly, amazingly, the pseudodragon turned into the shaman right before Mika's startled eyes.

The man's face was set in a grim frown, his attitude unimproved by the fact that Mika's hand was still resting heavily on top of his head.

"Uh oh," gulped Mika as he began to brush the shaman down, whisking non-existent dust off the man's wolfskin cloak. "I've been looking for you, honored one."

The shaman struck Mika's hand aside and drew himself up to his full height, his dark, beady eyes flashing angrily. "What do you want?"

"I need to replenish my supplies. All of my healing herbs and potions were destroyed," Mika replied politely, knowing that he must not lose his temper. "I worry about the safety of my party, traveling with my medicine pouch empty."

"From what I've heard of your skills, your party will be immeasurably safer without them," said the shaman, his wattled neck quivering with anger.

Mika stared at the man in bewilderment, unable to figure out why the shaman seemed to dislike him so much.

"I am not that bad," he said cautiously.

"That is not what my brother says," sneered the shaman.

"Who is your brother?" Mika asked, mystified.

"Whituk, shaman of the Far Fringe Clan," said Oban, watching Mika's face to measure the impact of his words.

He was not disappointed. Mika blanched and the blood left his face at the mention of the hated name. Whituk! The mealy-mouthed assistant who had become shaman and magic-user upon the death of Mika's father, thus casting Mika out of the clan without a hearth to call his own. Whituk! Whituk who had always been jealous of him. No, he would find no help from these quarters.

Mika turned on his heel without a word and made as if to go. The shaman's voice rang out again. "Why have you come to see me?" he asked harshly. "Do not speak of potions and healing herbs. These things are helpful, but you have a spell book. With the gem to aid you, you do not need such things. What is the real reason you have come? Speak truthfully, with none of your guile, and mayhaps I will help you."

Mika hesitated, desperate for guidance from one skilled enough to know the answer. The man hated him, that was clear, but he was a professional; his impressive laboratory spoke more eloquently than any words. His pride in his calling might cause him to help solve Mika's terrible problem. Deciding that he had little to lose and everything to gain, Mika turned to face the shaman. In an open and honest voice he told Oban about his encounter with the demon Maelfesh, sparing none of the details.

The three-fingered demon hand rested on the table between the two men, Mika's own two remaining fingers dwarfed by the larger, green digits; his palm seemed too small to accommodate such monstrosities. The shaman turned the hand over one last time and then set it gently on the table with a sigh.

"I'm sorry," he said, looking Mika straight in the eye, all sign of his earlier hostility gone. "There's really nothing I can do. It's a clear cut case of demon digititis. The prognosis is not good. The possession will continue to advance, finger after finger, then hand, arm, and so on."

"You mean . . . all of me?" Mika said in a small voice. "I—I could turn into a demon? Isn't there anything you can do to stop it? And how come the demon knows every thought I'm thinking the very heartbeat that it comes to mind?"

Oban, now just a harmless old shaman forced to deliver bad news to a patient, sighed again and rubbed his eyes. "I don't know how the demon knows. It could be any one of a number of devices; something that you possess, carry with you always, must be acting as a window and enables the demon to know what is happening. It could be some article of clothing, or something as mundane as your knife. But even without the window, the demon would still be all but invincible, for his powers far outweigh those of any mortal."

"Then what am I to do?" Mika asked in desperation.

"You must do what the demon ordered," said Oban. "Go to Exag, find this king, and wait for further instructions. And when they come, follow them to the last dot or you will surely be demon fodder."

"But what are the chances of his releasing me unharmed, even if I do as he says?" asked Mika.

"Not great," admitted Oban. "But what are your chances otherwise? I know of only one thing that will undo the damage."

"What?" asked Mika, gripping the table tightly.

"Something or someone of greater power," answered Oban.

"What about the stone that matches this one?" asked Mika, holding up the magic gem. "Would the two of them together be strong enough?"

"Perhaps. I do not know what their properties are, what they are capable of," Oban replied. "But it would certainly be worth trying. Just remember one thing: the demon will know the very instant you deviate from his instructions, and he will act accordingly."

With those words hanging heavy in his heart, Mika left the shaman's dwelling, his pouch swelled to overflowing with an abundance of healing potions, ungents, herbs, and tinctures, none of which could assuage his problems.

With the revelation of the dread demon fingers, Oban had lost his earlier hostility; he watched Mika go with a look of pity on his face, knowing that the man was as good as dead. Whituk would never have to worry again.

Chapter 19

MIKA'S GROUP LEFT THE NOMAD CAMP on the following morning, laden with enough supplies to see them as far as Exag and then on to Dramidja, if the Great She-Wolf granted them her protection.

Hornsbuck and Lotus Blossom hung from their saddles, bidding farewell to those who had become friends during the short interval of their stay. Lotus Blossom's pouch hung heavily at her belt, and it seemed obvious that her formidable and somewhat devious skill at knucklebones had not diminished.

RedTail was looking plump and well-groomed, having eaten his fill and been brushed till his thick coat gleamed like burnished bronze. Tam had spent the remainder of their time in the camp slumbering contentedly on Starr's hearth. He hadn't declined the tasty treats she had offered him, even though Mika himself sat morosely before the fire, staring at his gauntleted hand.

It was the princess, however, who was the most affected by their stay. No longer did she glower and snarl at wolf and man alike, but appeared content in her wolven form. More than content, she strutted proudly and even swaggered about, her head aloft, blue and green eyes flashing, and her tail arched high above her back. An admiring retinue of male wolves followed her wherever she went, and far from discouraging them, she led them on with coy glances and swaying hips.

Mika alone was despondent, for he had risked the demon's displeasure by stopping at the nomad camp rather than heading straight for Exag as he had been told. He had gambled on learning some bit of information that would help him fight the demon. Instead, he had gained a third demon finger and had learned absolutely nothing that would help him outwit and ultimately defeat the demon.

The princess had remained at Starr's side for the rest of the visit. The two of them had become nearly inseparable, and they constantly gave Mika the same cool look of hidden amusement.

That look had really begun to irk Mika, even piercing his great depression which they appeared not to notice. He wondered what they said to each other when they were alone, or how they even communicated at all. He wondered, but not enough to ask Starr, for he didn't really want to know.

Nor was he as disappointed as he would have been under normal conditions over his inability to get Starr alone, for he was unwilling to put his virility to the test again until he had found the red stone. He was actually relieved when it came time to wave a final farewell and take his leave.

Starr knelt next to Tam and the princess and

hugged them each in turn, though she squeezed the princess longer and whispered in her ear.

And there—there it was again! That look! The two of them staring at him as though they were laughing and sharing a secret! Suddenly infuriated, Mika felt the blood rush to his head. He kicked the roan hard, causing it to rear up on its hind legs and leap forward. Hornsbuck, Lotus Blossom, and the wolves were caught by surprise and were forced to race after him or be left behind.

The young boys, always ready for the opportunity to parade about and exhibit their fine horsemanship to the clumps of admiring girls, accompanied them past the edge of the forest and out onto the plains, yipping their budding wolf cries, waving their wolf-bannered lances, and causing their horses to rear dramatically. But even they were left behind, and the village disappeared from sight.

Once out on the plains, Mika felt the exhilaration of a new beginning and a sense of freedom from the clinging obligations that were always part of belonging. He looked over at Hornsbuck and saw the same look of excitement in his friend's eyes. Mika understood even more than before why a man might choose to live his life moving from one adventure to the next without the webs of personal entanglement.

The miles passed swiftly without incident, as did the days, growing colder with each new sunrise as they edged closer to the month of Sunsebb.

The grease bushes, the most common vegetation on the plains, were rimmed with an outline of ice that burned red with the rising sun. Their blankets were stiff and crackly when the companions rose with steaming breath from their bedrolls.

Tam and the princess had seemingly grown closer since leaving the nomad village. Mika was puzzled by this occurrence. He could not help but feel somewhat slighted, since Tam now spent more time in her company than with him, but upon reflection, he decided that he preferred the peace rather than the constant hostilities. If anything, the princess almost ignored him now, having eyes only for Tam.

The two wolves were together constantly, sometimes including RedTail in their forays, but seemingly content with their own company. They even slept together at night, curled into one tight ball, sharing body heat. Mika felt almost lost, sleeping without the weight of Tam at the foot of his cloak, but he told himself that the princess had never lived so roughly before. Tam had obviously taken pity on her and was simply being kind. It didn't mean a thing, Mika told himself. It did occur to him briefly that it was rather odd behavior for Tam, who was not given to kind deeds.

They hunted, they rode, they ate, they slept, and time passed smoothly. Yet Mika was never able to completely forget the curse that hung over his head, and he continued to guard against it, his exaggerated masculine persona now firmly in place. His every waking and sleeping moment was spent thinking about the curse, his hand, and the demon, and wondering what he was going to do about them all.

One night, as they were sitting by a fire built of carefully metered charcoal chunks, Mika was telling some wild story involving himself and three mermaids.

Finally Hornsbuck put down his mug of honeyed-ale and looked at him. Mika's voice faded away under the older man's steady gaze.

"Mika, I like a good story as well as the next man," said Hornsbuck, "but you've got to stop. Pretty soon you'll be believing these tales yourself."

"But, but . . ." sputtered Mika. "It's true! I swear it!"

"Mika!" roared Hornsbuck as Mika continued to protest. "No man, not even you, could do half the things you've told me. You've barely been out of the village on a score of occasions. How could you have bedded all those lasses in that short time?"

"Maybe it's true, Hornsbuck," Lotus Blossom said with a hearty laugh. "I remember you at that age. Seems to me there's not much difference between what the boy here says and you did." She eyed him speculatively and rolled a thick braid between her fingers. "Give him to me for the night, and I'll find out what kind of stuff he's made of."

"Hush, woman," Hornsbuck said with a dismissive gesture, his green eyes never leaving Mika's face. "Leave off your fooling."

But Mika paled, for he had seen the keen look of interest in Lotus Blossom's face, the same look that Tam wore when he was ready to devour a terrified rabbit. He knew that Lotus Blossom was deadly serious. The thought of being bedded by her sobered him more quickly than Hornsbuck's words.

"No more, Mika," Hornsbuck admonished. "Tell me what this be all about, and tell me the truth. And in your own voice, please. I'm tired of listening to you croaking like a bullfrog and watching you act the fool. Tell me what's going on, or I'll give you to Lotus Blossom and let her shake it out of you."

Looking into his bright green eyes, Mika knew without a doubt that he would.

Mika sighed and leaned forward, his elbows on his knees, his face hidden. He sighed again.

"It's a curse," he said in his normal voice, which sounded small and thin to his ears. "From the gem. It's a female stone, and if a man uses it, he starts to change into a woman a little bit at a time, each and every time he uses it."

"Are you sure?" asked Hornsbuck with a gasp. "That's terrible, lad!"

"Yes, I'm sure," Mika said miserably. "There were just little signs at first, but then . . . then with Starr, I found that I couldn't . . . couldn't!" There was an awkward stretch of silence.

"But—but—that's terrible! I'd kill myself if that ever happened to me," rumbled Hornsbuck. "Oh, uh, just a matter of speech, lad. Forget I said that."

"Don't be silly, boy. There's lots of other important things to do with your life!" Lotus Blossom boomed in her normal, hearty manner, but Mika could see the pity in her eyes and knew that her heart was not in her words.

"But there is a way out," muttered Mika. "It seems that there's a red stone, a male gem that will reverse the damage and make me as good as new. In fact, the two stones together are twice as powerful. When I'm done with this demon business, I'm going to get that stone."

"Of course you will," Hornsbuck said loudly, leaning over to pat Mika on the knee, abruptly drawing his hand back. "I'll even go with you, lad. I know you'd do the same for me."

"Oh, Hornsbuck, what'll I do if . . . if . . . ?" Mika said tremulously as he raised his head and looked at Hornsbuck with tormented eyes.

"Don't worry, lad," said Hornsbuck, so overcome by compassion that he actually placed his arm around Mika's shoulders. "I promise to see you through this, er, mess. You can depend on it."

"Oh, thank you, Hornsbuck," cried Mika. So great was his relief at sharing the fearful burden with someone that he leaned his forehead against the older man's shoulder and sobbed; Hornsbuck patted him on the back.

"Hornsbuck! What be you doing? The pair of you be acting like sniveling maids!" shouted Lotus Blossom.

Mika and Hornsbuck leaped apart as though stung by bees. Mika brushed his eyes with the back of his hand and blinked furiously. Hornsbuck jumped to his feet and began stoking the fire, which was perfectly fine as it was.

They busied themselves with a flurry of activities to cover their embarrassment and avoided looking at each other. After a short time they took themselves to opposite ends of the camp. Bidding each other good night in loud, masculine voices, they pulled their cloaks up over their heads.

It seemed to Mika that Hornsbuck and Lotus Blossom were more vocal than usual in their nightly frolic. Tam and the princess looked at each other through dark, slitted eyes and shared silent laughter. They fitted their long, lean bodies around each other till they were meshed, head to tail, and then they, too, closed their eyes and slept. The camp was quiet, with only one pair of human eyes remaining to stare at the stars in silence.

Chapter 20

THEY HAD CROSSED THE RIVER and entered the rough foothills of the Yatil Mountains without incident. Mika and Hornsbuck had regained their earlier camaraderie, and only occasionally did Mika catch the faintest glimpse of pity in Hornsbuck's eyes.

Lotus Blossom remained her usual coarse self and at times seemed to look for opportunities to pinch his bottom and tell him crude jokes. At first Mika thought she was doing it out of cruelty, and he found himself all but hating her.

She continued unchecked, but the constant crude comments began to lose their effect, and he found himself able to return them in kind. After a time Mika ceased hating her, and he found himself actually looking forward to the repartee, which was far easier to take than Hornsbuck's pity. Mika began to truly appreciate Lotus Blossom for the first time, feeling her gusto and enthusiasm for life rather than merely observing it.

Tam and the princess had grown even closer, running side by side and sharing dark glances. It seemed that Tam was teaching the princess all the things that a wolf should know.

So close was their friendship that Mika began to brood. It was he and Tam who were supposed to be bonded, best friends for life, not Tam and the princess. How could Tam take her seriously? After all, the princess was only a female!

Mike even tried to talk to Tam, to tell him how he felt, but Tam merely looked at him with blank eyes and quickly returned to the princess's side. Mika's ears burned, and he wondered if they, too, were somehow talking about him.

Of late, it seemed that Tam scarcely ever left the princess's side. Once, he even bared his fangs and growled at RedTail when he ventured close. RedTail stared at him blankly, then turned aside and thereafter kept to himself.

Time seemed to lose its meaning in the beautiful, crisp, cold days. Hunting was good, and they decided to make a short excursion up onto the lower slopes of the mountains to hunt the wild dass sheep that sported massive, curled horns and dense, oily coats.

They made camp in the mouth of a cave at the base of a steep ravine that cut into the mountain. They collected broken bits of wood, deposited throughout the dry steam bed running in front of the cave, and built a large fire, basking in its warmth.

They were fortunate enough to kill an unwary antelope. After filling their bellies, Hornsbuck relaxed the rules that usually controlled his behavior while on a mission, and he and Lotus Blossom drank a full skin of honeyed-ale. Soon they were wrapped in a beery embrace, asleep in front of the fire. RedTail had shared in their ale, and he lay soporific in front of the fire as well.

Mika was restless, having had no desire to partake of the ale, unusual in itself. It seemed that Tam and the princess were restless, too. They milled about and stood at the mouth of the cave, sniffing the cool night air and whining, high shrill sounds that spoke of yearning and wishes unfulfilled.

Mika watched them, envious of their togetherness, unhappy at being left out. It seemed that everyone had someone except him. Hornsbuck had Lotus Blossom, Tam had the princess, and RedTail had Hornsbuck. Only Mika was alone. He felt his loneliness keenly.

He grieved for himself and tried to remember what it felt like to be happy, to be in love. He tried to remember what it had been like to have fun. He was tired of brooding and feeling bad. Mika was miserable.

Suddenly, he knew what he had to do. It wasn't right that everyone else in the world was having fun and friends while he suffered so. He wanted to have fun again and feel as though someone liked him, and by The Great She-Wolf, mother of them all, he would! Picking up his shoulder pouch, he pawed through it until he found his spell book. He drew it out and leafed through it until he came to the right page. A beatific smile lined his face as he anticipated the wonderful time to come.

A sense of urgency filled him, and he shed his clothes quickly, save for his magic gemstone. He picked up the book once more, his eyes racing over the page, committing the difficult words and the complex rhyme to memory.

For a moment he thought about using the stone to ensure that the spell was said properly, but he quickly rejected the idea, having used the spell successfully twice before without benefit of the stone.

He knelt in front of the fire and, under RedTail's phlegmatic gaze, began to recite the words to the spell.

The flames leaped in front of his eyes, a crimson curtain on which the words were written as he uttered them clearly and carefully, enunciating with precision. Concentrating. Conscious of the fact that the smallest of mistakes could be disastrous.

The words to a spell were like those of a recipe. If the recipe were not followed exactly, the result could be very strange indeed. If one got the words wrong and were lucky, nothing would happen—the spell would simply not work, and the user would have to memorize the words all over again. For the words of a spell were magical, and once used, they vanished from one's mind completely and had to be relearned to be reused.

It was when one said the spell wrong and it worked in spite of being wrong that the real trouble began. In some extreme instances, the complex magical properties exploded catastrophically in the attempt to mesh two or more properties which were not compatible. When this happened, the user was generally killed or maimed in the process.

Sometimes, however, the result was worse than death, mixing separate components and producing a ghastly, hybrid mistake.

Mika had had such an experience himself when he first attempted the polymorph spell. He had turned himself into a great snowy owl, yet he had retained his human feet. This mistake, while looking rather silly, had not been fatal and had actually been of some help. However, it quickly became apparent that he had made another error somewhere in the recitation when he returned to human form—his arm had remained an owl's wing for several days.

Fortunately, the arm eventually returned to human form. But Mika had learned his lesson and now made very certain that he learned the spell thoroughly before speaking the words. Still, polymorphing was not something that one did lightly. Were Mika not so miserable, he would never have attempted the change.

The words spoken, Mika stared into the leaping flames and waited. The now familiar dizziness and nausea swept over him; he closed his eyes and felt the ground shift beneath him.

The flames were still blurred when he opened his eyes and looked down. His lips twitched in a lopsided grin. It had worked; he had become a wolf!

RedTail's eyes grew large and he stared at Mika, watching him intently. Mika stretched, feeling the long, hard muscles move beneath his sleek, black pelt. He shook himself, enjoying the feeling.

Mika abruptly looked down at his paw and saw that he had not lost the demon hand in the transformation; it had merely become a green, scaly, clawed demon paw. His dewlaps dropped in despair. Somehow he had almost convinced himself that the demon hand would not transmute itself and he would be normal as a wolf. Blackness closed in around him, and he felt like throwing back his head and howling. Madness seized him, and he glared at the hated append-age, snarling as though it were a sentient thing that had chosen this course of action. Hatred overcame him and he bit at the paw, as though he might solve the problem by ripping it from his body.

Pain, real pain, brought him back to his senses. He blinked the tears from his eyes and licked at the offending paw, soothing the ravaged nerve endings. Fortunately the scales were extremely tough and had not been broken by the force of his teeth, protecting him from himself.

This is crazy, thought Mika. I changed into a wolf so I could have fun, not bite myself on the paw—hand. Paw. Whatever. I could have done that as a human. Forget the paw. I'm a wolf, and I'm going to do some howling—have some fun! Kill a deer! Run! Play! No more grim thoughts. No more being crazy! Having delivered the lecture to himself, Mika leaped to his feet and hurried off to join Tam and the princess with tail wagging and a smile on his dewlaps.

Their reception was anything but what he had expected. The last time he had polymorphed into a wolf, he and Tam had experienced a deep joining of spirits, an intense feeling of brotherhood that had strengthened their bond of friendship, even after he returned to his human form.

Now, Tam turned to him with cold eyes and, extending his head stiffly with hackles standing on end, sniffed him from head to tail, slowly and careful-ly, as though he were an enemy!

Mika stood very, very still, watching the flat, black

pupils of Tam's eyes. They were hard and unfriendly and looked on Mika the wolf with open hostility.

The princess was far friendlier, extending her black nose in an open, curious fashion, her busy, silver-tipped tail wagging back and forth. She sniffed him all over and then coyly slid alongside, presenting her own body to be sniffed in turn.

Not wishing to be rude, Mika carefully lowered his head and sniffed the princess's neck in a perfunctory manner, all the while keeping his eyes on Tam, whose upper lip seemed to be quivering over his canines.

The princess slid past Mika, her small, lithe form pressing against his muzzle. Her slender back passed under his nose and then her tail brushed across his face, obscuring his vision, blocking out the sight of Tam.

And then the most exciting scent he had ever smelled hit Mika. A powerful yet elusive scent, it exploded in his brain like a bolt of white lightning. His body felt as though it were charged with electricity, and his world shrank until it contained nothing other than himself and the princess.

Tam's presence lingered on the fringes of his mind like a black cloud on the horizon, but it no longer mattered—nothing mattered to his frenzied mind but the princess.

The elusive fragrance crept into his nostrils, coated his tongue and palate, and saturated his brain. It was a siren song of obsession and lust and madness. His tail arced high over his body and he rose on stiff legs and pranced forward, drinking in the addictive scent until his maddened mind reeled under the impact and his body demanded that he act.

Suddenly something hard crashed into his chest, bowling him over. A sharp pain streaked across his muzzle, and hot, salty blood filled his mouth.

He staggered to his feet in time to see Tam leap from the mouth of the cave into the darkness that lay beyond. The princess looked back at Mika over her shoulder. It was a laughing, mischievous glance that challenged yet invited him to follow . . . if he dared. Then she, too, was gone.

Mika staggered to his feet, stunned, overwhelmed by forces he could not comprehend. He stood in the mouth of the cave and looked out into the dark night, whimpering softly, his tail wagging uncertainly.

Then he caught it, a brief message on the air, an invisible trail that could not be seen but could be followed. Without further thought Mika leaped from the cave and thrust himself into the night, trusting his senses in this all but unknown world.

His feet found the trail that led up the mountain at a precipitous angle. Sensitive footpads were forced to read every inch of the trail like a map, or a wrong step could end in death. The demon paw proved to be surprisingly helpful, the long, curved claws biting into the rock and gaining Mika purchase.

The moon had not yet risen above the bulk of the dark mountain. A cold wind swept down from the higher elevations, filling his nostrils with the smell of snow and ice and a thin thread of oily warmth that he somehow knew were sheep.

He also caught the rank scent of kobold, those horny-skinned, non-human dwellers of subterranean chambers. But the scent was old and carried no feeling of immediate danger. He ignored everything but that which spoke of the wolves who had gone before him.

He took joy in the power of his body, felt the strength in his muscles and the rising exhilaration that filled his mind. He ran on, more certain with each step that he would find the princess and that she would be his.

The more he thought about it, the more he tried to convince himself that there had been some misunderstanding earlier. Tam couldn't *really* be angry with him. After all, what had he done other than become a wolf? He and Tam were friends, bond brothers, pals. And all he wanted was to have fun and forget his problems. He would find Tam and explain it to him, and then everything would be fine.

Having reassured himself, Mika continued on, leaping from boulder to boulder, ascending higher and higher into the steep ravine, the demon paw helping him climb with ease.

The sound of water grew louder and as he reached a small plateau. High on the flank of the mountain, he found himself standing beside a small pool of water that trickled down from the snow-covered peaks above. Soon the flow would cease as winter locked its grim hold on the mountains, sheathing them in ice until the turn of the year.

But he knew that Tam and the princess had been here. Mika lowered his head and drank in the taste of her, which rested lightly on the smooth surface of the icy, black water. Her flavor inflamed his brain, driving out all thoughts of friendship and fun, driving him on in great leaping bounds, ever higher on the mountain.

He howled, a wild, joyous sound that poured out of his throat like liquid fire. Far away, a small band of brigands, outcasts of the city trying desperately to stay alive on the wild and dangerous plains, heard the sound and shivered, drawing closer to their tiny fire, clutching the handles of their knifes in fear.

Just ahead of him he saw a flash of silvery tail. He stretched out his body and felt his paws grab the stony earth and pull it toward him. He gained rapidly on the two wolves—and then he was upon them.

Tam stopped and turned to face him, lips bared in an open snarl. The princess sat down abruptly and stared from one to the other, her tongue lolling from the side of her mouth in a most provocative manner.

Mika crawled forward, whining plaintively, head lowered, body nearly scraping the ground, tail wagging back and forth slowly, almost begging to be accepted.

Before the princess could even react, Tam leaped at Mika, landing in a stiff-legged crouch a mere handspan away on the narrow trail. His head was lowered and his upper lip was drawn back completely, revealing his black gums and sharp white teeth. He snarled ferociously, the slaver glistening on his teeth.

Mika saw red. Anger clouded his mind like fog, and he lost all sense of reason. This wasn't fair! This wasn't fun! All he'd wanted was a good time, and instead his best friend was threatening to kill him. All right! If Tam wanted a fight, he'd get a fight that he wouldn't soon forget, Mika decided angrily.

Mika felt his own hackles rise, standing out around his neck like a stiff collar. The rage built in his chest, and his mouth fixed itself in a grimace of hate. He felt the remnants of his love and friendship for Tam wash away like the cold, sleeting rain that had begun to fall.

Tam snarled, a deep rumbling sound that rose from somewhere deep in his chest, and Mika answered with one of his own.

Tam moved then, rushing forward and striking Mika squarely in the chest with the full force of his body. Mika was not prepared for such an action; he tumbled from his feet and landed in the middle of the icy current which flowed beside the trail.

The shock of the frigid water brought him to his feet, trembling, angered that he had been taken off guard. He lowered his head and surged out of the water, striking low, mouth agape, snapping at Tam's front legs.

Tam leaped aside and attempted to grab Mika by the back of the neck, but Mika's rush carried him out of Tam's reach.

Then the fight began in earnest, each of them jockeying for position, trying to seize the others' neck. Teeth flashed, snapped, clashed. Blood flew from slashed muzzles, torn lips, and ripped ears. Heavy bodies slammed into each other, pushing, shoving, jostling, struggling for dominance. And through it all, Mika was conscious of the demon paw; the claws ached, almost rising on their own to rip through Tam's throat, but somehow, in some tiny portion of his mind, Mika kept control, knowing that to use the claw would be to wreak certain death. He was angry with Tam, angry and hurt, but he did not wish to kill him, only steal the princess and win the night.

217

And all the while, the princess sat calmly on the bank, observing with interest the mayhem she had created, daintily moving aside every now and then to avoid actual contact with the raging combatants.

In the end physical exhaustion won out, for so evenly were Tam and Mika matched that neither could gain permanent ascendancy.

They stood, flanks heaving, breath rasping in their throats, tongues hanging, and stared at each other, locked in an impasse that could not be broken by strength.

Then the princess made her move. Flowing sleekly down the trail, she moved past Mika without even the slightest of glances and crouched down in front of Tam. Whining shrilly, little high-pitched wolven sounds of solicitude and concern, she began licking Tam's face, licking away the blood and spittle that stained his dark fur. The princess had made her choice.

Tam straightened, his head rising in an imperious manner as the princess continued to bathe him with soft licks and tiny whimpers. Casting a cold look of victory at Mika, Tam draped his head across the princess's neck in a blatant gesture of ownership and victory.

Mika watched them depart, his head bowed low, exhausted in spirit as well as strength. He began to shiver as the rush of adrenalin that had sustained him throughout the battle deserted him and the cold, pelting rain penetrated his thick fur.

They were gone; he could see them no longer. It was raining harder now, a freezing rain that slashed down on his unprotected body like tiny blows. He stood a moment more, dejected and forlorn, feeling more alone than ever, depressed beyond belief over the outcome of his evening of fun.

Turning slowly, he began the long descent back to the cave, retracing the trail that he had climbed such a short time earlier in high spirits, entertaining high expectations.

The dizziness took him when he was but halfway down the side of the ravine. Losing his footing, he bounced down the trail striking head, hip, elbow, and tailbone—sharp blows that would bruise and be felt for days to come.

When the dizziness lifted, Mika lay sprawled on the trail and felt the rain coursing off his naked shoulders, realizing with a further sense of despair that he had returned to his human form.

The descent seemed endless in that dark night, for the rocky path was far more difficult to traverse as a human than it had been as a wolf. Stones and obstacles that he'd leaped in a single, graceful bound now required careful maneuvering by cold, clumsy fingers and toes. But the demon hand proved as useful on the way down as the paw had on the way up, digging in and holding tight in awkward and dangerous spots where a man might easily fail. For the very first time he actually found himself appreciating the demon hand, and that in itself was scary!

The moon was hidden by heavy clouds that released their contents directly over Mika's head. The storm intensified; thunder crashed and echoed from side to side in the steep ravine, and lightning bolts flung themselves at him as though they were spears and he the quarry.

Mika reached the cave as the last of the storm crossed the peak and drifted away, as though it had no further reason for staying once he was out of reach.

He looked to see if his absence had been noticed, but neither Hornsbuck nor Lotus Blossom had moved from the spot where Mika had left them. It seemed entirely likely that they had slept through the entire deluge. Their rumbling, baritone snores filled the cave with a thunderous discord rivaled only by the storm.

RedTail opened his eyes as Mika limped into the cave and tottered over to his bedroll. He dried his cold, aching limbs and tried to rub some warmth back into his body as he stood next to the remains of the fire. He wrapped himself in his blanket and laid down beside the glowing embers, too tired to care about anything anymore. "No more fun," he mumbled to himself. "Another fun night like this would kill me." He was asleep almost before he closed his eyes.

Chapter 21

"WHAT IN HADES HAPPENED TO YOU?" roared Hornsbuck all too early the next morning. "And where are Tam and the princess?"

Mika rolled over, and memory came flooding back along with the pain. He groaned. He moaned, feeling sick. Every single bit of his body either throbbed, burned, or just plain hurt. He raised his hand to his aching head and saw that his fingernails were all broken and the tips of his fingers were ripped and torn. He moaned some more. Only the demon fingers were undamaged. He slipped the gauntlet back on, unwilling to look at the awful hand.

Using his other hand, he felt his face gingerly and discovered a long, deep cut across the bridge of his nose. A second slash had ripped across one of his eyebrows and stopped just short of the eye itself. A piece was missing from the the tip of one ear, and the base of his tailbone hurt where Tam had clamped down on his tail . . . when he still had one.

Mika slowly crawled out of his blanket, groaning

constantly, and discovered that the back of his neck was stiff and bruised where Tam had gripped it in his powerful jaws. His entire ribcage was tender to the touch, and it hurt to breathe. Further, his feet were swollen, and the soles were cut and torn from heel to toe.

"What on Oerth!" exclaimed Lotus Blossom. "Hornsbuck, this boy's a mess! Mika, how did you get in this shape?"

As Mika attempted to hobble toward the fire, she scooped him up in her immense arms as though he were a child and deposited him gently in front of the blaze.

"Best fix you up or you'll be dyin', and then that demon would come looking for us," muttered Lotus Blossom. "What've you got in that there pouch?"

Fumbling in Mika's pouch proved too much for Blossom's thick fingers, and in the end she emptied it out on the floor of the cave.

"How about this?" she asked, holding up a vial of clear green fluid.

"No, that's for removing warts," Mika mumbled between cracked and swollen lips. "This'll do," he said, reaching for a stoppered horn filled with a thick, healing salve made from mullein flowers, powdered golden seal, ground gentian root, oil of hemlock spruce, and thick, yellow bear fat.

"Gimme," said Blossom, grabbing the horn out of Mika's stiff fingers. There was no point in arguing with the huge woman, as she could easily ignore his futile protests and have her way with him. Sighing deeply, he gave himself over to her ministrations, determined to suffer through them as a form of added penalty for his stupidity.

Blossom slathered the stuff everywhere, even on places that showed no signs of injury. Surprisingly enough, her immense hands were both deft and gentle, and Mika felt strangely soothed by her touch as well as by her gruff concern. And she only pinched him once.

"Well, now," said Blossom after she was finished. "It seems as though we missed something last night. Care to fill us in? And for starters, where are Tam and the princess?"

"I only wanted to have a little fun," Mika mumbled defensively. "You have Hornsbuck, and the wolves have each other, and all I have is this horrible hand. I thought that maybe if I were a wolf, just for a little while, I could have some fun, too. But it didn't work out like I thought it would. Tam was mad at me for some reason. The princess liked me, but that only made matters worse. They left, and I followed them. Tam and I fought, and then he and the princess ran off. I don't know where they are now."

"I should have known," rumbled Hornsbuck, more to himself than to Mika. "I should have recognized it. Tried to stop them, did you, lad? Not a wise move. Looks like you fell down the mountain while you were at it."

"It felt like two mountains," Mika said ruefully, trying to find a comfortable position. A thought suddenly came to him. "What did you mean, 'you should have recognized it'? Recognized what?"

"It's her time, Mika. Couldn't you see it coming?"

"See what coming?" asked Mika, feeling rather

stupid.

"She's in heat, boy," Blossom interrupted, annoyed at Mika's denseness. "In heat. Her and Tam are off together, and unless we can think of a way to find them and separate them, your little miss princess will be having a litter of pups before long."

"Pups! Oh, no! That can't be!" said Mika, sitting up straight on his blanket. "What will we tell her father the king, and what about the demon? How can I possibly explain a litter of wolf pups? Hornsbuck! Lotus! What will they look like? Will they be human or wolves, or—or both?" he asked in a strangled voice.

"I don't know, lad," Hornsbuck said heavily. "Only time will tell us that."

"Could be kinda interesting," Blossom said brightly. "And I don't see what you two are carrying on like this for, anyhow. Why would her father care? Way I understand it, this guy traded his own daughter to a demi-demon. I don't think I'd worry too much about his opinion. And why should the demon care? You told me his business was with the king, not the daughter. Seems like it's her problem now. Stop worrying."

Mika groaned and sank back down on his blanket, suddenly too miserable to think about the dilemma any more. He didn't know how it mattered to the king or to the demon, but with his luck they would probably both be furious.

Blossom started to say something, but Hornsbuck, realizing that there was nothing that they could do or say, rose and took Blossom with him, leaving Mika to his own miserable thoughts.

Tam and the princess were gone for more than four days and nights. By then Mika had become more or less resigned to the situation, realizing that there was nothing else he could do.

As a matter of fact, the union of Tam and the princess was perhaps preferable to what might have occurred had Mika emerged the victor. The wide variety of physical possibilities of the future offspring simply boggled his mind. The mere thought frightened Mika so much that he broke out in a nervous sweat.

It was possible that their offspring would be born all wolf. Or all human. Or multiple combinations of both. Or werewolves, appearing as human most of the time and turning into wolves periodically. Or wolven most of the time and turning human periodically. Mika found himself sighing a lot.

Tam and the princess were curled around each other, sleeping soundly, when Mika, Hornsbuck, and Blossom wakened on the morning of the fifth day.

The two lovers' paws and legs were muddy, and their pelts were streaked with dirt and leaves, and they slept, deeply exhausted. Neither even twitched a whisker when RedTail inspected them from head to frazzled tail with widespread nostrils and great, snuffling breaths.

The three humans did not need RedTail's heightened sense of smell to know what Tam and the princess had been up to.

When the two wolves finally woke, they ate the last of the antelope and then looked for more. Satisfying their hunger with chunks of mealybread, they curled up and went back to sleep again.

225

Mika sat by the fire while they slept. Hornsbuck, Lotus Blossom, and RedTail hunted for fresh meat to replenish their dwindling supplies.

Mika sat and watched Tam's sleeping form. Despite everything, he admitted he was glad that his wolf had returned. Mika had missed him sorely. It was not Tam's fault that they had clashed over the female—such things were a madness beyond reason.

Abruptly Tam opened his eyes and looked directly at Mika. They stared at each other in silence, and Mika read a reflection of his own thoughts in the warm amber of the wolf's eyes.

Hornsbuck, Blossom, and RedTail returned some time later with a brace of plump rabbits and three fat guinea hens. Mika sat down and helped pluck and gut the catch. Hornsbuck quirked an eyebrow at Mika, knowing that the younger man had something on his mind.

"Hornsbuck, I don't want to go to Exag," Mika said finally, frowning down at the guinea hen in his hands. "I'm afraid that once this demon has me where he wants me, he'll kill me."

"Be you afraid?" Hornsbuck asked in astonishment.

"Wouldn't you be?" countered Mika.

"Never! Wolf Nomads are never afraid! We welcome danger! We wrestle with fate! We laugh in the face of death!" shouted Hornsbuck as he thumped himself on the chest, his eyes growing glazed, overwhelmed by his own propaganda.

"Oh, Hornsbuck, come off it," groaned Lotus Blossom. "That Wolf Nomad mumbo-jumbo is going to rot your brain or get you killed yet. I love a good brawl, same as the next man, but I stop short of dying.

"The boy's got a point," she continued. "He doesn't want to get killed on account of some stupid code of manhood. Isn't there some way he can get rid of the princess and duck out on this demon? What good is honor if you're dead?"

Mika looked at Lotus Blossom with admiration, his heart singing as she expressed his very thoughts with eloquence. He heard a choked noise and looked up to see Hornsbuck, his face suffused with purple, his eyes nearly starting from his head, clutching feebly at his chest.

"Hornsbuck! What's the matter!" cried Mika, leaping to his feet to grab Hornsbuck by the shoulders, supporting him as the huge man's knees threatened to buckle.

Hornsbuck's breath rasped in his throat and the big man slowly sank to the floor, his hand still pressed to his chest.

"Woman, you know not of what you speak," he said in a gravelly voice, giving Lotus Blossom a cold stare.

"Wolf Nomads would sooner die than live without honor. We be different than other folk, our code means more to us than life. I would sooner die than live without the code, and I would kill any Wolf Nomad who diminished the honor of the clan by cowardice. You must wipe out cowardice as you would blight on a tree. All Wolf Nomads think as I do, even Mika. Be it not so, lad?" Hornsbuck said in a voice that was thick with tension. His green eyes drilled into Mika, waiting for his answer.

"Of course," Mika said with barely a pause, even as his heart plummeted within his breast. "I welcome danger! I wrestle with fate! I laugh in the face of death! On to Exag!" he cried, his voice ringing hollow in his ears. "Let the demon beware!"

Hornsbuck looked at him with pride and Lotus Blossom gazed at him with a bemused expression, but Mika saw none of it. His heart hung frozen, impaled on the quivering dilemma of his fear and the inflexible Wolf Nomad code of courage.

They set off early the next morning, before the fog had left the ground, their horses anxious to travel after being hobbled for six long days.

They swung south, paralleling the River Fler on the narrow strip of land that separated it from the Yatil Mountains. Traveling was good. The land was flat, with ample grazing for the horses. The mountains held back the winds from the east and created a massive barrier that deflected the worst of the winter storms.

Game was plentiful and even though Hornsbuck distrusted water, they spent a pleasant afternoon fishing on the shores of Lake Quag before turning east toward the Mounds of Dawn.

"I do not know much about Exag," said Mika as they left the fertile lakelands behind them, the land growing drier and stonier as they advanced. The mountains bordered them on the north and rose before them to the east.

"No one knows too much," said Hornsbuck. "They be an unfriendly and uncivilized bunch of barbarians. Pah!" he exclaimed, spitting to the side to show his dislike of the Exagians.

"I hear that they don't even gamble," Lotus Blossom said in disbelief.

"Pah!" spat Hornsbuck. "Religious dogbodies, that's what they are. Spend all their days looking up at the sun and all their nights gazing at the stars and the moon.

"They say that everyone has a destiny that's foretold in the stars. Your entire life be planned out for you by the priests depending on when you were born.

"They even make human sacrifices. If you be born under a particular star, you live knowing that you must die, sacrificed to the Goddess of Dawn."

"Why?" asked Mika, his flesh crawling at the thought.

"Because they are uncivilized barbarians, not cultured folk like ourselves," Hornsbuck explained patiently. "When you've traveled as long as I have, you'll learn that we Wolf Nomads be far superior to everyone else."

"Hornsbuck, why would the demon want me to come here?" Mika asked nervously, not at all reassured by what he had heard of the citizens of Exag.

"Not afraid, are you?" Hornsbuck asked suspiciously, tilting one shaggy eyebrow.

"Me? Afraid of a bunch of uncivilized barbarians who sacrifice their own? Hah!" exclaimed Mika, who was very much afraid.

"*Good!* Nomads never run from danger! Nomads love a challenge!" roared Hornsbuck. "What is life without danger?" He stood up in his stirrups and howled. "Come on lad, you don't want to grow old and die in your bed, do you? A nomad lives only to die!" Roaring out the last words, Hornsbuck kicked his horse into a gallop and rode off across the harsh land, howling and brandishing his spear above his head.

Mika and Lotus Blossom watched him ride away.

"Die in my bed . . . I don't think that's likely," Mika muttered. Feeling as though his own life was as preordained as the unlucky Exagians, he howled his own cry and galloped after Hornsbuck, the wolves trailing at his heels.

Chapter 22

THE LAND THEY CROSSED WAS HARD AND DRY, the color of ochre, and studded with large boulders. They had seen no water for the last two days, and their throats and bellies were begging for relief when they caught their first glimpse of Exag.

It appeared low on the horizon; a series of squares and pyramids, built of the same red ochre that they rode upon.

As they came closer, they saw that the curious shapes were enclosed within a high adobe wall that appeared to encircle the city without a single visible break. The strange geometric shapes within grew out of a series of low rises, actually an extension of the mountains that rose up behind the city like a dark curtain.

There was no sound coming from the city, no sense of the bustle and activity that normally marked any great gathering of people. In fact, the walled city seemed to exude an ominous air that sent a chill of foreboding creeping over Mika.

It soon became apparent that all traffic—what little there might be—entered the city through a single, tall, narrow gate, seemingly the only break in the wall that towered over them for more than ten man-heights.

Looking up at the great expanse, Mika could not even imagine how the immense wall had been built or, for that matter, by whom, since there seemed to be no junctures in the smooth surface, no indication of human construction. It seemed to rise straight up out of the hard ground itself.

Turning to ask Hornsbuck about the wall, he discovered that the older man's face was sharp, his watchful green eyes alert and focused on the gate.

"Watch your tongue, lad. Let me do the talking," said Hornsbuck quietly. "I be better skilled at this sort of thing."

Mika had his doubts as to Hornsbuck's diplomatic skills but did as he was bid.

They had trotted within hailing distance of the wall when Mika noticed that two men stood watch at the foot of the great gate. Their skin was as red as was the soil they stood on. So still did they stand that Mika mistook them at first for statues. But as the clansmen advanced, one of the guards stepped out to challenge them.

"What business have you here?" a guard demanded, his small eyes suspicious.

"Our supplies be low, guardsman, and we wish to reprovision," said Hornsbuck with great civility, his hands far from his weapons.

The second guard stepped up and stared at Mika and Lotus Blossom, then returned to examine Mika

232

more closely. Mika silently returned his stare.

He saw a tall man, taller than himself, who was slightly more than six feet. His hair was black and straight, cut square over the eyes and falling to the point of the jaw where once again it was cut squarely around the nape of the neck.

The guards' features were nearly identical, with high-beaked noses and narrow-lipped mouths. Beneath their hard, glittering black eyes were sharp cheekbones that appeared to have been chiseled out of stone.

They wore strange armor, comprised of overlapping circles of reddish-colored metal. It covered them from neck to knuckle to knee and clanked as they moved. Mika guessed that it was effective but heavy. Beneath the armor, bison-leather boots and leggings were visible.

They were well-armed, carrying broadswords slung in sheaths between their shoulder blades, knives at their waists, and powerful crossbows in their hands.

Evidently Mika, Hornsbuck, and Lotus Blossom passed their inspection, for after a few additional questions—most specifically, the dates of their births—the gates were opened, and they were allowed to enter the city.

Mika was stunned. Exag was like no other city that he had ever seen. It was laid out in precise and careful lines, each block divided into an exact number of buildings, all of which conformed to the same size and shape. The city could have been stamped out of a mold.

As could the people. As Mika stood and watched,

he saw a score or more different groups of people, each distinguished by the color of their garb.

One caste seemed to be comprised of a handful of elderly men who wore nought but white robes, affixed at the left shoulder, leaving the other bare and falling ungirded to the ground. They wore no cloaks, even though the days had become quite cold. Their heads were clean-shaven.

Mika thought the men looked quite ordinary but suspected that they belonged to the highest caste and held positions of importance because they were accompanied by a full complement of guards outfitted like those at the gates. A host of lesser creatures dressed in muddy brown robes hurried ahead to scan the ground for obstacles and push the crowds back out of the way.

Mika and Hornsbuck stood aside to watch such a procession pass them, noting the frantic, fearful movements of the brown-robed minions. All around them, the throngs of shoppers and passersby averted their eyes and bowed low in silence, seemingly stricken by the same mixture of fear and awe exhibited by the brown-robes.

Not wanting to call attention to themselves, Hornsbuck, Lotus Blossom, and Mika also bowed low, keeping their silence. But then, with a sickening feeling in the pit of his stomach, Mika realized that the procession had stopped in front of them; that one of the white-robed, shaven-headed men was looking directly at them! Mika hoped that the attention did not bode ill, but as the dark eyes traveled over him, he couldn't keep from shivering.

As though reading his mind, the white-robed man

lifted his arm and pointed at Mika. Instantly, the crowd fell back, leaving a wide circle around Mika, Hornsbuck, Lotus, and the wolves. The expressions of fear on their faces, along with relief that the finger had not been pointed at them, bore out Mika's own certainty that something awful was about to happen.

"What the . . . ?" muttered Hornsbuck as he gripped his sword, ready to pull it from its sheath.

"I don't know," replied Mika, drawing his own sword and noting as he did so that Lotus Blossom had nocked an arrow. The huge woman stood ready to let it fly, the muscles of her arm taut with the tension.

He also noted with satisfaction the expressions of concern on the faces of the brown-robed minions as they attempted to close in on the armed trio without any weapons of their own. Evidently, they were unaccustomed to opposition.

An angry expression crossed the face of the white-robe, whose hand still pointed at Mika. He yelled at his underlings, demanding that they seize the armed trio. As the brown-robes inched their way closer, Mika saw that the guards, who were most definitely armed and looked as though they knew how to use their weapons, were closing in as well.

"There's too many, Hornsbuck," whispered Mika. "What are we going to do?"

Just at that moment, a tiny voice sounded behind Mika.

"Psssst!"

Mika slide his eyes sideways, trying to see who it was, but was unable to see anything. Then someone yanked on the hem of his cloak, directing his focus downward.

"Hurry! Get in here, quick!" said the voice.

Even as the guards pushed the brown-robes aside in order to get at him, Mike glanced down and saw a small face. It was topped by a thick thatch of dark hair, and two sharp eyes looked anxiously out at him from a narrow space between two buildings. The boy appeared to be around twelve summers of age and, unlike all of the other inhabitants of the city, wore a hodge-podge of clothing, not belonging to any one caste.

"Stop staring and get in here fast, you big dummy," hissed the boy, grabbing hold of Mika's arm and jerking it with unexpected strength.

Mika, not expecting the boy's action, all but toppled into the dark passage. "Hornsbuck!" he yelped at the last minute. Hornsbuck, thinking that Mika was being attacked, wheeled and, brandishing his sword, followed him into the thin passage. Lotus Blossom, not understanding but unwilling to be left behind, followed on his heels, drawing the horses with her. The wolves slipped between the horses' feet, and the small passage was thus effectively blocked.

"Follow me!" cried the boy. "I can get you out of here!"

Hornsbuck nodded at Mika, signaling his approval, for even though Hornsbuck was the last person to run from a fight, he was wise enough to realize that they were badly outnumbered in an unfamiliar walled city that would be difficult to escape.

A cry rang out, the words indistinguishable, but the meaning and the intent were clear. Stop! Halt! It was the harsh sound of authority; the same in all languages the Oerth over.

236

The boy began to run, a dark shadow dissolving into the darkness, and the small group followed him as best they were able. Mika's heart beat faster as he struggled to keep the boy in sight, afraid that they would become lost and easy prey for those who followed.

The dark spaces were made for small boys at best, cats and rats more likely, and never intended for large nomads. The passage twisted and turned, leading into a complex warren between the buildings.

The sound of pursuit soon faded, though the boy's pace did not flag. He darted across one wide thoroughfare and then led them into the dense maze of the marketplace, teeming with smelly stalls and raucous shoppers. A multitude of eyes watched them as they followed close on the boy's heels.

The boy suddenly ducked into a dark space behind a stall that sold old, wrinkled fruit and vegetables, fit only for consumption by uncaring animals.

Once again they found themselves in a narrow, dark passageway that wandered throughout the innards of the marketplace. It was a complicated labyrinth that could easily confuse any but those who knew it well. All Mika and the others could do was follow the boy and try to keep some idea of their bearings.

The walls were composed of various bits of wood and plaster, occasionally brick, as generation after generation of vendors had added on to their establishments without benefit of skillful builder or knowledge of construction.

The corridors were open to the sky, and more than once Mika looked up and took comfort from the clouds that passed overhead and the occasional bird that hove into view, reassuring himself that the world still existed.

And then they stopped. The passage ended in what appeared to be a solid brick wall, which was all but covered by a mound of moldering debris. Mika, seeing no way for them to continue, wondered suddenly if the boy was a purse thief who thought to rob them! Well, if that was his intent, he had a surprise in store! Mika's hand crept toward his knife.

But the boy did not even look at the nomad. Bending down, he reached into the pile of garbage and fiddled with something. There was a nearly silent exhalation of air as the brick wall swung aside, revealing only darkness beyond.

The boy looked up at the rooftops nervously and scanned the passage behind them as though expecting to see some sign of pursuit. Then he quickly gestured them forward, urging them to enter. Hornsbuck readily passed the boy and entered the darkened doorway, followed quickly by Lotus Blossom and the wolves. Mika, though, hesitated. He glanced back and saw a contemptuous grin on the boy's face. Swallowing his fear, he glared down at the urchin, gripped his knife more tightly, and entered the chasm, leaving the horses behind.

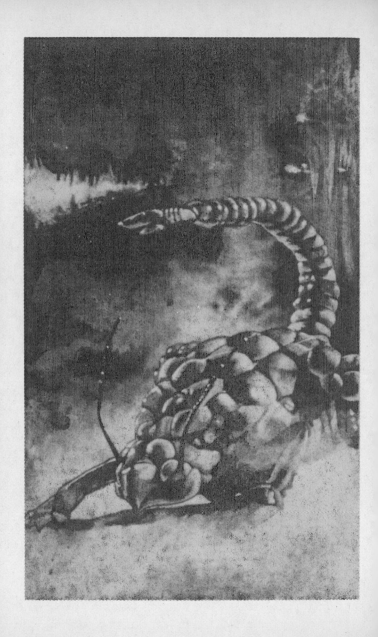

Chapter 23

MIKA HOPED THAT THE BLACKNESS would not really be as dark as it seemed. But it was. It was stygian, without even a hint of light. His heart began to thump against his ribs and his throat closed tight as the door closed behind them.

There was a scratching sound, and then another. Mika's eager senses caught the scent of smoke, then a tiny pinpoint of light. Mika focused on the small flame and sighed deeply, relief flooding his mind like rain on a parched land.

"Where are we?" asked Hornsbuck, his deep voice echoing emptily.

"Shh," whispered the boy. "We're not safe yet. A little while longer."

The diminutive flame showed them brick walls on three sides and a lowering clay roof above them. The boy moved forward, and Mika saw the tiny candle dip. With a sinking heart, he realized that the path they must take lay underground.

Mika was not fond of underground passages. He

had traveled them before when necessary, but nothing good had ever come of them. Monsters and ghosts and other horrible things lurked in such places. He silently loosened his sword, promising himself that he would not be taken unaware.

As though sharing his feelings, Tam and the princess pressed close against his legs, evidently no more enamored with the dark passage than he was.

But Hornsbuck and Lotus Blossom, untroubled by the darkness and what it might conceal, followed the boy closely. Mika grasped his sword more firmly and ventured forward, fearful of a trap, but even more afraid of being left behind.

The path underfoot was clay, hard-packed as though trampled by many feet. It led down a gentle angle and then leveled off after only a short descent.

Mika sensed that the walls had drawn back and that they were now passing through a large open space. The boy carried the only light, and it illuminated only a small area directly around him. Mika guessed that even that meager beacon was more for their benefit than the boy's, because the urchin seemed quite certain where he was going.

Another wall appeared, this one consisting of rotting bales of hay, no longer of any use as feed. The boy moved a bale to one side and manipulated something concealed behind. Once again the wall swung aside, carrying the bales of hay with it and revealing a large, low-roofed room. Astonished, Mika realized that it contained a large number of people in various attitudes of repose.

A sharp cry rang out and the peaceful scene erupted into violent action. Men raced for their weapons, women and children rushed out of sight, mothers dragging tiny gaping children away by force and scooping babes off their blankets.

Mika, Lotus, and Hornsbuck stood in the doorway, the boy before them, holding up his hand and shouting words that no one stopped to hear. Their wolf companions bristled in readiness, for friend or foe.

Women and children tucked out of sight, the men turned to face them, shifting nervously and waving an odd assortment of weapons, wooden broadswords whose edges were nicked and chipped, spears with stone points, and a variety of staffs and heavy cudgels.

Mika stared at the men, then relaxed his grip on his sword as he noted that few of them appeared to be in their prime. Most were very old or very young and seemed far more afraid of the three of them, even though they numbered several score.

"Father, they were about to be taken by the priests," cried the boy, interrupting the tense standoff. I brought them here, for surely they need our help."

Slowly, the men lowered their weapons and glanced at each other, still very anxious and uncertain over the presence of armed strangers in their midst.

"It's true, what he says," boomed Lotus Blossom, as she unstrung her bow and placed the arrow back into its quiver. "We arrived in Exag but a short time ago and almost immediately found ourselves surrounded by old men in white robes and guards who meant us harm, although we did nothing to offend them. This boy appeared out of nowhere and showed us a path of escape, bringing us to this place. You have no cause to fear us, but if our presence offends, my friends and I will leave."

The men seemed to waver. One by one, their weapons were lowered, and then one who seemed in charge drew near, studying them carefully all the while.

"You have arrived only this day?" he queried sharply.

"Aye," said Hornsbuck, "but a short time ago. We entered the gates and had no more than turned to watch the procession when all the trouble began."

Low murmurs broke out among the men as they spoke among themselves.

"Why did you come to Exag?" asked the apparent leader as the boy moved to his side.

"It's a personal matter," said Mika, unwilling to discuss the demon and the king with strangers, despite their timely assistance.

The man, whom Mika took to be the boy's father, stared into Mika's eyes, judging his words. He was small, rising no higher than Mika's shoulder, and was dressed, as were they all, in a ragbag of nondescript clothing obviously culled from the cast-offs of others or the garbage heaps.

He appeared none too healthy, his hair lank and dull and hanging about his shoulders in ragged clumps. His ribs were clearly visible as were the knobs of his shoulders and elbows.

His dark eyes had the hot, burning intensity of a zealot or a man who had not eaten adequately for a long time. His skin was pale and unhealthy looking with a single bright red spot in the center of each cheek. It was obvious to Mika that the man was in very poor health and he thought it unlikely that the fellow would make old bones.

The man looked at them with a puzzled expression. "Only fools and those wishing to die come to Exag," he said slowly, shaking his head and staring at them as though trying to decide which category they fit into.

"Why?" asked Hornsbuck. "Is it not a city like any other?"

The man laughed, a brief choking sound that contained no humor. "Exag is like no other city that I know of, excepting perhaps in Hades. Come, my poor unfortunates. Come sit by the fire and I will tell you what you have gotten yourself into."

"I knew I was right," muttered Mika, more to himself than to anyone else. "I knew I didn't want to come here."

The man led them to the center of the room, where a large fire burned in a wide fire pit. Here was the heart of the place. A number of cooking containers, mostly broken or dented in some manner, sat atop flat rocks at the edge of the fire, their contents simmering and bubbling quietly.

Tattered rugs and forlorn little toys lay scattered around the edges of the pit. As the women and children crept back to claim them, Mika could see that none of them, not even the babes in arms, appeared in much better condition than their poor possessions.

"What is this place, and who are you people?" asked Hornsbuck. "Why do you live underground like starved rats rather than bask in the sun above?"

"Better to live underground like a starved rat than feel the sun on your face and die," said a thin man with a twisted leg. "Soon you will be one of us and you will understand."

"Understand what?" roared Hornsbuck, shaken. "Are you all crazy?"

"Crazy? Perhaps," said the boy's father as he sat down on a broken chair close to the fire and gestured at them to seat themselves. "But mostly desirous of life. We do what we can and perhaps it will not always be like this. We have plans."

Lotus Blossom seated herself on a low stool that creaked beneath her weight as Mika and Hornsbuck hunkered down on their heels, waiting for the man to explain.

"We, all of us whom you see here, except for some of the children, were chosen ones." He looked at them expectantly, waiting for them to understand.

Mika, Lotus Blossom, and Hornsbuck looked at each other blankly to see if the others had understood, then looked back to the man, no sign of understanding on their faces.

"Chosen ones?" said Mika. "I guess we don't understand what you're trying to tell us."

"Here in Exag we worship the sun god," the man said patiently. "Every day, one whose birth was on that day is sacrificed to the sun god so that he will find pleasure in us and shine his beneficence down upon us. However, others who have been unfortunate enough to offend the priests are often chosen, as well."

"How—how, do they know when you were born?" Mika asked with a dry mouth.

"The citizens are forced to wear tunics that designate the month of birth," said the man. "And the very worst time is now, as we approach the time of the dawnstar, when the sun is eaten by the moon at daybreak on the last day of Sunsebb.

"Here in Exag the dawnstar is also known as the deathstar, for all those born under its sign are born for death. It is they whom the priests sacrifice to make certain that the new year turns in its cycle."

"The dawnstar does that? Surely you are mistaken," said Mika. "Everyone knows that it is the Great She-Wolf, mother of us all, who sees to the turning of the new year."

"Here in Exag, the dawnstar is given that honor," the man said with a wry smile.

"I, uh, I was born under the sign of the dawnstar," said Mika in a low voice.

"I know, I heard!" the boy said excitedly. "That is why I brought you here. I, Margraf, heard you tell the guards the date of your borning. Did you not see the look that passed between them?"

Mika was forced to admit that he had not. Nor, in fact, had he seen the boy. He wondered briefly if his powers of observation were slipping as well as other manly abilities.

"Not only was he born under the dawnstar," cried Margraf, "but I heard him boast that he was born during a sun-eating!"

There was a sharp intake of breath and then excited murmurings broke out all around him. Margraf's father raised his hands and shushed the crowd.

"Is this true?" he asked, his eyes glittering brightly.

"Yes, it's true," Mika said shakily. "Is there something wrong with that?"

"Not if you are ready to die," said the man. "You must know that there will be another sun-eating this turning. The priests have been unable to find one who was born on such a day. The whole city is in an uproar, for the priests say that unless such a person is found, the cycle will not turn and the world will surely end."

"But, but, that's nonsense," stammered Mika, looking at the circle of pitying eyes. "And besides, if it's true, why did they just let me pass like that? Why didn't they say something or grab me then? Why would they let me wander around loose?"

"And where would you go?" asked the man. "You and your friends stick out among us like dragons among sheep. Do you think that you would be difficult to find? Had Margraf not brought you to us, you would have been theirs for the taking."

"We are not that easy to take, little man," growled Hornsbuck. "We can fight our way out of most anything, and failing that we could always go over the wall."

"There are many more of them than there are of you," observed the man in a soft voice. "And the wall, no, I do not think so, for it is no ordinary structure of stone or clay. It cannot be climbed."

"All walls can be climbed," said Mika.

"This wall cannot be climbed," said a little weasel-faced fellow with bright, glittering eyes. "It's a trapper wall!"

Mika turned to Hornsbuck for explanation and

saw that his friend's normally ruddy face had paled noticeably.

"Hornsbuck?" he said softly. "What's a trapper wall?"

"It be a foul thing," said Hornsbuck, his forehead breaking out in a sweat, "usually found in subterranean places, caves and suchlike. Trappers mimic walls and floors and ordinary things that you would never suspect. Then, when you step on them or pass them by, wham, they grab you and crush you to death.

"Swords and weapons don't hurt them, not much does, save magic. I've never heard of one able to stand the light of day, but I suppose anything be possible. One almost got me once . . . it was a close call." The big man shuddered.

Mika looked away, deeply disturbed at the sight of Hornsbuck's distress. Never before had Mika seen Hornsbuck exhibit fear. If Hornsbuck were afraid, then Mika was doubly so.

"This wall," he said tremulously, "has no one ever climbed it?"

"Never," said the weasel-faced man. "We who know stay far away from it. The priests see to it that it gets a fair portion of those sacrificed each moon, but it is always hungry and satisfies itself whenever it chooses by grabbing those who pass too closely. You could not even get near it, much less climb it in safety."

"What are we to do?" Mika asked Hornsbuck in a low tone. "I have no wish to spend the rest of my life hiding under the ground like vermin."

"Patience, Mika, patience," cautioned Hornsbuck. "We can learn much from these people and when the opportunity comes, we will be ready. And do not forget, there is always the stone."

"How could I forget?" muttered Mika, his hand going to his neck. Then, his eye was caught by a sideways, scuttling movement. Mika wondered briefly what it was, but it was not repeated and he soon returned to the matter at hand.

"I am known as Lufa. I, or rather, we, as I have said, were all chosen ones, those picked by the priests to feed the hunger of the gods," said Margraf's father. "We chose not to die and so we have made our home here, fighting the priests as best we can. As you see, the world has not yet come to an end, despite our actions."

"Are you the only people who feel this way?" asked Hornsbuck.

"Everyone but the priests feels as we do, but they are afraid to act. If a person speaks out against the priests, he is chosen to be sacrificed when the right moon comes. Many who would join us are afraid to do so for fear of what might happen to them and their families," said Lufa.

"Well, then, what we need is a really massive revolt," said Mika. "Maybe we can convince people to turn against the priests and really change things around here."

"Great!" said Margraf, his eyes sparkling. "How are we going to do it?"

"Uh, I don't know," said Mika. "The usual, I suppose. We'll create a diversion—noise, fire, something like that. Then, while the priests' attention is on that, we get the people on our side and revolt! It's simple."

"The usual? Have you ever done anything like this before?" asked Lufa.

"Uh, well, no," said Mika, "but how hard can it be?"

For a moment there was silence and then a babble of voices broke out, each striving to be heard above the others.

"Quiet!" yelled Lufa, holding his hands up. Turning to Mika, he said, "It would have to be a massive diversion. We are still few, and the soldiers of the priests are many."

"Do you want to live better than you do now?" replied Mika in challenging tones. "Anything would be better than this."

"And get rid of that damn weird wall and let folks come and go in Exag as they please. And free enterprise, got to have that, a few taverns, gambling pits, dog races, liven things up a bit," added Lotus Blossom.

"Yes, the wall," murmured Lufa. "It is a symbol of our repression. But how can we get rid of it?"

"Fire," Mika said with a grin. "We'll destroy it with fire."

"Fire," mused Hornsbuck. "Yes, fire would do it, I think, if the blaze be big enough."

Slowly, smiles crept over the faces of the adults as they began to believe that their freedom might indeed be in sight. The children, unused to expressions other than depression and grim-lipped determination on the faces of their parents, suddenly clapped their hands and laughed. All appeared happy except for the little weasel-faced man who watched them with a look of suspicion and cunning in his dark, skeptical eyes.

The women, perhaps unable to express their joy in any other manner, turned to their meager supplies and made themselves busy with much clanking of pots and rattling of pans. Soon, good smells rose from the cooking fires.

Later, over pipes and tiny allotments of home-brewed honeyed-ale, Hornsbuck and the leaders of the underground people worked out the final details of Mika's plan, which they had decided would be carried out the following night. At last, even the weasel-faced man seemed persuaded, and the assignments were given out with enthusiasm. The underground people smiled at each other, knowing that if their plan succeeded, Exag would never be the same again.

As they made ready for sleep, unrolling their cloaks next to the fire, Margraf called out, "Good night, Mika. Sleep tight, and don't let the rusties bite!" All around the large room others echoed his words.

Mika smiled, thinking it some quaint local saying, and nodded in agreement. Tam and the princess curled up near the fire at his feet and were soon sound asleep. RedTail slumbered next to Hornsbuck and Lotus Blossom, who were locked in their usual embrace. Mika placed his sword and knife alongside his cloak as was his custom, readily available should there be trouble in the night. Soon, he, too, was fast asleep.

Sometime in the middle of the night Mika began to dream of birds. Or maybe it was crickets. Or locusts.

The sound so troubled him that the dream state passed away, leaving him almost unconscious, wrapped in his cloak, more than half asleep but listening to a peculiar chirping noise that fit no category he could identify.

He lay there for a moment more, half listening to the soft, chittering noise. It was a happy, non-threatening sound, almost like a pleasant murmuring carried on with oneself while occupied in a pleasant task. Sort of like humming. Mika almost fell back asleep, so pleasant was the sound. Then he heard the scuttle of feet and the rasp of metal on stone, and the soft sounds began again.

Mika's eyes blinked open. Feet. Movement. Metal. He whirled over, his hand reaching for the hilt of his sword. His hand met with something else. Something hard and chitinous. There was a moment's pause, and then the thing squeaked in alarm and scuttled away, chittering loudly.

Mika groped for his sword and knife, cursing audibly as the strange little creature made its escape. Mika had never seen anything like it before in his life. Since he seemed to have frightened it away, he gave up searching for his weapons and watched as the creature disappeared into the darkness.

The thing was about the size of a wolf but rounded, its body a mass of something that closely resembled metal-plating. Two long antennae protruded in front of the creature's body and waved back and forth as it trundled along on four bony limbs. A long segmented tail arched over its back and ended in a strange windmill-like protuberance.

Mika watched it go with a bemused smile on his

face. What a peculiar little thing! The last of its alarmed squeaks had all but faded away when Mika turned to look for his sword. But it was nowhere to be found. Nor was his knife. He leaped to his feet in alarm and threw the cloak aside, thinking that perhaps he had rolled over the weapons in his sleep. But there was nothing to be seen except a small pile of rusty detritus.

Tam and the princess got to their feet and snuffled among the folds of the cloak. Tam sneezed and sat down on his haunches and yawned. The princess merely looked puzzled, curled up on the cloak, and closed her eyes.

"Great protector you are!" Mika yelled at Tam. "Someone sneaks in here and steals my sword and knife right under your nose, and you sleep through it. What good are you? Why are you here? All you do is make moon eyes at that stupid princess. I wouldn't even be here if it weren't for her. Thanks a lot, friend. I get the trouble and you—you get the girl!"

Mika was working himself up to a fine rage, almost beside himself at the loss of his weapons. Nervous enough about being trapped underground against overwhelming odds with nought but a bunch of half-starved losers to help him, the loss of his weapons seemed the final blow.

"Sir! It is not the wolf's fault," said a small voice. Mika looked down and saw Margraf standing at his side. All around him were wakeful, watchful eyes. Looking around him, he saw with embarrassment that his diatribe had awakened nearly everyone in the room.

"It was the rusties, sir. I warned you about them,"

said Margraf, his small face looking up at Mika with an earnest expression as though Mika might blame him for the loss of his weapons.

"Rusties?" asked Mika, remembering now that the boy had warned him not to let the rusties bite. He had thought it but a quaint colloquialism.

"Yes, sir. Rusties. Rust monsters," Margraf said helpfully, peering up at Mika. "They live down here, sir, and they eat metal, turn it to rust, they do. It's almost impossible to keep them from it. That's why none of us has a metal weapon."

Mika looked down at the tiny heap of rusty flakes, the remainder of his sword and knife, and groaned. Only the fact that he had been sleeping with his hand tucked beneath him had protected the gauntlet. So that was what he had seen; the peculiar little creature he had frightened away was a rustie.

A terrible thought struck him and filled with panic. He rushed over to Hornsbuck and began running his hands over the nomad's great, blanketed bulk.

Lotus Blossom wakened with a screech and Hornsbuck with a snort, his snores halted abruptly. His arm shot out, and he grasped Mika with a powerful hand.

"It's me! Mika!" squalled Mika. "Where's your sword?"

"My sword? Why, it's right . . . right . . . Why it's not here!" mumbled Hornsbuck. "What's this damn dirt doing in my blankets? Trouble with caves . . . dirt everywhere . . ."

"It's not dirt," Mika said in despair. "It's rust. Something called a rust monster lives down here. Eats metal, so it seems."

"You mean we've no weapons?" roared Hornsbuck. "Damn its mischief. I'll kill it if I get ahold of it. Where is it?"

"It's gone, Hornsbuck," Mika said wearily. "Saw it run away myself. Didn't realize what it was or what it'd done. Wouldn't have done much good if we had. What would we have done, stomped it to death?"

"I'll fix you up with a club in the morning, sir," said Margraf. "Clubs work real good, and the rusties don't like 'em."

"Clubs," muttered Hornsbuck. He growled at RedTail, who closed his eyes and yawned, not at all disturbed by the rage of his bonded companion.

But curse though he did, it made no difference, the weapons were gone to rusty flakes. Lotus Blossom did her best to coax Hornsbuck back to sleep, to the relief of the goggle-eyed underground people.

After a time, Mika lay back down and, sighing deeply, managed to fall asleep once more.

It seemed that he had barely closed his eyes when he heard Tam barking and a second wolf, probably the princess, yapping shrilly. He opened his eyes, thinking that perhaps the rust monster had returned for a second course when he felt something sharp poke into his throat. His eyes opened wide and there, standing over him, was a guardsman! He started to rise, but the point of the sword pricked him painfully, convincing him that it was better to lie still.

All around him Mika heard the sounds of defeat, curses, frightened cries, and the sobbing of women. The wolves continued their harsh barking, and then there was the sound of a blow. Shrill "ki-yi-yiing" echoed through the cave, ending in a tiny whimper.

Mika stared up into the black eyes of the guard,

feeling the hate building within him, knowing that the princess had been hurt, but not knowing how badly. All thoughts of past angers dropped away. In that moment, the princess became one with him, an extension of him as was Tam, Hornsbuck, RedTail, and probably even Lotus Blossom. He knew that whomever had hurt her would pay for it.

But that seemed very unlikely at the moment. The guard motioned him to his feet and herded him together with the rest of the inhabitants of the underground room.

It was so easily done, reflected Mika. They had been captured with no chance of resistance, betrayed by the little man with the weasely face. It had taken no more than two score of guards. But the guards appeared in good health and were well-armed. Sitting with the rest of the men, hands on top of his head in front of the dying fire, Mika saw that their plan had been doomed from the first. They would never have succeeded. But he would rather have tried and failed than to be captured while sleeping.

The guards had no such problems, however. Using a lightweight, silken cord that Mika knew would be nearly impossible to break, the guards took special care binding the nomad, Hornsbuck, then Lotus Blossom. Prodding the underdwellers to their feet with none- too-gentle jabs, they started them walking along the trail that would take them to the surface . . . and to certain death.

Chapter 24

IF THE WEASEL-FACED MAN had thought to benefit by his betrayal, he was wrong. From their cells they heard him screaming and begging for mercy. But his life ended at daybreak with one terrified shriek, followed by others that were equally horrible and mind-chilling.

"It's like this every day," said Margraf, who had been thrown into the cell with Mika. "The screams are the worst," he whimpered, hiding his face in his hands. "I don't want to die," he said in a tiny voice. "I'm scared to die. They rip your heart out with their hands. I'm scared, Mika."

Mika was scared, too. The thought of having his heart ripped out was absolutely the worst thing he could think of. There were probably other worse things but, at the moment, having his heart ripped out was at the top of the list.

He supposed that he should try and comfort Margraf, but he frankly wished that there were someone to comfort *him*.

Margraf stopped crying, and Mika looked over and saw the princess licking the boy's face. Margraf threw his skinny, little arms around the wolf's neck and hugged her tight. She looked pained but made no attempt to free herself from his grasp.

Mika was startled beyond speech, for it was far from the normal behavior he had come to expect from the princess. The princess glanced at Mika briefly, as though feeling his thoughts, and then her eyes fell away. Mika grinned at her embarrassment, pleased that she was consoling the boy, and pleased as well that she had not been hurt by the guard.

Mika had been surprised when the guards threw all three wolves in the cell with him. It was a lapse in their judgment that he intended to capitalize on. Perhaps with the boy's help they could free him from the bonds which were so tight he could no longer feel his fingers.

"Boy, do you think you can help me get out of these ropes?" asked Mika. "We would stand a better chance of escape if I could use my hands."

Margraf wiped his eyes and his runny nose with the back of his arm and hand, then hurried to Mika's side. He plucked at the ropes, pulling and yanking, but nothing worked.

"Tam can do it," said Mika. "Tam, come here."

Tam nosed the ropes and then nibbled on them with his sharp canines. Strangely, the ropes resisted even those efforts; Tam sat back and whined in frustration.

Mika looked down at the ropes and saw that they were totally unaffected by Tam's teeth. Mika realized with a sinking heart that the ropes had to be enchanted. There was no way to remove them unless the enchanter released the spell or Mika used a spell to counter it.

He could feel the gemstone rubbing against his chest. His captors had searched him roughly for weapons, but they had not noticed the gemstone. Maybe there was hope yet, much as he did not want to use the blasted stone. But even a curse was better than having your heart ripped out.

Mika tried to remember his spells; whatever he did, he would have to do it from memory. He still had the pouch that contained his spell book—he never took it off anymore, not even when he slept—but he could not get to it because of the ropes.

Mika closed his eyes and concentrated. He thought he remembered the spell, a fairly low-level one he had learned early on but never used. Actually, he had used it just once; he'd been five years old when he tied Celia to a tree and made her eat the "magic" potion he'd whipped up out of berries and bugs, grass, and dirt. He smiled at the memory.

Looking down at the ropes, he began to speak the words softly under his breath. It was working! He could actually see the ropes writhing, starting to move. Soon they would start to loosen, to fall away from his body. There! Now they were moving! Were they pulling tighter? Yes, tighter! And still tighter! Damn! He'd gotten the spell backward!

"Mika! What's the matter? Your face is all red, and you look funny!" Margraf cried in alarm.

"Wsshfxx! Blrgle!" Mika spluttered as he tried to say the words, to get them out as the rope pulled itself tighter around his chest, squeezing his lungs, cutting off his air and making it virtually impossible to speak.

Somehow with his very last breath he whispered the combination of words that would reverse the spell. As he toppled to the ground he felt the ropes unwind and fall from his body.

Mika lay there for a moment with everyone clustered around him; Tam, RedTail, the princess, and Margraf. The princess even licked his face, which, while he appreciated the sentiment, he could have done without.

Finally he crawled to his feet, one hand pressed against his aching chest, and sat down on the hard stone bench that was part of the wall of the cell.

"I didn't know you were a magician," said Margraf, wonder and awe apparent in his voice. "Can you do other tricks like that?"

"That wasn't a trick, boy," Mika said, his chest still aching. "I wasn't trying to amuse you."

"I mean, if you can do that, you can do something that will get us all out of here, can't you? You'll save my dad and the others, won't you?"

Mika looked down at Margraf, saw the frailty and the pallor of his skin, his eyes bright with hope, believing in him. Mika looked away, not having the courage to tell the boy that although he was a magic-user, he wasn't a very good one and that the odds were more in favor of him getting a spell wrong than right. He was an unlikely choice for a savior, but it seemed as though he was the only hope they had.

"I'll do my best, boy, I'll do my best," he said with a sigh. Margraf beamed up at him as though he had promised him the world.

Shaking his head, wondering how they had gotten

into this mess, Mika looked around and tried to work out some sort of plan.

It had been dark out when they'd been dragged out of the underground passages. Mika did not have enough knowledge of the city to know in which direction they had been taken. They had traveled through much of the city, through narrow streets and open squares, ending at the foot of the tall pyramid they had seen while still far out on the plains.

Every city block contained a single tall tower silhouetted against the starlit sky, one that was twice as high as the buildings surrounding it. Mika had been perplexed at their purpose, but with the first light of dawn voices rang out in sing-song chants that were vaguely melodic and utterly compelling.

"It is the priests calling the faithful to prayer," Margraf had explained.

"Who goes?" asked Mika.

"Everyone," Margraf had replied, "but they don't go anywhere, they just kneel wherever they are and pray." Margraf had further explained that the call to prayer occurred four times a day and was always obeyed.

Now, a germ of an idea began to form in Mika's mind.

The prison at the foot of the pyramid was small and square and built of the same red ochre adobe as the rest of the city.

It seemed that the mountain blocked the rainfall. What little there was fell on the higher elevations to the east and never reached the city. Water was a scarce and precious commodity found only by means of deep wells. Water was rationed out by the priests—and may the gods help anyone who offended a priest.

Margraf and Mika had been placed in one cell along with the wolves. Hornsbuck and several others, including Lufa, had been put in a cell somewhere along the hall that divided the low, one-story building. The windows and door were heavily barred with thick metal rods. Mika examined them carefully and knew that he would never be able to break them or even bend them enough for Margraf to squeeze through.

Once they'd locked the prisoners in their cells, the guards had left the building, confident that there was no way for them to escape. Just before dawn broke, the priests had come and taken Weasel-face and several others away, paying no mind to their screams or their cries for mercy.

Further conversation with the boy revealed that the sacrifices were held both morning and night, every single day of the year without fail.

Shortly after freeing himself from the rope, Mika noticed that the princess had positioned herself against the bars of the door. Her ears were pricked forward, and she was growling. Mika walked over and looked through the bars but other than a cell directly across the way, he could see nothing. Nor could he see the inhabitant of the cell. Shrugging, he turned his mind to other matters. Escape would be difficult.

Along about mid-day, Mika heard the tramp of feet approaching the building. He moved to the small, high window and looked out, but all he could see was the pyramid.

"Quick, tie me up again!" Mika said, fearful that if he were found unbound, he would never get the chance to put his plan into effect.

Margraf tied him with the silken rope, and Mika wedged himself in a corner of the room, feigning a look of sullen misery that was not far from real.

Imploring cries poured out of the cells as footsteps pounded down the corridor and stopped at Mika's cell.

Margraf had been over-eager in obeying Mika's orders. By the time the door swung open and the guards entered, followed by a clean-shaven man with piercing blue eyes and high cheekbones, Mika's fingers were numb from lack of blood.

"Your date of borning?" demanded the priest, his eyes fixed on Mika's.

"The tenth of Harvesttime," answered Mika.

"You're lying," snapped the priest. "I can see it in your eyes."

"That's pain you see in my eyes," growled Mika. "Why would I lie? I know my date of borning."

"You would lie to save your pathetic life," said the priest, "but it will do you no good. You will die, as will all these others, given unto the honor and glory of Exag the Magnificent. Say your farewells to this sad Oerth and rejoice, for it is a far better world that you go to."

"Do I get a choice?" asked Mika.

"You should be happy to leave this painful world of sorrows behind," said the priest as he leaned forward and looked into Mika's eyes, attempting to convince him. "Your heart should be filled with joy knowing that through your sacrifice you will enable the world to turn to yet another cycle. Without your body, the sun would eat the Oerth and all would die. Does that not gladden your heart, my son?"

Mika stared into the priest's eyes, almost overcome by the intensity of the man's gaze. He blinked and drew back abruptly, suddenly more fearful than he had been before. The man was the most dangerous of all opponents, a religious fanatic who truly believed in his own dogma.

"Do you really think that it is so?" asked Mika, knowing that the only way to gain any latitude was to pretend to believe the nonsense that the priest was spewing. Denial would only infuriate the man.

"Of course," said the priest, his eyes shining with the light of true madness.

"Then if it will serve my brothers and the world, maybe it won't be so bad," said Mika. "Can you promise that the next world will be a better place?"

"I know it to be true, my son," said the priest. "Has not the great Exag himself given us his word? It is a great honor to die for Exag. I wish that I were able to do so myself."

"Then why don't you?" asked Mika, and he was rewarded by seeing the light of reason and caution creep into the man's eyes. So the fellow was not completely round the bend after all.

"Would that I could, my son," intoned the priest, "but my duties lie here. Also, I was born under another moon, and there are always many, many others who volunteer to take my place on that date."

I'll bet there are, thought Mika. I'll bet you make very, very sure of that.

The two men stared at each other, taking each other's measure.

"Untie him," said the priest with a gesture. "The turning is on the morrow. Let him spend his last day and night in comfort, preparing himself for the great honor that is to come."

The guards stripped the rope from Mika's body. At a gesture from the priest, they turned and left the room.

Mika had hoped that they would leave the rope behind, but it was not to be. As the last of them exited the cell, Mika and the priest were left gazing at each other.

"Do not think to escape," advised the priest, "for there is nowhere to go. My men are everywhere, and the building is stout. Best ready yourself for the morrow."

After a last moment's pause, the priest followed his guards. As the door opened, the princess made a dash and tried to push her way through, but the priest kicked her in the chest and slammed the door in her face, locking the metal door behind him.

"Good try, girl," said Mika as he helped her to her feet and rubbed her ribs. "You didn't stand a chance, but it was a good try."

The princess turned her head and looked at Mika as though he were a dolt. The look stopped Mika short. His hand froze in mid-pet as he tried to figure out what he had said to warrant such a look. The princess got to her feet and paced over to the door, where she stood growling. Mika followed her and looked through the bars in an attempt to discover what it was she was growling at, but all he could see was the occupant of the cell across the hall, a large, white-haired man who stood with his back to them.

There was something regal in the stance, something imperious—no, arrogant—that was it! Could it be? A wild thought came to Mika, and he stared down at the princess who stood with teeth bared, growling in a menacing fashion. It was! It had to be! It was the king, the princess's father!

"Are you the king of Dramidja?" Mika called to him in a low voice.

After a long moment the figure stirred and turned to look at Mika. Mika pulled back in astonishment. The man was very large, his huge head set on a thick neck. His chest was barrel-like and tapered into a narrow waist, with slender hips and legs that seemed too small to carry the immense bulk. It was immediately apparent that he was the king, for aside from the haughty gaze above the narrow, arched nose, there was the evidence of his eyes. One was blue, the other green.

The king cast his regal gaze over Mika, the wolves, and the ragged child, and dismissed them as unworthy of his time. He turned his back on them once more. The princess began barking angrily.

That single look, that single action, drove Mika into an instantaneous rage. "Don't you turn your back on me!" he hollered, gripping the bars between his hands. "It's your fault I'm in here!"

The king turned to look at Mika, only slightly curious. He did not speak, but quirked a single eyebrow.

"Don't even recognize me, do you?" Mika said in a cold tone. "My name is Mika, born to the Far Fringe Clan of Wolf Nomads. I have nearly come to death and have suffered grievously on your behalf. More than two score of my men and blood kin died for you, and you do not even know of our existence or care."

"You're right," the king said in a laconic tone, stroking his mustache with his forefinger. "I do not know who you are, and since I have no idea of what you speak, how can I possibly care?"

"Do you know where your daughter is?" asked Mika.

For the first time the king seemed to lose his poise. He paled, a flush of red appearing on the high bridge of his nose. He stood next to the bars and really looked at Mika for the first time.

"What do you know of my daughter?" he asked sharply. "Where is she? What has become of her?"

"You don't care about her! What you really want to know is whether or not the demi-demon Iuz got her as you planned," said Mika. He had the satisfaction of seeing the king's face go tense with shock.

"How—how do you know about Iuz?" he asked in a whisper.

And Mika told him.

"Then it is all over," the king said, sinking to the bench and burying his face in his hands. "All over."

"Don't you even want to know what happened to the princess, your daughter?" asked Mika, unmoved by the king's sorrow for his own failed plans.

"What does it matter now? All is lost," muttered the king over the rumbling growls of the princess.

"How could you have sent your only child—your daughter—to a certain and hideous death at the hands of a demon?" asked Mika, trying to give the man the opportunity to explain himself.

"You don't understand," said the king, slowly straightening to lean his head back against the bars. "You couldn't possibly understand what it means to rule, to have power. Or what it means to lose it."

"You're right," replied Mika. "Nor do I understand sacrificing a daughter to a demon."

"It was the price of power," the king said with a dismissive slice of his hand. "And besides, she was a sharp-tongued wench who would not marry. There was no pleasing her no matter what I did. I grew tired of her constant demands. She was just like her mother, always at me for one thing or another. I was glad to give her to Iuz. It was the easiest part of the bargain. The hard part was playing the grieved father. Yes, tell me. I want to know. What happened to the wench? If still she lives and Iuz didn't get her, who did?"

"I did," answered Mika, his heart gone cold inside his breast. "Here she is," he said, standing aside and gesturing with an outstretched hand toward the princess, whose growls emanated deep within her chest and issued between slavering lips.

The king gaped at the wolf and then stared at Mika. He turned his gaze back to the princess, who began to fling herself against the bars. Finally the king threw back his head and roared with laughter, great guffaws that echoed throughout the building, momentarily silencing all other sounds.

"You mean that . . . that wolf is my daughter, the Princess Julia, heir apparent to the throne of Dramidja?" asked the king. Tears filled his eyes as he clutched his sides and laughed till he collapsed against the bars, too weak to stand upright.

"How did you do it?" he asked at length.

"With the stone," Mika replied stiffly, holding out the gem.

The king stiffened and got to his feet, his eyes cold and hard, all vestiges of humor vanished.

"The stone," he said, thrusting his hand between the bars. "It's mine, give it to me. There might be a chance that I could . . ." His words faded away, and his eyes grew crafty.

"Escape? Forget it," Mika said harshly, willing to inflict as much pain as possible. "You have no hope of getting out of here. Iuz was but a middleman. His boss caused you to be imprisoned and sent me here as well."

"Maelfesh? Maelfesh!" whispered the king.

"Big guy with a kind of fiery personality," said Mika. "The kind of guy who stands out in a crowd."

But the kind did not reply. Once again he buried his face in his hands and whispered, "All is lost, all is lost."

Chapter 25

THERE WAS NOTHING MORE to be gained from trying to speak with the king.

Mika stroked the princess's head, far more sympathetic to her than he had ever been. With a father like that, no wonder she turned out as she did. She did not even seem to notice the gesture. Mika left her to her growling to speak briefly to Tam, RedTail, and Margraf and then contemplate his own situation. In the face of the priest's overwhelming confidence and the king's fear, Mika's plan no longer seemed quite so brilliant.

He stood by the window all the rest of that long day, looking up at the sky and wishing that he were free. The sky was the soft, clear shade of winter, empty except for a time when a few large and ungainly shapes flapped across his narrow bit of vision.

After he had stared at the strange forms for a long while without conscious awareness of them, their peculiar shapes penetrated his depression; he looked at them and wondered what they might be. They were certainly not songbirds—too big. Nor eagles nor hawks, still larger and far too bulky. They seemed to be flying in a direct line behind a lead bird or whatever it was. He wished with all his heart that they would just swoop down and take him away with them. A peculiar tingling whiteness filled his head, and he felt dizzy and faint.

He put his hand on the stone sill and steadied himself. After a heartbeat, the feeling passed. He pressed his face against the cool bars of the window just in time to see the last of the odd creatures cross the width of the tiny window and disappear from sight. He felt even more depressed once they were gone.

Prayers were called at midday and again at mid-afternoon, when still more unfortunates were dragged up the steep stairs to the top of the pyramid where, outlined against the angry red of the falling sun, they donated their lives to the demanding Exag.

Their terrified screams rang in Mika's ears long after the last call to prayer echoed through the city shortly after dark.

Mika had kept to himself, thinking throughout the long day. The king had withdrawn into a tight-lipped shell and had not even looked their way since morning. The princess had finally given up her vigil of hatred at the bars. She, along with Tam and RedTail, had paced and slept and now stared up at Mika as though expecting him to do something. Margraf watched him as well, though after his one outburst of tears he had not lost control of his emotions.

"The rusties," said Mika, turning to Margraf. "You say there are a lot of them. How many?"

"I dunno," said Margraf. "More than I can count.

There's lots of 'em. I can never figure out what keeps them alive. Father says that there are even bigger ones that live in the lower depths, some as big as buildings, but I think that's just a story made up to scare the little kids into behaving. I've never seen a big rusty, just the little ones that come foraging for metal. We hardly have any metal left, but there's always lots of them. I guess they must be pretty hungry."

"I certainly hope so," Mika said fervently. "I hope they're hungrier than ever before in their lives because I'm about to give them a banquet."

Margraf stared at him as though he had lost his mind. Mika chuckled, opened his shoulder pouch, and took out his book of spells.

"It will take a combination of spells if it is to work," Mika muttered, stroking his beard with his gauntleted hand. Mika had enough trouble accomplishing only one spell and doing it right, much less two. He would need to use the gemstone for certain, but at this point it no longer mattered. The curse and even his demon fingers seemed but a trifle compared to his approaching death.

Hornsbuck had been calling to him all day, but Mika had not answered, racked with self doubt and weighted down by the responsibility he felt for all of the others. He smiled to himself grimly, thinking about the king. Surely this was what it was like to rule, holding the lives of others in your hands. He was determined to do a better job of it than the king had. As the darkness grew, somehow he knew he would succeed.

He moved to the doorway and pressed his face

against the bars.

"Hornsbuck," he cried in a hoarse whisper.

"Aye," came the sullen reply.

"I think I've got it figured out," Mika said. "Everyone be ready to run for it. It will start around midnight. Be ready."

"Mika! What are you going to do?" Hornsbuck whispered hoarsely. "What's going to start around midnight?"

"Just trust me, all right?" said Mika. "I'll do the best I can, and then it's every man for himself until we get to the wall. The plan is fire; grab torches and whatever else that will burn and pile it against the wall. We'll burn our way through the damned thing and leave this cursed city behind!"

A ragged cheer broke out. Mika sat down again and began reading words from his spell book, trying to commit them to memory, all the while wondering if the horses were quartered somewhere nearby or if he had lost his faithful roan forever. He also thought about the king and the demon, wondering what would happen, but he no longer really cared. If his plan worked, he would take his chances, and if it didn't, well, a man could only die once. He hoped.

Midnight came almost too soon for Mika, although none too soon for the restless wolves and the rest of the prisoners.

"He's starting!" piped Margraf as Mika faced toward what he assumed to be the center of the city and began to chant, his gauntleted hand wrapped around the gemstone, the other pointing down toward the heart of the labyrinths that underscored the city.

For what seemed a long time, a very long time, although in truth it was merely a matter of heart-beats, nothing happened. Mika did not cease in his incantation of the magical spell, repeating it over and over.

Then he heard it. At first it was no more than a soft, scuffling sound, the barest of murmurs, like the sea lapping against the shore on a hot summer's day. But the sound grew. Louder and louder it became until it sounded like the beat of scores upon scores of antelopes pounding across the dusty plains.

One might have missed it if one were not listening for it, but Mika was. A broad smile creased his face, making it difficult to repeat the spell. But still he kept on.

And now the sound was even louder, the trampling of feet, many, many of them, and all heading unerringly toward Mika.

The sound of them grew louder and louder and *louder* still! They thundered toward the prison, chittering and squealing and squeaking. For the first time Mika felt fear, and the incantation wavered.

Screams broke out on the far side of the building, and Mika was afraid that his fellow prisoners would panic. But then he heard a ragged cheer go up, and laughter as well.

"They did it, they got the guards! Squashed 'em flatter than a mealybread!" shouted someone on the opposite side of the corridor.

Mika forced himself to hold his concentration until he knew for certain that the spell had worked.

The noise grew even louder. The wolves milled

around the cell restlessly: the princess whined, Tam growled, and RedTail panted heavily. And there! There in the window were the waving antennae of a rust monster! No, two! No, three, four, five sets of antennaes flicked across the bars of the window! Tam flung himself at the bars, barking hysterically. It was all that Mika could do to hold the two male wolves back. The princess seemed to have no liking for the rust monsters either and contented herself with angry barking.

Cheers rang throughout the building. Mika guessed that the strange little creatures were swarming over the prison, tasting each of the bars. Mika hoped, no, prayed, that there were enough of them to do the job.

Mika broke off chanting and sat down wearily on the floor. The casting of spells was a difficult business, mentally as well as physically hard on the caster. Mika felt as though he could sleep for a fortnight, but he knew that it was not possible if he wished to live.

The window was totally obscured now by a mass of wriggling, squeaking creatures who nibbled, licked, chewed, and crunched on the closely spaced bars.

Tam whined nervously, and the princess's voice grew hoarse. RedTail stared fixedly at the window with narrow, slitted eyes.

Abruptly Tam looked up at the ceiling and whined. Mika glanced at him and wondered what he sensed.

Tam cocked his head to one side and whined more insistently. Mika stood up and walked over to him, wondering what was the matter. Then he heard it too. Creaking. And felt it. Kind of a trembling.

A bit of red clay trickled down onto Mika's head,

and then a dribble of larger bits cascaded down his back. And even as he watched, it seemed that the entire ceiling buckled and bulged downward into the room, until Mika had to pull back to avoid being struck by falling bits of clay.

A shout came from the center of the building, then a loud crashing noise, the sound of falling adobe and timbers. Mika heard squeaks and the rush of tiny feet! He saw antennae in the corridor, weaving back and forth across the face of the door, excited murmurs of rustie joy as they fell upon the bars of the doors.

The roof groaned above Mika. He gathered everyone into the farthest corner. Mika hoped that every rustie in Exag had answered his call. They would undoubtedly eat their way through the metal bars of the windows and doors. The only real question was whether or not the building would collapse under their weight, killing everyone in the building before they could escape.

The roof collapsed with a loud crash. Mika and Margraf and the wolves were showered with broken adobe, wooden beams, and a mass of wriggling rusties.

"Mika!" screamed Margraf as he tried to fight his way clear of the mass of clay and timbers, only to be trod upon by a throng of chittering, squealing rusties fighting each other to be first at the metal door.

Mika struck out with his fists, but as his knuckles crashed into the rust monsters' hard exoskeletons, he realized that striking them would do little good. He plucked one rustie, who was in the process of stepping on Margraf's head, up by its tail and slung it through the newly opened window. It struck two others who were attempting to climb in and knocked them off.

Mika pulled Margraf out of the debris and dropped him through the circle of waving antennae which once more framed the window. The wolves followed on the boy's heels, the princess whining and stepping high as though loathing the touch of the creatures. Tam and RedTail contented themselves with growling at the metallic creatures who did not even hesitate in their steady progression.

Finally Mika himself slipped over the sill, stopping only to pat a rustie who was too small to climb and was squeaking with frustration as it threw itself hopelessly against the bottom of the wall. Mika lifted the tiny creature onto the sill, where it trilled happily before slipping into the writhing mass that filled the broken remains of the room.

Mika was extremely fond of rust monsters at that particular moment. It was almost a sense of paternal pride, and he found himself wondering if they could be trained or would cohabit with wolves.

He viewed the building—or what little could be seen of it—with satisfaction. The entire structure quivered with rusties as they climbed, crawled, slithered, and fought each other to reach the metal that was their goal.

As Mika and Margraf watched the amazing sight, more and more rusties pushed inside the building, and more and more humans fought their way out. Soon they were surrounded by Lufa, Hornsbuck, Lotus Blossom, and the majority of others who had not run off or been killed by the priests. There was no sign of the king, nor of the huge rusties that Margraf had spoken of.

Ah, well, one couldn't have everything.

"Good going, lad," said Hornsbuck, an amused glint in his eyes as he bent down to thump RedTail on the flanks. "Never would have thought of such a thing myself. Best get going, though. This bit of nonsense is bound to raise someone, and then we'd be done for. Come on, let's head for the wall. Lufa, take us to the point nearest the mountains!"

"Aye," agreed Lufa, a wide grin on his face as he hugged Margraf to his side. He pointed east and headed off at a fast trot.

Mika turned to follow, when all of a sudden his hand began to tingle. He opened his mouth to shout, to cry out for help, when the pain seized him. It was worse this time, worse than before. Mika rolled over on the ground, hugging the hand to his chest and crying aloud, his voice drowned out by the madness around him. He felt hands on him and heard sounds of concern. Tam whimpered, and the princess nuzzled him. He tried to speak, to beg, to implore someone, anyone, to make the pain go away, but the agony was overwhelming, too much to bear. There was a loud roaring in his ears, and he felt himself falling into a flaming vortex that ended in darkness.

Chapter 26

MIKA WAKENED TO FIND HIMSELF ringed by anxious faces: Hornsbuck, Lotus Blossom (who smoothed Mika's hair back from his forehead), all three wolves, Lufa, and Margraf. His glove was off his hand, and one brief glance showed him what he already knew: the demon had given him yet another green-scaled, taloned finger. The pain was gone, save for the pain in his heart. He sighed, drew the glove on, and accepting Hornsbuck's arm, climbing shakily to his feet.

Very little time had elapsed since the onset of his collapse. Ascertaining that Mika was able to travel, the group set off, with Lufa leading the way. Mika, Hornsbuck, Lotus Blossom, and the wolves followed immediately behind. The remainder of the underground people brought up the rear.

They traveled through dark streets and empty squares, meeting no one, yet Mika could not shake the feeling that something was wrong. Their escape seemed too easy. Why? Where were the soldiers?

Where was the king? What was the demon up to? And why, why did he feel as though he were being watched?

Mika tried to cast off the sense of unease, telling himself that they would soon be at the wall and would breach it with flames and make good their escape even if his entire hand and arm turned green. But he still felt the nagging sense that something was wrong.

They found a torch burning low in its bracket at the base of a tower. A low murmur of protest and fear rose from the more easily frightened by the audacity of taking something that belonged to the priests. Then, a giddy sense of boldness seemed to seize them and they fought each other for any torches they found thereafter.

An almost festive mood carried them to the foot of the great wall, where the shadow of the mountain fell on them like a bad omen.

Upon closer inspection, the wall appeared to be constructed of normal adobe. Mika began to wonder if Lufa were wrong, if it were all just some giant hoax perpetrated by the priests to keep the inhabitants of Exag in line. Well, he would soon find out. He gestured for all of those who held torches and those who had gathered pieces of wood along the way to join him at the wall. Following his instructions, they piled their bits of wood close to the base of the wall yet not actually touching it, hoping to avoid triggering the mechanism that would bring the wall to life. When the wood was stacked, Mika looked around him one last time at the circle of hopeful faces, all of them believing in him, trusting in him for the miracle of freedom.

Margraf left his father's side and slipped his small hand into Mika's, his bright eyes shining with admiration.

Mika smiled, a grimace really, and hoped that the boy had not misplaced his faith. Turning to the others, he gave a signal and tossed his torch on the small pile of wood. The other torches followed, arcing through the dark night like falling stars and landing on the wood with a shower of bright sparks.

The wood burned quickly. Mika eyed the row of shuttered buildings closest to the conflagration and hoped that the flames would not waken anyone who might raise an alarm.

The fire bit into the wood, crackling as it leaped higher and higher. As the last of it caught, the men used whatever lengths of wood and metal they had been able to arm themselves with to tip the whole fiery pyre over onto the wall itself.

For a moment nothing happened. Mika strained to see past the glow, to see whether or not the wall was burning. Then he smelled it, an awful stink, like that of burning feathers. The wall began to ripple, attempting to pull itself away from the fire. A hole appeared, small at first, but one that grew larger and larger before their eyes.

And then the wailing began, a thin, eerie, high-pitched lament that shivered on the nerves and made one's teeth ache. As the hole grew larger, the screaming became louder.

Mika looked around nervously. He knew that it would be but a short period of time before the guard was alerted and they would be discovered.

"Quick! Get through—leave!" he whispered,

pushing Lufa toward the hole.

"We can't! The hole's too small!" cried Lufa. Mika turned back to the wall and examined it. As Lufa said, the hole was still too small for even the smallest adult.

Mika began to kick and push the burning wood against the wall, forcing it into the hole, hoping that it would eat its way through more quickly. But as the hole grew, so did the screaming. And then the wall began to move all over, not just the one small area that was being burned. It rippled for as far as the eye could see. It shook. It heaved. Cries of alarm came from distant locations. Mika could only assume that the wall was reacting similarly along its entire length.

The fire was burning with great intensity now. Huge sheets of flame concealed the opening, and the underground people pulled back from the heat reluctantly, realizing that there was no way that they could pass through the flames in safety. Fearing the flames, the wolves huddled together at the edge of the buildings.

It was an amazing sight. The wall undulated up and down as the flames bit into its great expanse and spread as far as the eye could see. The screaming grew louder and louder as the pain drove the nearly inanimate wall almost insane with previously unknown pain.

The wall began to disintegrate, bits and pieces of it, wrapped in flames, falling off, sizzling on the ground. The pieces fell like fiery meteors, sometimes exploding and landing far from the wall itself.

Mika gestured for his small group to fall back even further, and they watched in awe as the wall burned.

A large chunk exploded out of the wall and landed on the awning of a mercantile located a few paces from where they stood. The awning burst into flames immediately and soon spread to the building itself.

Fortunately, no one lived in the building. But residents of the area soon flooded the streets wrapped in various forms of night garb and stood staring at the fire with awe-struck eyes.

Indeed, it was an amazing sight. Mika congratulated himself on a job well done. He had done a fine job. For a moment he almost forgot about the king and the demon.

The entire wall was blazing now, shooting sparks and flaming pieces of itself onto the nearby buildings and into the crowds that filled the streets. It lit up the entire sky, illuminating the area almost as brightly as daylight. Mika looked around and saw that the prison escapees were virtually indistinguishable from the rest of the crowd, most of whom had dressed hastily and presently wore a coat of the soot and ashes that rained down from the sky.

But Mika also noticed something else: the look of joy on most people's faces as they watched the burning wall. A few people rushed about, throwing water on their buildings and stamping the flames, but most just watched as the fire consumed the hated wall.

The wolves were extremely disturbed, pacing in the darkest of shadows, whining high-pitched, nervous sounds, and panting loudly. They were clearly fearful, and that more than anything brought Mika back to reality, reawakening his sense of danger.

The underdwellers might now be safe, able to blend in with the rest of the crowd and make their way to the safety of friends, or even out of the city itself, but he and Hornsbuck and Lotus Blossom were far from safe. Their appearance and their wolves drew attention like lightning rods. Already a number of people were staring at them with as much interest as the fire. It would only be a matter of time before guards arrived on the scene. Mika placed a hand on Hornsbuck's arm and pointed toward the wall. Speech was virtually impossible over the roar of the conflagration.

And then it happened. As if from nowhere, he suddenly appeared before Mika. The king.

His eyes were alight with rage and madness. His hair was wild and stood out around his head in a spiky aura. He swung a massive, two-handed broadsword in front of him, cleaving a space through the crowds as he approached Mika.

"You!" he screamed. "You are the cause of my ruin! You foiled the demon and aborted the bargain! You caused me to be imprisoned! You dared get in my way, you nobody, you filth! I shall kill you!"

He advanced on Mika, driving him back steadily until he could go no further, his back against the wall of a building.

The crowd gasped and hovered, drawn, in the manner of crowds everywhere, toward the drama that threatened to spill someone else's worthless blood while sparing their own precious supply.

Mika started to draw his own sword, then remembered that the rusties had eaten it. A quick glance at Hornsbuck told him that he, too, was still disarmed. Hornsbuck and Lotus Blossom, grasping the situation instantly, began pushing through the crowd, searching for a sword. But by the time they found one, it might well be too late.

When help came, it was from an unexpected source. Tam had slipped in and crouched at Mika's feet, looking for an opening, when suddenly, there was a dark streak and a short scream. The princess! While the king's attention was focused on Mika and Tam, the princess had flung herself at her father, driving him back with the force of her attack. As he fell, she clamped her jaws around his throat. There was a short, burbled scream, and then it was done. The king's limbs thrashed and then he lay still, blood pouring from the gaping hole in his neck.

Mika stared at the princess, stunned. And then he lifted his gauntleted hand and saluted her. The man had been her father, but he had treated her as though she were a slave or an inhuman pawn. He had deserved to die. The princess acknowledged his gesture and then stepped back from the body, lifting her feet delicately as though stepping over a bit of overripe carrion.

A complement of guard hurried into the street leading several frightened horses hitched to wagons carrying huge barrels of water and sand.

Mika pressed himself into the shadows of a building and was quickly joined by Hornsbuck and Lotus Blossom.

"Thought you was a goner, that time, boy. You got more lives than a displacer beast," chuckled Lotus Blossom, eyeing him with respect.

"We've got to get away," said Mika. "Or we'll all be needing extra lives. Those guards will spot us soon."

"I don't think so, lad. They've got their hands full with the fire. Listen to that wall scream, will you? I've never heard anything like it," said Hornsbuck.

But Mika wasn't interested in the wall anymore; it could longer provide them with the means of escape. Its shrill screaming only aggravated him now and made him nervous.

"I don't like it; I wish it would stop," said Mika.

"Then our troubles would really start," said Hornsbuck. "Don't you see, lad? Those fellows have more than they can handle as it is without looking for us. We're safe as long as the fire keeps burning. That screaming is music to my ears. Look there, some of these folks feel like I do."

Mika followed Hornsbuck's finger and saw several guards attempting to force a group of citizens to help put out the fire. But it was obvious from their slow, reluctant movements and their sullen expressions that the citizens were not eager to help.

Just as Mika was beginning to think that Hornsbuck was right and that they were safe, he looked up and saw the high priest standing not two paces away, his bright blue eyes searching the crowd.

"Oh, Mika, isn't it exciting?" Margraf piped, his shrill little voice carrying as clear as bell. The priest turned and looked straight into Mika's eyes. He smiled, and Mika's heart sank.

"Hornsbuck," said Mika, never taking his eyes off the priest.

"Hmmm?" said the huge nomad. Mika felt him turn before grunting, "oh," as though Hornsbuck had tasted something unpleasant.

The priest motioned, and a full complement of the guard moved into sight, positioning themselves behind the priest.

"Make no struggle," said the priest. "Or it will go hard with your friends."

"What friends? I've got no friends here! Get away from me, kid, you've been nothing but trouble since we met!" Mika shoved Margraf away from him as hard as he could.

Margraf looked up at him with wide, disbelieving eyes, and tears began to make streaks down his soot-stained cheeks. Mika did his best to frown, but Margraf stood frozen in place and looked as though Mika had struck him. His stricken face twisted a knife in Mika's heart. Lowering his head, Mika winked broadly at the boy and jerked his head to one side, telling him to go.

Margraf smiled, his eyes lighting up with understanding. He put his head down and bulled through the guard, taking them by surprise and making good his escape.

Mika, hoping to give the boy a better chance, yelled out defiantly, "Well, what are you waiting for, a bigger crowd? Come on, priest, let's see whose magic is stronger, your god's or mine!"

Hornsbuck looked at Mika as though he were mad and tightened his grip on the length of wood he had used to prod the fire. Lotus Blossom clenched her mighty fists, and the wolves bared their teeth and crouched low, ready to spring.

The guards moved to either side of the priest, outflanking them neatly. In an open area the situation might not have been so serious, but Mika's group had been caught in the narrow space between two buildings that ended in a solid adobe wall, a cul-de-sac with no exit other than the one blocked by the priest and the guards.

"Tam! On the ready," murmured Mika. The wolf bent low, ready to hurl himself at whomever Mika directed. RedTail and the princess took up their positions on either side of him.

"Come," the priest said pleasantly. "Put down your weapons and do not think to fight; you have done more than enough damage tonight."

"Hah! We haven't even started!" roared Hornsbuck as he leaped at the priest, striking hard with the length of wood. But as he came thundering out of the cul-de-sac, two men, both hidden from sight on opposite sides of the buildings, struck out. One clubbed him on the head with a massive cudgel and the other pounded his own club down on Hornsbuck's length of wood, forcing its point into the ground. It happened so quickly that Hornsbuck had no time to react; he sank senseless to the ground like a heavy sack of grain.

All the heart went out of Mika at that point and he signaled Lotus Blossom and the wolves to surrender, not wishing any of them to be killed. The guards seized them roughly and dragged them through the crowd. People moved away and eyes turned aside as he passed, even those whom he recognized as having rescued.

The city was deserted. But it seemed different in some other way . . . off kilter. Even the guards noticed it, staring around with wide eyes, nudging each other. Over to the left, a building seemed to sag to one side, and the door was lying on the ground. To the right, the window to the wheelwright's shop was wide open, the shutters lying on the ground, apparently ripped from the wall hinges and all.

The guards took out their sense of unease by handling their prisoners roughly. Mika tried to endure it stoically.

He could see that the sky was beginning to lighten, and his spirits dipped. Was this the morning of his borning? Was this really the way his life would end? It seemed quite possible unless he could think of something to forestall the inevitable. He searched his mind for something, anything that would work. A spell of any sort that would free him from the priest. But no matter what he thought of, he either did not know it well enough to recite from memory or it would not free his companions, too. And like it or not, he could not convince himself to leave them behind.

A building shuddered on the right and then slowly collapsed in a rumble of bricks and creaking timbers. Underlying the noise was a soft chittering as familiar forms scurried by him and rushed off down the street to disappear into the next building.

There were more people in the streets now, none of whom gave them a second glance. More than a few were inebriated, women as well as men, and some were in various stages of undress, screaming and yelling with joy and drunken abandon. At any other time Mika would have cheered with them, but now that his life was at stake, he cursed them blackly.

He caught sight of a towering form outlined against the dawn sky. A rust monster as tall as a two-story building ponderously pushed its way into a building, grinding the girders under its immense feet and grazing contentedly on spikes and nails.

Joyous shrieks and boisterous laughs mingled with the crash and rumble of falling buildings and the distant crackle of the burning wall. A naked, giggling woman ran past them, pursued by an amorous admirer. The city was going to pieces.

No one realized the situation more acutely than the priest. He kicked at one of the rusties and cursed as he banged his toe on its hard exoskeleton. Mika grinned in spite of himself. He could have told him as much.

The rusties became more and more numerous as they approached the section of town that held the pyramid. They were everywhere, large and small, fat and thin; they rushed in and out of buildings, chittering and squealing, squeaking and waving their antennae. They munched on hinges, chewed on doorknobs, licked torch posts, and nibbled on nameplates.

As they came within sight of the pyramid, Mika saw more than a few of them lying belly up in the middle of the road, legs stiff, and he wondered if they were dead, victims of their own gluttony, or merely drunk on overindulgence. He smiled, proud of the havoc he had created almost single-handed. Maybe the priests of Exag would kill him, but, he reflected as yet another building collapsed, they wouldn't have much of a city left to show for it.

Chapter 27

DAWN WAS BREAKING OVER THE CREST of the mountains, the sun a small red crescent, when they arrived at what remained of the prison. The roof and walls had collapsed, leaving only a pile of rubble to show where it had once stood.

The priest, his face white with fury, his thin lips compressed in a tight line, mounted the pyramid's narrow stairs, which seemed too small for human feet. But that did not deter either the priest or the guards, who dragged Hornsbuck and Lotus Blossom up the entire steep length and prodded Mika before them at spear point.

The priest glared at Mika from time to time, his nostrils pinched and his fingers opening and closing convulsively as though anxious to wrap themselves around Mika's heart.

Mika hung as heavily as he could in the guard's hands, his feet dragging on the steps. But the guards' muscles were made of iron, and Mike was lifted above the level of the steps and carried as easily as a parent would a reluctant child.

Tam whined. Mika turned his head and commanded him to leave, but the wolf ignored him, as did the princess and RedTail, all of them staying out of reach of the guards' spears. They continued to follow.

In spite of desperate ploys, none of which worked, they came at last to the very peak of the pyramid. It was not pointed at the top as Mika had thought, but flat, with enough room for a large, white, stone altar.

The altar had a deep groove cut in one side, and it was darkly stained. Blood, thought Mika. My blood soon.

The guards wrestled him forward, holding Hornsbuck and Lotus Blossom one level lower. Hornsbuck was only just regaining consciousness. A trickle of blood coursed down his face, and he wobbled unsteadily between his captors. Lotus Blossom still struggled against the four guards who held her, throwing one, then another off balance, but they managed to hold her. The wolves circled behind, growling and snapping at the backs of legs, drawing blood and causing distraction.

Mika fought as best he could, struggling to stay away from the awful altar for as long as possible. He believed for the first time that there was nothing and no one to save him.

The sun was rising, more than half of the blood-red orb visible above the mountainous horizon. Dark, flat clouds streaked its surface, coloring the sky around it a sickly, ominous shade of sulfurous yellow.

The guards dragged Mika to the edge of the altar and ripped his doeskin tunic from his body, revealing the gemstone suspended from its gold chain, glittering blue and then green in the sullen glare of the rising sun.

The priest reached up and, though Mika twisted and turned and nearly hurled himself and the two guards off the platform, he attempted to rip the gemstone from Mika's neck. As his hand closed around the stone, Mika felt a surge of power course through his body. The priest stiffened, his back arching, hair standing out all around his head, eyes and tongue protruding. He stood poised on the tips of his toes for an endless heartbeat and Mika dared to hope that he was dead, but the priest's hand opened and he dropped the gemstone. Mika himself was unharmed and equally stunned at the strange occurrence.

At that moment, with the priest still groggy, Mika sensed the princess crouching to spring. He cried out, "No, stop! They'll just kill you!" The guards were still alert, spears held at the ready for such a maneuver. The wolf hunkered at the edge of the step, her leg muscles quivering, dewlaps twitching.

At the priest's command, the guards wrestled Mika face-up onto the altar, spread-eagled, holding his arms and legs down at all four edges of the altar. Mika pulled and strained against them, but they were strong and had performed this duty many times before. His muscles creaked with the strain, but he knew in his heart that it was hopeless.

The sun had cleared the horizon now, larger and redder than ever he had seen it. It rose above them until it seemed to Mika that it would surely strike the pyramid as it passed overhead. Mika stared at it, nearly hypnotized with the immensity of it.

Suddenly, he thought he saw a face!

Yes! There it was, an eye, no, two eyes like glowing carnelian, a nose wrapped in flames, and a mouth like a seething cauldron, opening, opening wide to eat him whole! Mika shrieked, struggling against the bonds as the mouth opened to consume him!

And then, seemingly out of nowhere, a ghostly apparition drifted toward the angry crimson orb, closer and closer with every heartbeat. It was the moon, wrapped in shimmering, gossamer, ethereal streamers that softened its outline and made its familiar shape somehow strange and otherworldly.

The raucous laughter and cheerful screams of those in the city below mingled with the rumble of falling buildings and rose to underscore the desperate scene.

"Great She-Wolf, mother of us all, help me. I promise to marry and be a better person if you'll only help me now. Please!" Mika prayed between gritted teeth.

"It is nearly time," intoned the priest as he watched the shrouded moon approach the swollen sun. He turned to the edge of the altar and palmed something that Mika could not see; then he turned to face Mika, placing himself on Mika's left side and waited. His eyes glittered coldly, and he permitted himself a thin smile as he looked down on his victim.

The moon had begun to encroach upon the sun, seeming at first too small to affect it in any way, like a gnat nibbling on the toe of a giant. But it was relentless in its progress and soon, almost unbelievably, the sun was but a gibbous protuberance at the edge of the darkened moon.

The red glow faded, dulled bit by bit, until the air

around them grew gray. Silence fell, along with the darkness, as even those in the crumbling city below became aware of the awful advent. Only the words of the priest were heard, unknown words, a litany of death in an unknown language. Raising his hand above his head, the priest chanted aloud, his words ringing harsh and clear in the gray, murky air, an offering—an appeasement—to the conflict above them.

As the moon continued to engulf the sun, driving the world into greater darkness, the priest's words rose to a shriek howled out against the wind, which had sprung up with no warning. The turbulence beat against the priest, threatening to topple him from his precarious perch, but he held fast, screaming the words into the dark wind. Now, now it came! As the moon moved into its final phase, devouring the slim sickle that remained of the sun, the priest's arm began to descend.

And then, magically, like winged saviors, the same strange figures Mika had seen from the window of the prison began to circle above them. But there was something familiar about them. He strained his eyes to watch them, avoiding looking at the movement of the priest's arm.

"Harpies," yelled one of the guards who held Hornsbuck, following Mika's gaze. "They take what is left of the offerings to Exag, the hollow bodies after the heart is gone. They cannot help you, my friend. Harpies help no one but themselves."

The priest's hand continued to slice downward as the moon ate its way into the sun. Everything seemed to move in slow motion. As the priest's arm

299

descended, Mika saw the flash of something bright, something metallic held in the man's hand.

But Mika was barely watching the priest, even though the nearness of his death could be measured in handspans. All of his attention was focused on the harpies, for now he was almost certain of something. The lead harpy was accompanied by a much smaller figure, and suddenly Mika knew that he was right.

He closed his eyes and concentrated as never before, his mind striving to remember the words to the mind-meld. In a burst of inspiration he added the charm spell, one he had used often on wavering maidens.

He forced his lips to utter the words, and then it was there, the blinding white flash, the link, the magic connection, and he was looking down at himself spread-eagled on the altar. Part of him saw himself through his own thoughts; the other part viewed the world through the thin, nictitating membrane of the circling harpy, felt the rush of cold, thin air through widespread feathered wings. A cold mind, harsh thoughts. Greed. Blood. Death. Thoughts of ripping flesh from bones. His flesh. His bones.

Then the charm spell struck and there was a second blinding, silvery flash filled with other thoughts, cartwheeling together in a melange of sexual ecstacy. Mika recoiled, shrieking 'no!' in his mind. But the other half of him cried 'yes!' and spiraled downward in a frenzy of anticipation.

The priest's hand was drawing closer, still gripped in the strange distortion of time.

"Save me!" Mika cried, all but screaming the message into the cold mind of the harpy. "Save me, as I saved you and yours when no one else would help! Save me and mine! This I ask you in the name of honor and all that is fair!"

He felt the harpy hover undecided; then, as the priest's hand began its final plunge toward his heart, the harpy dived, too, plummeting like a rock, straight for the altar.

The knife point actually scored Mika's chest before the harpy struck, knocking the priest sideways, striking him full on the back of the neck. Mika heard the spine crack, saw the man's head fall to one side, still alive, but unable to control the body which no longer responded to his mental commands.

The guards were thrown into confusion and fell back from the huge, flailing wings and evil gaze. The harpy sliced Mika's bonds with her razor-sharp talons and then, gripping him by the shoulders, rose almost as quickly as she had descended.

The harpy rose vertically into the gray darkness, the sun now completely engulfed by the dark, viscous moon.

Mika writhed in the painful grip of the harpy's claws. His heart quailed, although still inside his breast, for which he was immensely thankful. As he watched all those who were dear to him shrink in the distance, he wondered whether or not he had exchanged one horrible death for another.

Chapter 28

THE PYRAMID GREW SMALLER and smaller beneath them. Mika watched Hornsbuck and Lotus Blossom for as long as he was able, watched as they used the coming of the harpies to wrest themselves free of the guards, then attacked and killed them with their own weapons, abetted by the wolves.

Mika tried to keep his mind off the trickle of blood that inched its way down his body where the great talons gripped his shoulders.

The wall of the city below had been almost completely destroyed; a charred and smoking line of blackness ringed the city. Where the wall still stood, citizens had gathered and were throwing burning brands on the pitiful remains.

Destruction was rampant throughout the city; buildings lay crumbled and collapsed, while rusties of all sizes rummaged in the rubble, only now, with the advance of the sun, starting to withdraw.

Chaos prevailed over most of Exag. Here and there lone priests were being chased by angry citizens, but for the most part it was disorder of a simpler, happier sort. The Exagians, long denied freedom of pleasure, were making up for lost time with zealous excess that would bring headaches on the morrow: they ran naked through the streets, downing alcoholic beverages in great quantity, and frolicked with the opposite sex. Even as Mika was borne away, he felt a gladness grow in him that he had been able to bring about the collapse of such a repressive society.

Finally, the city—or what remained of it—was lost to sight as the harpy carried Mika high into the mountains. The blood had ceased to flow and his shoulders ached immeasurably where the creature gripped him, but pain was preferable to death. He did not complain.

As they circled even higher, Mika felt the tingling begin for the fifth time, as he knew it must. This time it was not quite so bad, though almost bearable in its intensity. Perhaps it was because he was expecting it. After all, if destroying a city didn't deserve a demon finger, what did? Or perhaps it was because he was growing used to it. Whatever the reason, he was able to remain conscious throughout the horrible process. Or maybe it was even part of the demon's plan for tormenting Mika, for he was able to remain alert and watch as the harpy, accompanied by her child, now fully feathered and flying alone, carried him to a dank, depressing aerie high on the flank of the mountain overlooking the city.

The harpy looked at Mika, her eyes dark and blank and filled with cold cunning, tempered by another emotion Mika struggled to identify.

Mika tried to find some shred of warmth, some slightly human emotion to relate to, but there was nothing. He tried to avoid looking at the harpy's body, which was grotesque beyond belief. The face was hideous enough, cold, dark eyes bereft of the slightest vestige of warmth. The mouth was slack and wet, and sharp teeth, accustomed to the taste of human flesh, glinted in the light of the newborn sun. The hair that covered her head was brittle and lacklustre, and it stuck up at odd angles like hay from an ill-made stack. The flesh was white and pale, chapped and rough from exposure to the elements, and bore little resemblance to the soft, clean, sweet-smelling flesh of women he had known in the past.

The carrion stench of the ugly creature was enough to gag a weaker man. Mika was forced to admit that he *was* a weaker man, so he took care to breathe through his mouth. The body was an awful carica-ture of all that was meaningful in Mika's life, the withered, pendulous breasts a parody of feminine beauty.

Below the waist, the harpy was less difficult to look at since her nether regions were rounded and feath-ered, ending in powerful wings, gigantic thighs, and chickenlike legs with three immense, taloned toes.

The youngling, whom he had to thank for his life, was only slightly less ugly. Already tiny breasts were beginning to form on the narrow chest, and her feath-ers were a soft and silky gray. Her face was not terri-bly unattractive if you squinted, and her hair would have been almost decent with a good wash.

Mika smiled at the youngling and began to wonder why one never heard of male harpies, when the elder female shrieked in his ear and shoved him toward the edge of the aerie.

"All right, all right!" said Mika, wondering how it was that mothers always knew what you were thinking, whether or not they were able to mind-meld.

Then the female reached out and grabbed Mika with a powerful grip, pulling him toward her in spite of the fact that he was digging in his heels, resisting.

The harpy smiled at him and cooed gently, spittle drooling out of the corner of her mouth. She batted her eyelids coyly. With a terrible shock Mika identified the strange look in her eyes as passion!

Mika was horror-stricken! Love with a harpy! Ugh! Ugh! Ugh! The thought was almost too horrible to contemplate, but he knew he dared not show his dismay or she would kill him outright.

What followed was a nightmare. The harpy drew him to her, enfolding him in her arms while pressing her body against his, nibbling on his ears and the back of his neck. She held him immobile with her powerful wings and ran her hands over his body. He struggled, but it was no use, she was just too strong. She played with him, her fingers alternately caressing, stroking, pinching, pulling, teasing. Racked with revulsion though he was, Mika found himself responding to her expert ministrations!

He cursed his body and pictured disgusting thoughts, like liver and onions, baby puke, and maggots, but nothing worked—his body continued to react, and for once the curse failed to do its awful work. He tried to push her away, but the wings pinioned his arms, holding him prisoner while the harpy continued to have her way with him.

"Stop! I'm the man! This isn't the way it's supposed to be!" shreiked Mika, but the harpy paid him no mind at all, nuzzling him and stilling his cries with her mouth. And his body, traitorous thing that it was, defied him, acting independent of and ignoring his loud mental protests.

At last he could fight no longer. Seduced from without, betrayed from within, he gave himself up to his fate.

The harpy played him like an instrument, strumming the low notes and then rising higher and higher, bringing him to the very brink of crescendo before pulling away and starting again. Over and over it happened, the harpy smiling blissfully, Mika nearly gibbering with the constant rise and fall of unrequited emotion. Intensely pleasurable though it was, Mika did not know how much more his poor body could stand and wondered if one could actually die from such efforts.

Once again it began. In desperation Mika decided that he would try a mind-meld again, only this time without the blasted charm spell, for that was undoubtedly the reason for the harpy's attentions. Hopefully he would reach whatever dark place passed for her mind and persuade her to let him go.

The passion started to build in him. Closing his mind to it, he clutched the magic gem in his gauntleted hand, the only item of clothing left to him, and began to chant the now familiar spell. As the last word left his lips, there was the feeling of floating, the feeling of empty space, of spiraling down, and then he was joined with the harpy.

The emotion took him then, swept him away, joining, combining both his feelings and those of the harpy. Higher and higher they rose, and Mika almost imagined he could feel the wind rushing past him, so intense was the passion. Then he opened his eyes and nearly fainted, for he *did* feel the wind rushing past him. They were airborne, circling higher and higher in the cold, thin air above the mountain!

Mika screamed and began to struggle, pushing against the harpy and wriggling wildly. It was more than either of them could bear; the harpy lost control and seized Mika tightly with her arms as her great wings beat the air in powerful, measured strokes, exploding in a white heat that blended with a brilliant kaleidoscope of colors more intense than anything Mika had ever experienced. As the ecstasy ripped through her and was passed along to Mika, he screamed aloud, his voice echoing off the mountains.

And then, incredibly, the harpy let him go! Her arms just opened and released him! The shock of falling brought him back to his senses, and he seized her ankles with both hands, gripping them tightly. The mind-meld was slipping, almost gone, but he could sense the feeling of satisfaction, of lust satisfied, of irritation that the man-thing was still hanging on. Suddenly Mika knew why there were no male harpies. There were no such things! This was how female harpies mated, and when they were done their human partners were simply discarded like so much garbage!

The link was gone. There was no way to reach her mind again unless Mika used the gem, but at the moment he did not want to take his hand off her ankle. The harpy began trying to shake him loose, flying up and down in erratic patterns. Mika held on tight. She tried to strike at him with her wings, but she lost altitude, dipping perilously close to the tree-tops. She tried to pry his hands loose, but he held on for dear life—*his* dear life. But his body was tired, and hanging on grew more and more difficult with every passing heartbeat.

The harpy, sensing his exhaustion, looped in the air and spiraled, trailing Mika behind like a strange banner. At the last moment she gave a great jerk, and he felt his grip loosen . . . and then slip away.

The great feathered creature flew down alongside the screaming man as he plummeted through the air. As she came level with him she plucked the shining gem that she had so admired off his neck and then flew away, back to her aerie, leaving the human to his destiny.

Hornsbuck and Lotus Blossom and the wolves watched and listened helplessly from many miles distant as Mika, a tiny speck in their eyes, fell through the air screaming.

They found Mika around mid-day, caught in the upper branches of a towering pine tree. There did not appear to be anything wrong with him other than extreme exhaustion and a multitude of bruises. He later explained to his companions that as he drew near the pine, the demon hand shot out of its own accord, seized a branch, and broke his fall. The magic gem was gone and Mika had acquired another demon finger, but that did not seem to trouble him greatly, for even though he seemed too exhausted to speak, he wore a huge, contented smile on his face.

Chapter 29

WITH LUFA'S HELP, a guide was arranged who showed them the way through the Yatil Mountains and across the western border of the Caliphate of Ekbir. Fortunately, their horses had been recovered, and the grateful Exagians made certain that Mika's group left with heavily laden supply bags.

Neither Mika nor Hornsbuck nor Lotus Blossom had any interest in encountering any of Ekbir's large army, and they did their best to maintain a low profile as the princess's time for birthing drew near.

They wintered in the thick of the Udgru Forest, enduring the cold of Fireseek and the brisk, damp winds of Readying and finally, the soft sweet breezes and gentle days of Coldeven, the land renewed itself and life was born, in a continuing affirmation of hope.

Two cublings were born unto the princess, easily and without much pain, for which Mika was eternally grateful. One was male, the other female, and both appeared to be entirely wolf. And yet . . . and yet there was that niggling doubt, for the female had blue eyes and the male green, and their limbs seemed slightly longer than was seemly for ones so young. Their pelts, while dense and sleek, felt more like hair than fur. Mika looked into the princess's eyes and wondered.

One bright morning in the month of Planting, Mika, Hornsbuck, Lotus Blossom, RedTail, Tam, and the princess and the two pups, who frolicked at her heels, stood on the shores of the Dramidj Ocean and looked across the blue waters draped with heavy mists toward the distant island that still, even now, held the answer to their lives.

There was still much to be done. The princess had a throne to claim and a kingdom to rule, as well as the problem of how to regain her human form.

Hornsbuck was committed by the code of the Wolf Nomads to see the mission through to its conclusion, no matter what was required, and RedTail would follow him to the ends of the Oerth.

Lotus Blossom was determined to follow Hornsbuck and prevent him from throwing his life away in the name of that stupid Wolf Nomad code of honor.

Tam was determined to follow the princess and the man to whom he owed his allegiance, hoping that their purposes—and their paths—did not differ.

And Mika . . . ah, Mika. Mika was determined to go to the island and find the magic blue and red gems that would return his hand to normal, restore the princess to her human form, and remove the curse that was slowly tainting his manhood. And, when that was accomplished, he hoped that the princess would finally show her gratitude for all that he had done in a most womanly fashion. After all . . . what would she have done without him?

Epilogue

THE DEMON MAELFESH was happy. He had been amused for a time, which was a very unusual occurrence. Why, he had actually laughed aloud several times! He couldn't even remember the last time he had laughed—maybe it was the time he had roasted that fat demi-demon over the volcano. He had screamed for several centuries before the demon finally died. That had been fun, but it had also been several eons ago.

He had forgotten how humorous humans could be with their silly machinations, always trying to affect the outcome of their short lives.

It was too bad that the gem had been lost; it had provided quite a nice mirror onto the life of the human. He didn't suppose there would be much to interest him in the harpy's cave. Still, one could never tell.

The demon was so pleased that he snapped his fingers and sent down a shower of flaming meteors that fell on some thatched cottages belonging to a village of poor peasants on the outskirts of Yecha, setting the buildings ablaze.

Yes, humans were definitely fun. Maelfesh made a mental note to look in on them more often. After all, even a demon deserved a good laugh every eon or so.

But demon Maelfesh was also angry. Very angry, and the more he thought about it, the angrier he became. He realized that the human Mika, that miserable excuse for a Wolf Nomad, had escaped his clutches. In fact, the more he thought about it, the more certain he was that he had been tricked. Maelfesh did not like being tricked. It made him angry, and when he was angry whole worlds trembled!

The demon scanned the Oerth searching for the man, Mika, knowing that he was alive somewhere, knowing that he would find him. When he did, the Wolf Nomad would remember the curse of the demon hand as belonging to the good old days.

ABOUT THE AUTHOR

ROSE ESTES has lived in Chicago, Houston, Mexico, and Canada, in a driftwood house on an island, a log cabin in the mountains, and a broken Volkswagon van under a viaduct.

At present she is sharing her life with an eccentric game designer/cartoonist, three children, one slightly demented dog, and a pride of occasionally domestic cats.

Other books written by Ms. Estes include nine of TSR, Inc.'s ENDLESS QUEST® series of books, as well as *Children of the Dragon* and *The Turkish Tattoo* published by Random House, and *Blood of the Tiger* from Bantam.

She wrote the best-selling *Master Wolf*, the first GREYHAWK™ book in the continuing adventures of Mika, shaman of the Wolf Nomads, and is hard at work on the next one.

NEW IN 1987 FROM THE CREATORS OF THE DRAGONLANCE® SAGA

LEAVES FROM THE INN OF THE LAST HOME

Compiled by Tika and Caramon Majere, Proprietors

"The Complete Krynn Source Book," as edited by DRAGONLANCE authors Margaret Weis and Tracy Hickman, brings together for the first time all the poetry, songs, recipes, maps, journals, legends, lost manuscripts, scholarly essays, time-line chronology, herbalism, numerology, runology, and artifacts of Krynn, in one loving and lavish catalogue that is a must for devoted readers of the DRAGONLANCE saga.

Now on sale!

THE ART OF THE DRAGONLANCE® SAGA

Edited by Mary Kirchoff

Collector's edition of new and previously published sketches and full-color paintings of the DRAGONLANCE saga as depicted by TSR's well-known staff of artists and other superb illustrators. Interviews with the series authors, Margaret Weis and Tracy Hickman, and the TSR artists, illuminate the creative process behind the magnificent visual interpretation of this fantasy classic.

Now on sale!

THE ATLAS OF THE DRAGONLANCE® SAGA

by Karen Wynn Fonstad

A complete atlas by a noted cartographer detailing the lands and places of the DRAGONLANCE® novel and game saga. Including extensive maps and descriptions of the world of Krynn, as created by Margaret Weis and Tracy Hickman. A unique and comprehensive gift book for serious fans of the DRAGONLANCE® fantasy series.

On sale in October!

ADVENTURES FOR TSR® ROLE-PLAYING GAMES

DUNGEON™ Adventures

A new periodical from the publishers of DRAGON® Magazine.

Edited by Roger E. Moore

DUNGEON Adventures features a collection of role-playing adventure modules in each issue. Included among these will be DRAGONLANCE® adventures for those interesed in continuing their journey through Krynn.

DRAGONLANCE books, adventure games, and calendars are sold through fine book and hobby stores. Or you may order directly from The TSR Mail Order Hobby Shop, P.O. Box 756, Lake Geneva, WI 53147. A complete catalog of TSR, Inc. products is available upon request. To place an order with VISA or MASTERCARD, call our toll-free order number: 1-800-558-5977. (Wisconsin residents call 414-248-3625.)